BIRDIE
ON THE
RHINE

Book 2 of the Birdie Abroad Series

HEIDI WILLIAMSON

Originally published as *Birdie at the Castle* under the pen name Heidi English.

Copyediting by The Blue Garret
Book Cover Design by ebooklaunch.com
Published by Flyaway Ink Creative

For Zach, Rachael, and Olivia
the original adventurers

Dozens of villages dot the banks of the Rhine River in Germany, many with castles or fortress ruins to explore.
—Marty McEntire, *Europe for Americans Travel Guide*

CHAPTER ONE

"Who made up this torture?" Birdie slid her sneaker across the dirt floor of the… what was it?

A classroom, she supposed.

But it was unlike any classroom she'd been in before. For starters, it was enormous, with windowless stone walls that climbed three stories to an arched ceiling overhead. The air was cold and damp, and what meager light there was puddled under electric wall sconces that flickered like candles.

Besides, it was summer, thank you very much. She shouldn't be in a classroom at all.

She rolled her eyes toward the sky, which had to be out there somewhere beyond the thick stones, blue and cloudless, the last of the morning rain chased off by an eager wind.

"I cannot believe this is happening." She slipped her pack

from her shoulders and dug for her jacket. She wasn't sure whether to laugh or cry.

"Oh, it is happening."

The voice cracked behind her, making her jump and nearly drop the pack. She hugged it close as a teenage boy marched past, clipboard in hand.

He was older, with blond hair and brown eyes that were set too close together in his gaunt face. His crisp shorts and a button-down shirt made him look like a walking ad for private school.

Where had he come from?

She scanned the room but saw only the medieval doors at the top of the stairs. A few minutes earlier, the woman from the ticket kiosk had used a skeleton key to unlock one of them, shown her inside, and then left, allowing the wooden door to drift closed with a thud, taking the sunshine with it.

Had he been hiding in the shadows?

"Come," he said, the word clipped and accented with German. "Follow me."

Birdie didn't move. "Where are we going?"

He raised a brow.

"And who are you?" she asked.

His straight shoulders slumped.

"We are going just there." He pointed across the cavernous room to a rough-hewn table that stretched nearly half its length. Skinny chairs lined both sides.

Empty skinny chairs.

As if signing her up for history camp at a ruined fortress in middle-of-nowhere Germany wasn't bad enough, her mother had dropped her off early.

She willed the dirt floor to split open and swallow her whole.

"My name is Friedrich. I am head counselor of Camp Rheinfels." He clicked on a penlight at the top of his clipboard and skimmed a sheet of paper. "There will be others, of course. They will arrive soon. Because you are early, you can begin by sorting the costumes."

"Wait. Did you say… costumes?"

Friedrich nodded once, crisply, but didn't look up. "Yes. But first, your name, please?"

"Birdie Blessing."

He glanced up from the clipboard then, lifting his eyes just enough to see if she was messing with him.

She recognized the look.

A name like Birdie always got looks.

His gaze was sharp as he took in her long dark hair, her hazel eyes, and her height, which was shorter than his by more than half a foot.

He must have determined she was serious because he twisted his lips and returned to his clipboard. He ran a mechanical pencil along the list of names on the sheet of paper. "Yes, here you are. The last one. Did you sign up just now?"

"Apparently."

"Age?"

"Fifteen."

He scratched it on the paper. "State?"

"Uh, Pennsylvania?"

He nodded, jotting again. Then he used the pencil tip to point to a pile of fabric at the far end of the table. "Start there. You must separate the costumes into types – dresses, pants, shirts, vests, aprons. There may be a bit of chainmail. I will return shortly."

He clicked off the penlight, then sprinted up the stone staircase. When he reached the top, he used both hands to open one of the heavy doors just enough to slink through.

Birdie caught a flash of blue sky and sunshine before the door thudded shut again, leaving the sconces as the only source of light.

A shiver ran up her spine as her eyes readjusted to the gloom.

What had this room been?

Did she even want to know?

She tried to visualize the map she'd seen in her mom's tour book, Marty McEntire's *Europe for Americans Travel Guide*.

Not the dungeon.

No, that had been on the other side of the fortress.

She turned in a slow circle, attempting to get her bearings. She'd been too mad about getting shuffled off to camp to take in the scenery on the drive up the hill. And once her mom dropped her off, she'd been ushered unceremoniously down here without so much as a *"Guten Morgen."*

Not that it had been a Guten Morgen anyway.

In fact, the Morgen had pretty much stank.

The morning had dawned gray as rain pelted the windows of their room, which was on the top floor of the family-run Hotel Flussufer overlooking the Rhine River. They'd overslept, and she'd had to hustle to shower and dress before the proprietor stopped serving breakfast in the restaurant downstairs.

"This is different," she whispered as she slid into a chair across from her mom and set down a bowl of cereal she'd collected from the buffet, where yogurt, pastries, and cereal shared space with lunchmeat, cheese, salmon, dinner rolls, and hard-boiled eggs.

Her mom nodded as she speared a sliver of cold salami with her fork. She appeared refreshed for once, relaxed and comfortable in a T-shirt and jeans. She'd pulled her highlighted hair into a messy bun and brushed on just the right amount of makeup to draw attention to her eyes, which were hazel like Birdie's.

They were tucked into a tiny table in the restaurant, which ran the length of the hotel's enclosed front porch and had tall windows that showcased the dreary morning. Despite a full house, the room was quiet. No music played, and the few conversations taking place were quick and hushed. Birdie noticed one other family with two kids about her age, but everyone else appeared to be well past retirement.

She thought back to the lively discussions they'd had at the communal table at the bed-and-breakfast they'd stayed at in Bruges. That had been their first stop on this summer-long trip through Europe. She'd met a boy named Ben at that table, along with his Uncle Noah, and an elderly couple – Harry and Helga – from Ohio. The caring owner, Mrs. Devon, had cooked omelets and bacon for breakfast, and they'd all eaten together and shared stories like a family.

That breakfast room had been lively, warm. In comparison, this place felt like a heavy, cold blanket.

The hotel's proprietor was a man named Herr Mueller, who had a pale face and a deeply receding hairline. He was working his way from table to table with a carafe of coffee, speaking quietly with each of the guests.

He stepped over to refill her mom's cup. "Ah, the beautiful Blessings. And what are your plans for today? We missed you at breakfast yesterday."

"Oh, thank you." Her mom reached for the cream. "Yes. We got an early start. I'm so sorry if you waited for us." She stole a quick glance at Birdie before continuing. "Today I'm planning to drive back to the castle on the Mosel River that we visited yesterday, Burg Eltz."

Birdie's eyes narrowed. They'd spent the entire afternoon at Burg Eltz. It was a magnificent place, to be sure, a perfect castle hidden in the forest with towers and spires that rose like something straight out of *Grimms' Fairy Tales*, but why make the drive and spend a second day when there were so many other things to see right here?

"Of course, of course." Herr Mueller nodded approvingly. "It is a splendid *Schloss* – that is our word for castle. The same family has owned it for nearly nine hundred years and, unlike many of the castles here along the Rhine River, it was never attacked."

"Yes, it's lovely. Today I'm taking my sketchbook. The owners were kind enough to grant me permission to explore the rooms that aren't on the tour."

They had? When had that happened? Birdie didn't remember a conversation like that at all.

"You are an artist?"

"A designer. I design clothing and home accessories and

I'm working on a new medieval-inspired line."

Herr Mueller cradled the carafe against his chest. "Burg Eltz is a perfect place for such research. The two of you will enjoy the day."

Her mom cleared her throat and wrapped both hands tightly around her coffee cup. "Actually, my daughter will spend her day here, in Sankt Goar. I'm driving her up the hill to Burg Rheinfels. There's a camp for teens there."

Birdie's eyes had grown wide in surprise. She thought Herr Mueller's had, too, but he recovered before she could be sure.

"Of course," he said. "The history camp for the tourists. Some of my guests send their children there."

He had not elaborated. He'd topped off her mom's coffee and given Birdie a sad kind of look before moving on to the next table.

And now here she was, at camp – history camp – alone, in a creepy… kitchen?

She glanced around.

Probably not. The dim space was far too big for that, and there were no signs of fire grates or kitchen gear. And it was chilly. She wished she'd worn jeans instead of shorts.

A storeroom?

She let her mind rest on that option as she crossed the dirt floor and slid into a high-backed chair behind the pile of old-fashioned clothes. She refused to let herself think about the ghosts that might linger in a place like this.

She had enough ghosts of her own.

She surveyed the pile, pulled out a blue quilted vest, and held it up to the light. It was small, with limp leather laces that held it closed.

She tossed it back onto the pile.

Why had her mom signed her up for this stupid camp? She'd seen it in the Fun for Kids section of the guidebook, but she never in a million years imagined her mom would register her for the thing. They were in a foreign country, for goodness sakes. What was she thinking?

Birdie sighed, the sound lost against the thick stone walls.

She knew what she was thinking.

That was the problem.

She was thinking that Birdie could not be trusted to be left alone.

Not after what happened in Bruges.

It figured. The one time in her whole life she'd done something wrong – really wrong – and it got her bounced into day camp like a first grader.

She rubbed her forehead.

The lump had gone down, but an ugly bruise had bloomed in its place, just below the swoosh of her long dark bangs. She'd noticed it this morning in the bathroom and managed to secure her hair in a way that covered it.

But covering a bruise was not the same as forgetting what happened, and her mom had definitely not forgotten that she'd snuck out of the bed-and-breakfast in Bruges and picked a fight with some other tourists.

At least that's what her mom thought happened.

She'd never believe the truth. Birdie barely believed it herself. It seemed like a dream. Except Ben hadn't been a dream, and neither had the other girl at the bed-and-breakfast, Kayla, or even Henri or his little sister,

Marguerite.

They'd been her friends, or at least as close to friends as she'd had in a while.

The quarter-size piece of aventurine glass, with its shimmering cinnamon color and golden speckles, hadn't been a dream, either. They'd slipped into the past with that piece of glass, and helped Henri and Marguerite find a book they'd lost, a book that meant the world to them.

The aventurine was safe in her pack, solid, smooth, and carefully wrapped in a soft cloth she'd found in Bruges. If she'd given it even an ounce of consideration, she'd have left it in the hotel room rather than bring it to camp. She'd been so rushed – and then so mad – that it hadn't even crossed her mind.

It didn't matter. She had no intention of taking it out of the pack or even touching it while she was here. She and Ben had found enough adventure for a lifetime with it, and she didn't want to find any more, especially alone in a ruined fortress.

Correction – a ruined fortress where she didn't want to be.

Her mom hadn't even given her the option of going back to Burg Eltz, or doing anything else. They could have spent the next couple of days together, exploring all the other castles along the Rhine River, but no, her mom had shut that idea down completely.

"You'll have more fun at camp," she'd said as they walked across Sankt Goar to retrieve their rental car from the public lot.

Doubtful.

CHAPTER TWO

A few minutes later, to Birdie's relief, the thick wooden doors opened again and this time Friedrich shoved stoppers beneath them so they would stay that way. The light from the beautiful late-June day splashed down the staircase, and fresh air filtered across the room to where she was sitting.

Friedrich positioned himself at the bottom of the stairs, clipboard upright and mechanical pencil poised. A teenage girl followed and took up residence across from him. She had a pretty face and sandy brown hair twisted into a single thick braid that rested softly against the front of her right shoulder. She stood just a few inches shorter than Friedrich and reminded Birdie of the girls on her high school soccer team at home – solid, sturdy, and eager to spend time outside.

"Guten Morgen, Louisa." He sounded rather formal.

"Hey, Friedrich. How many campers today?" A German accent just brushed the words.

"Six. Wait, no, that is incorrect." He tilted his head toward Birdie. "We had a late addition. Seven."

Louisa considered Birdie sitting alone at the long table and smiled, lifting her hand in a small wave.

She waved back, feeling slightly foolish.

"An odd number," Friedrich said.

Louisa shrugged. "It's not a big deal, is it? We will make it work."

Great, Birdie thought.

Friedrich switched to German but stopped speaking as shadows skimmed the doorway and voices carried across the room from outside.

American voices, she realized, and that made her relax a little in her chair.

"Mom. We passed it," a young man said.

"What? I thought it was in the dungeon."

"No. Back there. In the storeroom."

"Are you sure?"

"Yes."

"Your brother told me it was in the dungeon."

"That's because he doesn't want to go."

"So in here?"

The shadows reappeared and filled in a moment later with the shapes of four people.

"Yes, this must be it. Rich, you were right."

Rich's mom poked her head through the open doorway. She was a tiny woman with blond hair cinched into a stubby ponytail that poked out the back of a baseball cap. She called down to Friedrich and Louisa.

"Is this the history camp?"

"Of course," Friedrich replied. "Yes."

"Finally. I thought we'd never find it." She started down the stairs, her three children a step behind her. "This place is confusing. You should really install more signs."

Neither Friedrich nor Louisa responded.

"These are my children. They're registered for the full session. What are the hours again? When should I pick them up? Wait, do I need to pick them up? Can they take the train back to the bed-and-breakfast or do I need to sign them out?"

"Mom, give them a chance to—"

"Names?" Friedrich cut in.

"Hennessey. Rich, Raina, and Ryan." Mrs. Hennessey peered over Friedrich's clipboard as he scanned the list.

"Ages?" He addressed the kids, who'd formed a half-circle one step above their mother. They looked very much alike, with light brown hair, fawn-colored eyes, and the slender faces of athletes. Rich was clearly the oldest, his broad shoulders hinting at the man he would become, the sharp line of his jaw in stark contrast to his brother's boyish features. Raina reminded Birdie of the girls in her dance class back home, with her hair nestled in a perfect ballerina bun.

"Rich is sixteen, Raina is fifteen, and Ryan is thirteen," Mrs. Hennessey answered.

"American, yes?"

She nodded.

"State?"

"New York." She pointed to her cap. "Ever hear of the Mets?"

Friedrich didn't answer. He ticked some marks on his clipboard. "Camp Rheinfels ends at 16:00. Tomorrow ends at the same time, unless you stay for the optional lock-in, in which case we conclude at 9:30 the next morning. Campers are free to arrive and depart on their own. They are teenagers, so you are not required to sign them in or out. However, during camp hours, they must stay on the fortress grounds."

"When is 16:00 again?" Mrs. Hennessey turned to her children as two more campers entered the stairwell behind them.

"It's 4:00, Mom," Rich said.

"Okay, 4:00. Your dad and I are—"

"Ma'am?" Friedrich interrupted.

Mrs. Hennessey glared at him. She didn't look like a woman who enjoyed being interrupted or called ma'am.

"Please move into the storeroom to speak with your children so I can check in the others."

"Others? Oh, sure."

As Mrs. Hennessey moved away from the stairs to impart final instructions to Rich, Raina, and Ryan, Birdie recognized the boy and girl behind them from breakfast at the hotel. They both had dark, shiny hair, golden skin, and high cheekbones. They carried a little extra weight on their short frames, the boy more so than the girl. An image of her brother, Jonah, snickering and calling them pudgy, popped into her mind. She instantly felt guilty and pushed the thought away.

"Sophia." The girl skipped down the last few steps to stand in front of Friedrich as he consulted his list. She was wearing a pretty lavender shirt with tiny white dots on it.

"Sam," said the boy, who was in a green polo shirt and shorts. They were nearly equal in height, which meant they both had to look up at Friedrich.

"Fifteen," Sophia continued. "We're twins, and we're from Hawaii."

"Welcome to Camp Rheinfels." Louisa offered them both a warm smile. "You win the prize for coming the longest distance. You can join our early arrival at the table."

As Sam and Sophia made their way over, Friedrich lifted his eyebrows at Louisa and tilted his head toward Mrs. Hennessey, who was reciting some kind of safety checklist.

"Mom, we know." Rich draped his arm around her shoulders and turned her gently toward the stairs. "It's going to be okay."

"Your children are in excellent hands here," Louisa said as they approached.

"What?" Mrs. Hennessey drew her attention away from her children to consider Louisa. "Okay, then. I will see you later this afternoon." She took one last glance around the storeroom as if uncertain she really wanted to leave her children there.

"Mom," Rich said again. "It's okay. We're good."

She nodded. "Right, okay."

The siblings watched her jog up the staircase before joining Birdie, Sam, and Sophia at the long table. Birdie had yet to organize one costume. She picked up the blue vest again and held it to the light.

"That's a lot of stuff." Sam's voice was bright in the dim room. "What are you doing?"

"I'm supposed to be organizing the clothes into piles by type – pants, shirts, dresses. I haven't gotten very far."

He surveyed the pile. "No, you haven't. We'll help." And with that, Sam took over the entire operation with the efficiency of an assembly line captain, positioning the Hennesseys and Sophia along the full length of the table and passing clothes down the line, item by item.

Birdie was grateful for the help and impressed by how quickly they fell into a groove. Louisa clicked on a speaker, and the storeroom filled with classical music. Her mind drifted back to school and band practice, picking out the flute as she listened.

"I'm Sophia, by the way. I think we're staying at the same hotel." She handed Birdie a shirt.

"I saw you at breakfast. I'm Birdie."

At the far end of the table, Raina snickered.

Rich shot her a sideways look and she stopped.

"Birdie? Really? That's an interesting name." Sophia acted as if she hadn't heard Raina. "You probably get a lot of questions. I'm sure it gets tedious."

Birdie bit back a giggle. "You're right about that."

Sophia passed her a petticoat. "Why did you sign up for camp?"

"I didn't exactly sign up. My mom made me come."

"Really? Sam and I saw a sign about this camp on our tour here yesterday and begged our parents to let us come. They had this whole other day planned. We were going to tour vineyards, which would have been fine, I guess, but this seemed like more fun." She squinted at the sconce on the wall near the table. "Although it is a bit gloomy. I wonder if we'll be in this room all day."

"I hope not," Birdie said. She'd been in there long enough already.

"I was surprised they said yes, my parents, I mean," Sophia continued. "Mom runs a tight schedule, and this was a big shift."

"They were getting sick of us." Sam leaned in as he picked up another shirt from the pile.

"No, they were not." Sophia frowned. "Sam, really."

He laughed. "Let's just say they didn't put up much of a fight when we said we wanted to come here instead of tagging along to the vineyards."

Birdie looked down at the wool trousers in her hand and smiled. She thought of Jonah again, and how they used to argue all the time. Jonah wouldn't have been as diplomatic as Sam, though. He definitely would've called her a name. Maybe "loser." No, probably something worse.

Not that Jonah Blessing ever would have been forced to go to history camp. No way. Her dad would have put the kibosh on that.

A wave of sorrow caught her by surprise. She sat up straighter in the chair, willing away the tears that threatened to spring up and sting her eyes.

Not now. Please, not here.

Her dad and Jonah had been gone for more than a year and, although she knew she needed to move on, memories of how life used to be still crept up and rocked her.

"Are you okay?" Sophia asked.

She swallowed. She shouldn't have let her guard down.

"Our parents really do like us." Sophia's rich brown eyes showed genuine concern.

Birdie forced a smile and hoped it looked real. "I'm sure they do. I'm good." She passed the pair of trousers to Sam.

"Okay, finish up in the next three minutes and we will begin the activities," Friedrich announced from across the room. "The final camper has arrived."

Birdie glanced up as the last member of their group crossed toward them. She paused with a puffy white blouse in her hand. "Kayla?"

"Birdie?" Kayla squinted as her blue eyes adjusted to the light. She looked the same as she had in Bruges, with her long blond hair pulled up with a large clip and her feet wedged into sandals that had given her terrible blisters.

"You're holding up the line." Sam plucked the blouse from her grasp as Sophia handed her another item.

"What are you doing here?" Birdie asked.

"What are you doing here?"

"My mom made me come."

"My grandparents gave me this option or cuckoo-clock shopping."

"We did cuckoo-clocks on Monday." Sam caught Kayla's eye as he continued to work. "They're more interesting than you'd expect. The shops charge a lot of money for them, and they probably turn a good profit."

"Right." She bumped him over and took the seat beside Birdie. "This seemed cooler."

"When did you get here?" Birdie asked.

"Yesterday. We're staying in the next town down the river.

The people at the front desk told my grandparents about this camp. My grandmother looked it up in her Marty McEntire book and, voila, here I am."

"Why didn't you stay in your room if you didn't want to see the clocks?" She'd met Kayla's grandparents, Harry and Helga, and when it came to sightseeing they seemed to let her do whatever she wanted – which wasn't much.

"I suggested that, but my grandparents took my phone away for the rest of the trip. They said I spend too much time thinking about home." She pondered a vest that Birdie handed her and made a face as she passed it to Sam. "I didn't feel like sitting around all day watching TV in German. Luckily, this is our last stop and then it's back to the good old US of A."

"Ah," Birdie nodded. Kayla and her phone had been inseparable in Bruges. Was that really just a few days ago? One thing was for sure – she had not expected to see Kayla again. Especially here.

"This place is pretty rank." Kayla scrunched her nose and eyed the sconces on the walls. "The air smells like dirt."

"Dog dirt," Raina added.

They all shifted to look at her sitting at the far end of the table between her brothers.

She shrugged. "What? It does."

"I wouldn't go that far," Birdie said. "You get used to it."

"Okay, good job with the costumes." Friedrich strolled over and surveyed the table. "Now it is time for other activities. Pick up a chair and bring it to the center of the room. Arrange the chairs in a circle and sit down."

They did as they were told, except for Sam, who grabbed

the last handful of unorganized clothes and hustled around
the table to deliver them to the proper piles. When he was
done, he picked up a chair and came to sit in the circle next
to Sophia.

They gave each other a high five.

"Good job, Sam," Sophia said.

No – Birdie allowed herself a small smile – they were
nothing like her and Jonah.

CHAPTER THREE

"This is the schedule for camp." Louisa settled onto a creaky chair and handed them each a long sheet of paper.

Kayla grabbed the paper and skimmed it before tossing it under her chair. "Too bad Ben isn't here."

Birdie thought the same thing but remained silent. She hadn't known him long, but she missed him.

"I saw him again, you know, before we left Bruges. He and his uncle were packed and ready to go. Where were they going?"

"Berlin."

"Right. Berlin." Kayla smiled at Friedrich, who sat across the circle from them, clipboard in hand. "How far away is Berlin?"

He scowled at the question. "Berlin is in eastern Germany. It is the capital city. It is six hundred fifty kilometers from here."

"How far is that?"

"In miles, or—"

"No, like how long does it take to get there?"

"Six or seven hours by train."

"What's in Berlin?" Sam finished reading the schedule, folded the paper, and slipped it into the pocket of his shorts.

"A friend." Birdie leaned forward so she could see around Sophia. "Someone we met at the last place we stayed."

"Anyway," Kayla continued, "he was missing you. Or at least he was missing the aventurine. Did you bring it with you?"

"Shh." Birdie nodded toward Louisa, who was lowering the volume of the music so it was just audible in the background. "We're starting."

"Thank you, Louisa." Friedrich scanned the schedule on his clipboard one last time and then considered the group. "I am Friedrich."

He made eye contact with each of them as his gaze drifted from one end of the circle to the other. When he reached Birdie, she bit the inside of her lip to keep from giggling.

"I am head counselor at Camp Rheinfels. I am seventeen years old and this is my second year leading this camp. My assistant counselor this week is Louisa." He opened his hand toward her, as if giving her the stage.

"Yes, um, thank you, Friedrich." She sat up straighter, and her sandy braid slipped from her shoulder to nestle against her back. "I'm Louisa, as he said, and I'm sixteen years old. This is my first year at Camp Rheinfels, but I've been a camp counselor at a Schloss – that's how we say

21

castle – near my village for two years."

"Do you live far from here?" Rich was sitting beside Louisa and considering her with interest. He was much too big for his chair, yet somehow looked like he belonged in it.

"No, not far. Just a few kilometers up the river."

"That's cool. Is the other castle, I mean Schloss—"

Friedrich cleared his throat. "Louisa and I look forward to teaching you about this once-mighty fortress." He glanced at Rich and then down at his schedule before continuing.

A corner of Rich's mouth quirked as Louisa smiled at the floor.

"After you learn about Burg Rheinfels," Friedrich continued, "I will assign you a role in the annual pageant that takes place at tomorrow evening's festival. The pageant helps visitors understand the history of the fortress."

"A pageant?" Ryan's forehead rose and his lips parted. It was the first time he'd spoken since they'd arrived. He shook his head slowly as he turned to glare at his older brother.

"You mean like a beauty pageant?" Kayla leaned forward in her chair.

Friedrich tilted his chin.

"No," Sam said. "I think he means like a Christmas pageant, or a skit."

Friedrich nodded. "Yes. Yes, that is it. A skit. It will begin in the afternoon and conclude in the evening. You will each —"

"That sounds a little longer than a skit." Ryan tilted back in his chair and folded his well-tanned arms.

Friedrich's cheeks flushed. "Perhaps the word is incorrect." He cleared his throat again. "As I was saying, at the festival, you will each play a role. You will pretend to be people from the Middle Ages."

"Think of it like a role-playing video game." Louisa had regained her composure and was listening to the conversation with interest. "Today and tomorrow, you'll learn about the jobs people did at the fortress. Then you'll learn to do one of those jobs."

"Yes, that is correct. Thank you, Louisa." Friedrich shimmied in his chair. "Tomorrow afternoon and evening – if you stay for the optional sleepover – you will dress in costumes and act out those roles for our visitors. Maybe your parents will come to see you in this role-play?"

Kayla and Birdie exchanged glances. Harry and Helga would love this – Birdie was sure of it.

Friedrich reviewed the schedule again, then looked up at the group. "Now you may ask questions."

Everyone turned toward Rich, but Sam spoke first.

"Do you have a festival every week?"

"No," Louisa replied before Friedrich could answer. "Only during camp, so you're lucky to visit this week. We have two festivals, and therefore two camp sessions, each summer. One is at the beginning, so now, and it celebrates the failed marriage of Princess Elisabeth and the evil Prince Gunzelin. Then, at the end of the summer, we celebrate the wedding of Princess Elisabeth and Prince Helmbrecht."

"Two weddings?" Kayla asked.

"One, really. One fails. It is tradition," Louisa said. "Other questions?"

The silence stretched in the dim room until it was clear they wouldn't move on until someone else asked a question.

"What's the difference between a castle and a fortress?" Birdie had been wondering, sort of, and it seemed like as good a time as any to ask. "Are they the same thing, but one is bigger?"

"That's a good question." Louisa pulled her braid forward and played with the tassel of hair at the end. "Castles and fortresses are similar. At Burg Rheinfels there was a central keep, or castle, surrounded by other buildings and thick fortification walls. It was built to protect the entire village, not just the noble family who lived here. We'll see the remnants of it when we go outside. Anyone else?"

"What grade are you guys in?" Ryan lifted his chin a bit as he spoke, as if he were tossing them the question.

"Oh yes, grades," Louisa said. "In Germany we go to secondary school, like your high school, until age nineteen if we plan to go to university. So we are both in our eleventh of thirteen years."

"You have to go an extra year?" Ryan asked.

"Yes. But in this part of Germany it is normal."

"Do you at least have summers off?"

"We have six weeks for summer break," Louisa said. "And other breaks throughout the year."

"Okay." Friedrich checked the large watch on his wrist. "It is time now to learn about each of you. We will go around the circle beginning with" – he paused as he considered them, then pointed to Raina – "you."

She sat up in her squeaky chair. Ryan snickered in the seat next to her.

Raina was petite like her mother, her legs slender and tan in dark shorts with white flowers on them. Her features were delicate and, if she hadn't opened her mouth while they were sorting costumes, might have been mistaken for being sweet.

"Tell us your name, how old you are, where you are from, and an interesting fact about yourself," Friedrich instructed.

Birdie groaned inside.

Not an interesting fact.

She had many facts about herself, none of which she wanted to share with the group.

Her mind raced. What was she going to say?

She couldn't tell them about her dad and Jonah. Not yet. Probably never. Except for Kayla, these were strangers she'd know for two days. And she'd only known Kayla a few days longer than that.

She racked her brain to come up with something to share.

She couldn't tell them how she got the bruise on her forehead or about the aventurine. They'd think she was lying.

She thought about school but came up blank. Other than the fact that her friends had all started avoiding her, her school life was pretty boring. She played the flute. Woo-hoo.

"I'm Raina Hennessey. I'm fifteen and I'm from Brooklyn. That's a part of New York City. An interesting fact about me is that this is my first time out of the United States."

That was a good answer. Relevant but not too personal.

"Did you only just arrive in Europe?" Louisa asked.

Raina nodded. "Yes. We flew into Frankfurt yesterday morning and took a train here to a small town called" – she glanced at her brothers for confirmation – "Bach Rock?"

"Bacharach, yes." Louisa smiled. "That is near my village. Welcome to Germany. We are honored to be your first stop."

"Thanks." Raina leaned back in her chair.

"Next." Friedrich nodded at Ryan.

"Ryan Hennessey. Thirteen. Brooklyn. I play baseball."

"Baseball. I see. A true American sport. Do you hit the ball well?" Friedrich asked.

Ryan shrugged. "Well enough."

"Then we will have a job for you in our blacksmith shop, pounding the iron into swords and spears. And what brings you to Camp Rheinfels?"

Ryan poked his thumb at his brother. "Ask him."

"Ah yes." Friedrich sat back and gestured to Rich.

"Yeah, it was my idea to come to camp." He had a calm air about him, as if he spent a lot of time reading or conducting research. He was cute in a noble kind of way, like a knight of Camelot. "I'm into history and I thought it'd be cool to explore the ruins here." He glanced at Ryan and Raina. "I didn't think our parents would make them come too."

Ryan harrumphed, and Raina bumped his shoulder with hers. "Could it be worse?"

"Not sure how."

"Anyway, I'm sixteen, also from Brooklyn obviously, and I like to play video games like *Dragon Age* and *Skyrim*."

Louisa's face lit. "You'll enjoy the festival then. You'll feel like you're in one of those games."

"Sweet. And just so you know, my brother? He's more

than just okay at hitting. He's the best on his team."

"In our league," Raina added.

"And it's a big league," Rich said.

Ryan sat up taller.

"Okay, so now we know a bit about the Hennesseys," Friedrich said. "What about the two of you? You are brother and sister, too, yes?"

"Yes," Sophia said. "We're twins. I'm Sophia and this is Samuel, but he goes by Sam—"

"Tell us an interesting fact about yourself, Sophia," Louisa cut in gently, "and then Sam can tell us his."

Sophia nodded and Birdie noticed how pretty she was, her skin glowing in the dim light as if she'd brought a piece of the Hawaiian sun with her to Germany. Her black hair was long and glossy, while Sam's was short and neatly styled.

"My interesting fact is that I'm the president of our school's puzzle club," she said. "I founded it last year."

Another excellent answer. Birdie had never heard of a puzzle club, but if her school had one, she would not be its president or founder.

"Interesting," Friedrich said. "What kind of puzzles does your club solve?"

"All kinds," Sophia said eagerly. "Normal ones like crossword puzzles and jigsaw puzzles, of course, but we also study old puzzles. You wouldn't believe how many types there were – in fact, many of them were originally from Europe. Others came from China. I can go over some of them if you'd like me to."

"Maybe later." Friedrich held up his hand. "Sam?"

The twins were not tall, but when Sam adjusted his

posture, he seemed to take command of the room.

"I'm the president of the entrepreneur's club at my school. We figure out how to start businesses and make them succeed."

Of course he had a great answer too. It also explained why he was so good at managing the costume sorting.

Friedrich considered Sam. "You might be a good fit as our baker's apprentice. Herr Becker could use some business guidance."

Louisa barked a laugh beside him, then covered her mouth with her hand.

"Sure, I'll help," Sam said. "But why is it funny?"

Louisa's eyes grew wide. "Oh, I meant nothing by it. It's just that Herr Becker has a reputation for not being very nice to his customers."

"Got it. I can help him with that."

"I will mark it down," Friedrich said. "And now for our early Birdie."

Here it was.

"Yes. That's me. My name is Birdie Blessing and I'm fifteen. I'm from Bamburg, Pennsylvania and… something interesting about me?"

She paused.

Kayla sat back and raised her eyebrows, waiting.

That gave her an idea. "Something interesting about me is that I met Kayla earlier this week at a bed-and-breakfast in a town called Bruges in Belgium."

"You met in a different country?" Ryan shook his head slightly. "I thought you guys knew each other from home."

"No, we—"

"So, that just leaves me." Kayla leaned into the circle before Birdie could finish. "My name is Kayla and I'm seventeen, so older than all you shrimps except for Fred."

"Friedrich," he corrected.

"I'm from Akron, Ohio and my interesting fact is that when I met Birdie in Bruges, she took me back in time using a magical piece of glass that she is probably hiding right here – right now – in this very room."

CHAPTER FOUR

Birdie clenched her fists in her lap. Just what she needed. She should have known Kayla would pull a stunt like that.

Sam and Sophia exchanged a puzzled expression, as if trying to decide if they'd heard correctly. The others appeared equally bewildered.

Birdie wasn't sure what to do. Should she say something? But what could she possibly say?

Louisa chuckled, breaking the awkward silence. "So Kayla's interesting fact is she's a storyteller. We must all remember that."

Kayla sat back in her chair and examined her fingernails with a satisfied smile.

"Okay, very good," Louisa continued. "So now that we know each other better, it's time to explore the fortress." She surveyed the group, stopping at Kayla's sandaled feet. "Do you have trainers? Or sneakers? In America, you call them sneakers, yes?"

"Me?" Kayla flexed her feet so everyone could admire her strappy shoes. "No. No trainers or sneakers. But I'm good in sandals. Ask Birdie."

"You are sure?" Louisa didn't look convinced.

"I have nothing to change into, so yes, I'm sure."

"You may have trouble on the path with this morning's rain, but let's hope not, okay?"

Birdie was first up the stairs and out into the sun, soaking in its warmth after the chill of the damp storeroom. She followed Louisa down a path of crushed sand and through the stone archway that sheltered the ticket booth.

The woman who'd unlocked the storeroom for her earlier that morning sat in the booth on a barstool. Her dark hair was chopped short, with severe bangs that emphasized the slope of a long nose. She narrowed her eyes at each camper as they passed, as if trying to memorize their faces.

Louisa leaned toward Birdie. "Don't worry about Frau Hamel. She takes her job too seriously sometimes, they tell me."

"Who tells you?" Birdie dragged her gaze away from the woman.

"The people who hired me as camp counselor. They told me this is the normal way for her."

"Normal? You mean she studies everyone who walks by?"

Louisa shrugged. "Normal. She watches everyone like a hawk."

They followed the path until they were out of Frau Hamel's sight, passing a sprawling gift shop that was closed up tight. They skirted the main gate, where an idling tour bus waited to unload its passengers, and continued onto the paved parking lot, which felt modern and out of place among the stone ruins. A few cars were already there, parked at the very edge of the lot.

The sky was blue and clear, any remnant of the morning rain long since blown away on the breeze. Birdie took a deep breath of fresh summer air, grateful to be above ground.

She was aware of Kayla several steps behind her and made a point of keeping some space between them. How could she trust her after what she'd said during the introductions? She didn't want the other campers to paint her with the same brush, to think they were old friends when they barely knew each other at all.

Not that Kayla had lied, but no one else needed to know about the aventurine. That interesting fact was best kept hidden.

Louisa led them up a steep grade to the top of the lot while Friedrich brought up the rear, as if they were toddlers in danger of wandering off.

"Will we have time to check out the gift shop?" Sam called to Louisa. He was walking in the middle of the pack with Rich and Ryan.

She'd reached the remains of a low stone wall at the parking lot's edge and stopped. "Of course. We make time always for shopping. Now, everyone is here, yes?"

"They all made it," Friedrich announced from the back of the group.

"Okay, good." She fit her sneaker into a small hole in the crumbled stone and hoisted herself to the top of the wall. It was broad enough that she could stand without fear of falling into the woods below.

She towered there, facing the campers with her arms spread wide and her braid dangling down her back. "Now, please turn around in a circle, slowly, and tell me what you see."

No one moved.

"Yes, yes, I know this is strange. A very slow circle, please, each of you. It will be fun. I promise."

Ryan pivoted first. "A parking lot."

"Yes, of course. What else?"

"Treetops." Sophia pointed to the sprawling vista behind Louisa's perch. "And vineyards on the hills beyond them."

"Yes." Louisa glanced over her shoulder, then turned back to them. "All that land once belonged to the fortress. Even now, forest paths switchback down this mountain to a stream, and then wind back up to the vineyards. The servants climbed the paths, but they were too steep for horses, so the farmers used the main road." She pointed to the two-lane road that Birdie's mom had driven up, just beyond the gate where the tour bus idled. "They cut the road through the fields to bring the harvest to the fortress gates."

"What else do you see?" Friedrich had snaked through the group and positioned himself in front of Louisa, only standing on the ground.

Birdie turned a half-circle. "Destruction."

The bombed-out ruins begged to be explored, even though they were nothing like the elegant Burg Eltz she'd toured the day before.

"Yes." Friedrich bobbed his head approvingly. "From here, you can see the outline of the massive fortification walls that once surrounded the fortress. Some still stand, but Napoleon's troops destroyed the others in the 1800s."

"Why?" Ryan asked.

"This part of Germany switched from German to French control and back again many times," Rich explained to his brother before Friedrich could answer. "They destroyed the castles to show who had more power. But it was senseless."

"It's a shame that Burg Rheinfels was destroyed, yes." Louisa pointed to the heart of the ruin. "What's left of the original keep – or castle – is under the flags with the dragons on them. A few walls still stand, although you must try to imagine them several stories higher and joined by a gabled roof made of dark slate tiles. There were windows, too, outlined by red sandstone and dark wooden frames."

Birdie contemplated the piles of rubble, trying to imagine the fortress as it must have been.

"All the stone is now weathered and worn down," Friedrich added, "but the buildings were once painted bright white, with flags flying from the tallest towers. Everyone respected and feared the powerful family who lived here."

"As you imagine the white keep standing tall, notice the remnants of several other buildings in the courtyard. There was a busy village within these walls." Louisa pointed out each crumbled structure as she spoke. "That was a chapel. Next to it was an apothecary. Then came the brewery, and the kitchen. Then the blacksmith and the stables. The armory for weapons was there." She kept gesturing to sad piles of rubble that encircled the former keep. "On this side, there's a stack of old cannonballs, the guards' quarters, and the place where the dungeon once stood."

"Dungeon?" Ryan grinned. "When do we see that?"

"We will explore the grounds later," Friedrich said. "But it is important that you first understand what you are seeing." He gestured to the fortification walls again. "Back then, the fortress was heavily guarded. Soldiers patrolled these walls to be sure no one launched a sneak attack. Tunnels led from building to building. Some tunnels still exist, although most have collapsed with time. Important structures were underground, too, like the dungeon. We will visit each ruined structure later today."

"What else do you notice?" Louisa swiveled her hand so the group would continue its rotation.

"The river." Raina's back was now to Louisa. "It's way down there, beyond that fortification wall."

From high on the hill where they stood, the wide expanse of the Rhine River rippled like a ribbon between rocky cliffs and steep vineyards.

"The river was the whole reason Burg Rheinfels existed," Friedrich said. "It brought ships, and with them, gold and riches. The landowners along the river levied tolls on those ships and goods. It's why there were so many castles along the Rhine and why Sankt Goar was teeming with action back then. Crews moored their vessels at the docks and went into town to celebrate their safe passage through the Loreley."

"What's the Loreley?" Kayla asked.

"Do you see the sharp curve in the river?" Louisa tented her hand over her eyes as she peered upstream. "Many sailors met their deaths on the outcroppings beneath that steep slate rock. They blamed it on a fair maiden, a siren called the Loreley, whose voice drew them toward the rock and, of course, to certain death."

"She enchanted the men with her flowing hair, and they could not resist her song when she called to them," Friedrich added.

Kayla loosened the clip that held her hair, allowing it to fan across her shoulders.

"The Loreley is one of many legends about the river," Louisa said.

"The hillsides, too, would have been busy," Friedrich continued. "Particularly in autumn when it was time to harvest the grapes to make wine. This area of Germany was famous for its white wine – it still is – although some villages on the other side of the river insisted on making reds. No one trusted the villages that trafficked in red wine, and they struggled to compete. That led to wars, battles, marriages, and surprise attacks."

"Because the more land you had, the more of the river you controlled," Rich said, more to himself than to the group, as he studied the view below them. "And the more tolls you could collect from those ships."

"Exactly. And Burg Rheinfels was by far the largest fortress of them all," Friedrich said.

They stood at the top of the parking lot a few minutes longer, admiring the landscape as the cool breeze softened the heat of the mid-morning sun.

Far below them, the narrow village of Sankt Goar nestled in the gorge, the window boxes on its half-timbered houses overflowing with flowers. A two-lane road skirted the village and hugged the riverbank, separated from the water by a wide bike lane. On one end of the village, Birdie could just make out the municipal parking lot where her mother had left their rental car overnight, and on the other end, Hotel Flussufer.

Barges, laden with huge containers, and river cruise ships, laden with old people, slid past each other in the calm water.

"Where are they going?" Sam asked.

"The cruise ship? To Amsterdam," Louisa said. "They follow the Rhine from Switzerland and go all the way to the North Sea."

As Birdie listened to Louisa and Sam, she felt a prickle at the back of her neck. She didn't turn right away, hoping the feeling would go away and not wanting to know what might be behind her. Despite the warm sun, she shivered. It definitely felt as if someone were watching them.

She turned around slowly, peering past Louisa, who gave her a funny look, to the forest and the vineyards beyond. She scanned the treetops but saw nothing, not even a bird. Maybe there were hikers back there or workers. The ghosts of her brother and father were certainly not there, hiding beneath the trees, haunting her even here.

She was so focused on the woods that she didn't notice Kayla step up beside her until it was too late.

"Do you have the aventurine?" she asked, following Birdie's gaze across the treetops.

"No," she lied, keeping her voice low so the others wouldn't hear. "And what was the big idea bringing it up back there? No one else needs to know. No one else should know. They wouldn't believe it anyway."

"Where is it?" Kayla seemed unfazed.

"At the hotel." She turned away from the woods. The sensation of being watched had dropped away, allowing her to focus on shooing Kayla from her side.

"Why didn't you bring it?"

"Seriously?" She gestured to all the rubble. "Think about it. Would you really want to mess with that thing here?"

Kayla shrugged. "Why not? This camp is lame. Besides, we could see how Fred reacts."

"No." Birdie shook her head. "That would be ludicrous."

"Maybe." Kayla stepped back toward the others. "But you're no fun."

Medieval fortresses had towering castle keeps adorned by flags that presented the colors of the ruling family. Villages thrived inside their thick stone walls, and they made room to protect those who lived nearby during an attack. Their gray ruins are scattered across Europe, haunted by time and battles. —Marty McEntire, *Europe for Americans Travel Guide*

CHAPTER FIVE

The rest of the morning passed quickly as they explored the nooks and crannies of the ruined fortress, navigating the crumbling stairs to the top of the remaining fortification walls, tracing the patrol routes of the medieval guards, and marveling at the bird's-eye view up and down the river.

On the road below, rumbling buses came and went, delivering a United Nations of tourists to the grounds. Birdie and the others peered at them through slits just wide enough for an arrow to slide through and stuck their heads out of murder holes that had once been used to pour hot tar on invaders.

When they weren't up high fending off enemies or dodging camera-toting tourists, they went low, crawling through dark underground passages to reach other parts of the ruin. They visited the museum, too, a static collection of old cannonballs and glass cases filled with artifacts and maps.

By the time they returned to the storeroom two hours later, Birdie was dusty, hungry, and ready to sit down, no longer concerned about the cool, musty air. The lunch offering seemed like a feast on metal trays, and she wasted no time digging into a baguette lined with thinly sliced ham. She took a bag of chips and a small can of soda too.

Sam shoved the costume piles to one end of the table to give everyone a place to sit. Louisa clicked the music back on, and before long they'd emerged from tired hunger into lively conversation.

"I hate to break up the party," Friedrich said a while later, not sounding particularly sorry as he interrupted Sophia, who'd been describing what it was like to live near the beaches in Hawaii. "But only five minutes remain before we begin our next activity."

"You can finish telling me later," Birdie said.

Sophia nodded and smiled.

"What's next?" Sam asked as he reached for another baguette. "The gift shop?"

"Next, we determine your roles in the pageant," Friedrich said. "And we must go through the costumes and find one that is appropriate for each of you."

"Are they clean?" Kayla eyed the garments suspiciously. She sat at the far end of the table, a few chairs removed from the rest of them.

"Of course," Friedrich said. "We clean them after each festival."

"Good." Kayla pushed her chair back and stretched her legs out long, crossing them at the ankles. "And after we get our costumes?"

"Then you will learn more about the roles you will play," he said. "It is vital that you are believable. The festival is important to Burg Rheinfels and we must maintain its reputation. So, take a few minutes now to clean up and then we will start."

"I'll be right back," Birdie told Sophia, checking her watch as she grabbed her pack. She tossed her mini soda can into a recycling bin near the door as she made her way up the stairs and outside to the ladies room, which was across the path from the ticket kiosk.

To her relief, the booth was dark and there was no sign of Frau Hamel. A paper clock stuck to the window showed she'd be back after lunch.

Although the restroom had modern plumbing, the workers at Burg Rheinfels had tried hard to make it look like it was from the Middle Ages. To flush the toilet, Birdie yanked hard on a long wooden handle that was suspended from a chain in the ceiling. To wash her hands, she used an iron pump to push water into a massive stone basin.

She was turning to leave when she glimpsed herself in the wavy mirror above the basin and realized that the breeze during the walk along the fortification walls had not been kind. She pulled her brush from her pack and repositioned the swoosh of bangs over the bruise on her forehead. She considered the result.

Not bad. Not bad at all, really.

But… how could she look so normal?

This camp, this day, was so not normal. Nothing had been normal for a very long time.

Normal was swimming at the pool with her friends or

going to the library to get the summer reading books her teachers always assigned. Normal was going on vacation with her dad and mom and Jonah.

Normal was definitely not staring at herself in a creepy mirror in a foreign country, alone, after running around a bombed-out fortress all morning with a bunch of strangers.

So much had changed, and yet the same girl stared back at her from the mirror.

Voices outside broke her train of thought. She slipped the brush back into the pack and opened the door, smiling weakly at the mom and little girl waiting there.

She flung her pack onto her shoulder and headed down the sunny path to the storeroom. There were no trees in the stone ruins for shade, although she imagined that as the day went on, the walls would cast long shadows. She considered taking a side trip to the gift shop to find a pair of sunglasses, but then imagined Friedrich sending out a search party and thought better of it.

She was still thinking about the gift shop when a pinpoint of heat radiated against her back.

She stopped in the middle of the path and glanced up at the sky.

The heat couldn't be from the sun. It was too focused, too limited to one small spot.

She wiggled her hand into the space between her pack and her back, trying in vain to rub the spot. Her heartbeat quickened as she realized the heat was coming from inside her pack – and getting hotter. She swung it from her shoulder and, kneeling along the path, rummaged inside until she found its source.

The aventurine.

"No," she whispered as she pulled out the small piece of cloth. "Not here. Please, not here."

She glanced up and down the path. The nearest tourists were several yards away and hadn't seemed to notice her.

She carefully unfolded the cloth, revealing the quarter-sized piece of glass, its rich cinnamon hue enlivened by golden speckles. It was the first time she'd looked at it since she'd left Bruges and a wave of memories flooded back.

Ben trapped in the old bar.

Henri running from those awful boys.

The dead expression in Eva's eyes.

They'd escaped, but it had been close. It had been Kayla who'd come through in the end. She needed to remember that.

The small piece of glass was as beautiful as she remembered, its golden speckles swimming in the coppery background. The souvenir. That's what Ben had called it.

She ran her thumb over its surface, which was growing hotter.

She glanced around. Everything still seemed okay – the sandy path, the tourist group making its way toward a bus outside the gate.

But the speckles continued to swirl, glowing brilliantly.

Birdie knew what would happen next – they would slam together into a shape. A shape that was a clue. A shape that wouldn't change until she figured out what it meant.

"Bist du verloren?"

Birdie closed her fist around the aventurine, praying it didn't get any hotter. She looked up, her alarm growing at the sight of Frau Hamel.

Had she seen the glass?

"You are lost?" Frau Hamel switched to English.

"No, ma'am." Birdie stood and brushed the sand from her bare knees. "Er, *nein*. Sorry. I don't speak German. Just headed back to camp."

Frau Hamel eyed the storeroom door. "It will be cooler in there, out of the sun."

"Yes, ma'am."

She slipped the glass into her pack and hurried down the path, trying to process what just happened. As much as she wanted to be sure of what she'd glimpsed on its surface, she didn't dare take the glass from her pack again. She could feel Frau Hamel's hawkish glare on her back, and knew the woman wouldn't turn away until she was in the classroom.

But Birdie had seen the image as she closed her hand, if only for an instant.

It was a flower.

A beautiful rose.

CHAPTER SIX

"You are late." Friedrich checked his watch as he hovered near the table with a stack of papers.

Birdie paused at the top of the stone stairs, her heart pounding, as she waited for her eyes to adjust to the gloom. "Sorry."

She crossed to the table where the others sat looking bored. The music and conversation were gone.

She slipped into a seat between Kayla and Sophia and cradled the pack in her lap.

"Are you okay?" Sophia asked. "You don't look so good."

"It's hot out there."

"Do you need a glass of water?"

"No, I'm good. Thanks, though. Did I miss anything?"

Sophia looked concerned but didn't press the issue. "Not really. We're just getting started."

"Welcome back," Louisa said from her seat at the far end

of the table. "Friedrich, the character sheets?"

Birdie's fingers trembled as he handed her a sheet. She inhaled deeply and willed her nerves to settle as she set the paper on the table and clasped her hands on top of her pack.

Friedrich waited beside her.

She leaned forward and read the title. "A lady's maid?"

"Yes, that's right." Louisa couldn't hide the excitement in her voice. "You will be a lady's maid for me. They have selected me to play Princess Elisabeth this year. Don't worry. We'll have fun."

"Who selected you?" Sam asked.

"It was part of the interview. Camp counselors must also play roles at the festival."

"So what are you?" Kayla asked Friedrich.

Birdie would not have thought it possible, but somehow Friedrich straightened his spine even more. "I am the prince. Prince Gunzelin."

"Of course you are." Kayla twisted her lips. "That's the one who doesn't get the girl, right?"

"That is correct."

"Do you play the prince at the second festival, too? The one she marries?"

Friedrich shifted uncomfortably.

"No. There is another boy here who plays that role," Louisa said. "He normally assists Frau Hamel with selling tickets on busy days."

"Is he cute?" Kayla's gaze shifted from Friedrich to Louisa, whose cheeks flushed pink.

"That's a yes," Raina said from the other end of the

table, where she sat with her brothers.

Friedrich scowled and adjusted his papers. "Enough of that. As you know, you must learn to be villagers who work at the castle. You will each have a position of importance. You must stay in character throughout the pageant and" – he paused and glared at Kayla – "be nice to the tourists."

He crossed the room and rummaged in a large wooden box.

"What's he doing?" Birdie whispered, loosening her grip on the pack as the glass cooled. She was afraid it would activate again and prayed it wouldn't happen before she figured out how to get it out of there.

"No idea," Sophia whispered.

Friedrich yanked an enormous black hammer from the box and used both hands to lug it to the table. He plopped it down in front of Ryan with a thud. "As decided during introductions, you will assist the blacksmith."

Ryan snorted as he picked up the ridiculous hammer. "This is no bat." He positioned it to take a swing but a sharp look from Rich stopped him. "What? I was just gonna test it out." Ryan shrugged as he set the hammer back on the table with a clunk.

"And Sam will be the baker." Friedrich turned to the others. "Birdie is the lady's maid for Louisa as part of the duke's royal family. We still need a guard, a seamstress, and someone to manage the stables."

"You may have other roles to play, too, depending on how many local volunteers they have for the pageant," Louisa said.

"I'm still a little unclear." Ryan snatched up his character sheet and eyed it suspiciously. "What's going to happen exactly at this pageant?"

"It's like the finale of a play," Louisa explained. "It's a bit of a parade and a performance all in one, and all the reenactors take part."

"Can we pick the role we want to play?" Sophia asked. "Or are you assigning them all?"

"You can pick your role from the ones Friedrich just listed. Did you have something in mind?"

"Managing the stables. I love horses."

"They have horses in Hawaii?" Raina asked.

"Very well." Friedrich rustled through the sheets and handed one to Sophia.

"So that leaves Rich, Raina, and Kayla," Louisa said. "Do you have any preferences?"

"I'll go for the guard." Rich sat back in his chair. "No one would take me seriously as a seamstress. Will I get to wear armor?"

"Not heavy armor." Friedrich handed him the character sheet. "But we can see if there is any chainmail around."

"I saw some," Sam said. "When we were sorting the costumes."

"Cool," Rich said.

"I guess I can be the seamstress," Raina said. "But I don't know how to sew."

"But you know how to dance," Louisa said. "And that will come in handy for the pageant."

"Dancing?" Ryan scrunched his nose as if he'd tasted something rotten.

"I'll be the back-up princess," Kayla offered. "You know,

like an understudy."

"No. Friedrich and I play the roles of prince and princess. We'll find a role for you, don't worry."

"Frau Hamel may need help in the ticket kiosk," Friedrich said.

"Maybe you can be the executioner," Birdie murmured.

"Very funny. Hey, I have a question."

Louisa raised her eyebrows.

"What if we don't stay for the sleepover? Who plays these roles, then?"

"The lock-in is optional," Louisa said. "Most campers who don't stay overnight still take part in the festival and leave with their parents when it's done."

"Aren't you staying?" Raina asked.

Kayla shrugged. "Not sure."

"Okay." Friedrich checked his watch again. "Take five minutes to study your character sheets."

Ryan scanned his sheet and tossed it onto the table.

"That was fast," Sam said without looking up from his own paper.

"I'm an apprentice to the blacksmith. I hit things. What else do I need to know?"

"What to wear, for one thing," Sophia said. "And how you're supposed to behave."

Ryan rocked back on his chair, peering over Sam's shoulder at his sheet as he did. "The baker's apprentice is a good gig. At least you get to eat."

"Yeah, but you get to smack things. Besides, this says I'm not allowed to eat. At least not in front of the tourists."

"I'm sure you'll be able to sneak it. Maybe you can bring

me a piece of cake or something. I'll need some strength to deal with this hammer. It's heavy as—"

"A bat?" Rich glanced up from his own paper.

"Yeah, if they made it out of lead. See for yourself." Ryan dropped his chair forward with a thump and used both hands to push the hammer across the table. Rich lifted it with an effort, then passed it to Sam.

Birdie stared at her character sheet, unseeing.

Why hadn't she remembered to take the aventurine out of her pack, to squirrel it away in the hotel safe with her passport?

She tried to think of an excuse to leave camp, something that would give her enough time to hike down the hill to the hotel, hide the glass in her room, and get back. That would take at least an hour and there was no reason she could think of that would excuse her that long.

She closed her eyes, took a deep breath, and opened them again. She just needed to stay calm and she would come up with something.

In the meantime, she forced herself to study the character sheet, to read the words.

She was to wear a plain black dress made of wool over a collection of underskirts, and wrap her head in a white scarf. The scarf in the photograph had a weird bulge in the back, so her hair probably had to be in a bun. At least the fabric would cover her bruise.

She was going to sweat to death, she was sure of it. She was suddenly grateful they held camp in the storeroom, where it always stayed cool.

Except for that small spot in her pack, she realized with a

start. It had fired up again, and the heat radiated against her lap. She clamped her hand down over it and prayed for it to cool down. She peeked up and down the table, relieved to see that no one was looking at her.

A scraping noise across the storeroom drew her attention as a different world shimmered into view. It was hazy, as if superimposed on the real world around her.

Please don't do this here.

The scene was translucent, more of a reflection than reality. In the shimmer, the stone walls were lined with barrels and casks, with cinched sacks piled against them. A heavyset, bearded guard slouched at a table near the wall, his long leather vest hanging open as he snored.

Birdie drew in a breath when she saw the symbol stitched in gold thread on his chest.

A flower.

A rose.

As she strained to make out the details of the room, a thin girl drifted past the guard, her slippered feet barely touching the floor. She couldn't have been more than seven or eight years old.

She pushed a tiny hand into one of the sacks and wiggled her fingers to loosen the tie. She kept close watch on the guard as she retrieved a handful of something small, but he didn't wake. She moved like a ghost back across the storeroom, disappearing through a narrow opening in the far wall.

"Birdie?" Kayla's voice was barely a whisper. "Are you seeing this?"

She swallowed.

"You brought the glass here?"

"What is up with this glass you keep talking about?" Sam dropped Ryan's blacksmith hammer on the table with a clunk. "Or are you telling stories again?"

The guard grunted, waking as he faded away.

"More like lies," Sophia said under her breath.

Kayla and Birdie were silent, staring at the place where the guard had been.

"Hello?" Sam waved his hand in front of her face. "Kayla?"

She shook her head as she turned toward him, slowly coming back to reality. "I told you Birdie found a piece of glass that made magic." She glared at Sophia. "And it isn't a lie. The only one who lied around here is Birdie."

Birdie searched for a distraction. "Hey, Sam – is that your blacksmith hammer?"

"No." He sounded disappointed as he picked it up again with both hands and swung it around. "It's Ryan's. I'm the baker, remember?"

"Whoa, careful there." Friedrich made his way over to the table.

"It's heavier than it looks." Sam handed it back to Ryan.

Kayla ignored the boys. "Let me see the glass."

"No." Birdie slipped the pack onto the back of the chair and stood up. "We're not doing this here."

"I think we already have." Kayla gestured toward the place where the guard and the girl had shimmered into existence.

Birdie pushed her chair away from the table and crossed the storeroom. She ran her hand along the cold gray stone where the girl had disappeared and, sure enough, found an angled opening camouflaged along it.

That must have been how Friedrich snuck up on her that morning.

"Where does this go?" she called to him.

"To an office on the lower level of the museum. We use it for camp materials. How did you know it was there?"

CHAPTER SEVEN

Birdie stepped through the angled opening in the wall and into a narrow, curving tunnel. It was clean and level – unlike the dirt passages they'd crawled through earlier in the day – with round lights embedded in the floor to illuminate the path to the museum.

"Birdie?" Friedrich's voice sounded muffled as he called to her from the storeroom.

She pressed deeper into the passageway. Several yards down, the tunnel split into three sections, one leading to the museum and the others leading off in distant directions. She started down the one to the right, but stopped when she heard Friedrich again.

"Birdie!" He was shouting now, a note of warning in his voice. "Birdie! Come back here!"

She glanced heavenward. She really did not want to have to deal with Friedrich. She turned around and headed back to the storeroom.

"Are you ready for tomorrow, then?" He was hovering in the opening with his hands on his hips and had to take a step back as she exited.

"Not quite." She should have said *not at all*. She wasn't ready for anything.

At least now she understood how the girl, and Friedrich, had slipped in and out of the storeroom so easily, but that did little to ease her mind. She needed to get the aventurine out of the fortress. Its connection to the past was stronger in the storeroom than it had been outside, and she guessed it would continue to intensify, just as it had in Bruges. The last thing she needed was to disappear into the past with everyone watching.

And who knew what she would find if she did? This was an armed fortress, and she was a teenage girl in shorts and a T-shirt. Not good.

To make matters worse, Kayla had seen the guard and the girl, too, so if the aventurine activated, she'd be right there with her.

If only she hadn't let her touch the glass in Bruges.

"Better get busy." Friedrich was still speaking to her, she realized. "You have an important role."

"I'm a servant." She met his close-set eyes.

"Yes, but you assist Princess Elisabeth, so it is important."

"It is a good role," Louisa called, smiling from the end of the table where she was helping Raina and Rich figure out their costumes. "I promise."

Birdie returned her smile, but she didn't feel very happy. She made her way to her seat and picked up her character sheet. She might need to make herself throw up or get a nosebleed or something equally horrible. That was the only way out of this.

Kayla bumped her arm.

"What?"

When she didn't respond, Birdie twisted in the chair to face her. "What?"

Kayla held the aventurine in the air between her thumb and forefinger.

Anger flared through her. "Give it here." She pushed her chair back and stood with one hand outstretched. "I mean it. Give it to me now."

The other campers stopped what they were doing and stared at them.

"What is it?" Raina leaned forward.

"Should we go for a walk?" Kayla twitched the aventurine in her fingers so the gold caught what little light there was in the room. "See what this place was really like?"

"Give it back."

"It's getting warmer—"

"I said give it back to me. It doesn't belong to you."

Friedrich made his way over to stand between them. "There is a problem?"

She gritted her teeth. "Kayla stole a souvenir from my bag and I would like it back."

"Is this true?"

Kayla shrugged.

"Return Birdie's property," Friedrich sighed, not bothering to hide his irritation.

Across the room, the crates shimmered back into view,

barely there.

"Kayla." Birdie watched the crates become clearer. "We need to—"

"Sure, Fred." A slow smile spread across Kayla's lips. "Whatever you say." She lifted the glittering piece of glass on her palm and, with a flick of her wrist, tossed it to him.

"No!" Birdie cried. But it was too late.

Friedrich caught the aventurine in midair. "Ow – it's hot."

"Nice catch," Ryan said.

But Friedrich didn't respond. He was gazing around the storeroom. *"Was zur Hölle—"*

Louisa stood. "What is it, Friedrich?"

Birdie touched his elbow. "It's okay." She hoped the others wouldn't hear, which was stupid, since everyone in the room was watching them. "Just give me the glass and I will fix this."

The bearded guard emerged from the tunnel, very much awake. He was beefy and strong, and he started when he saw them.

"Um, Birdie…" Kayla scrambled back, knocking her chair to the ground. "I think he sees us."

"Give it to me now, Friedrich," Birdie urged as the guard drew his weapon.

Friedrich gaped at the burly man.

Birdie grabbed his thin wrist and shook it hard. He released his grip on the aventurine, and it tumbled into her hand as the other campers faded away.

The guard unsheathed his sword. He growled something in German, and the color drained from Friedrich's face.

The guard charged toward them, shimmering into better focus as he advanced.

"Run!" Kayla yelled. She darted up the stairs and yanked the heavy door open wide. Tourists and villagers shuffled by, completely unaware of each other.

Birdie shoved the hot glass into her pocket and ran after her as a clatter filled the air. She pivoted in time to see the guard fade off, the tip of his sword just inches from Friedrich's chin.

He stood frozen, his arms raised in surrender, staring into the empty space.

"I said, what is going on?" Louisa set down the mallet she'd used to smack one of the metal lunch trays. The sound had reverberated through the room like a gong.

Friedrich spun to her, completely flustered.

"Birdie? Kayla?" Louisa demanded.

"It's… nothing." Kayla let the heavy door swing closed as she jogged down the steps. When she passed Birdie, she smiled. "So sorry about your toy. I just, you know, found it on the floor. If it means that much to you, you should really take better care of it."

"Why are you doing this?" Birdie said. "I thought we were friends."

Friedrich had recovered enough to get angry. "Both of you. Outside. Now." He marched up the stairs.

Birdie followed him, but Kayla headed toward the table.

"You, too, Kayla," he said.

"Who died and made you boss?" She faced him and placed her hands on her hips.

"Go!" Louisa ordered from across the room, pointing to

the stairs. Beside her, Raina and Rich exchanged confused glances.

"Fine," Kayla huffed as she made her way back up the stairs.

Friedrich was silent as he marched down the path. He led them in the opposite direction of the ticket booth, away from Frau Hamel's hawkish eyes. Birdie sensed the anger rolling off him, as if it were taking all his strength to keep from whipping around and confronting them right there in the open air.

They moved deeper into the ruin, passing through the courtyard, which was thick with tourists, and past the crumbling structures they'd explored before lunch.

He continued until they reached the largest structure, which was the former keep. They hadn't entered it earlier – he'd said they weren't allowed inside because of its condition. Birdie could see why. The freestanding walls around them soared at least three stories high, with gaping holes near the top where arched windows had once protected the interior. The ceiling had long-ago lost its battle with the elements, or with cannon fire, and the blue sky was all that remained above them. The floor was carpeted with gravel, interrupted by patchy grass and weeds.

Despite the open air, they were quite alone.

"What is this place?" Kayla searched the sky as she did one final pivot.

"It was the great hall," Friedrich said. "In the keep."

"Not so great anymore."

Friedrich ignored her. "What happened back there?" he

asked Birdie.

Good question.

She thought about lying, telling him she wasn't sure what he was talking about, but that would be pointless. He'd seen the guard and the storeroom, and now he could never unsee it.

She started with the smallest amount of information she could.

"Kayla took my souvenir, and I wanted it back. She knew it was important to me."

"Yes, but what is that stone? It cannot be what Kayla says."

"It's not a stone. It's a type of glass called aventurine that was made in Venice in the Middle Ages."

Friedrich nodded. "I am familiar with the Murano Island near Venice. It is famous for glass. You bought it there?"

Birdie shook her head. "No. I found it. That sounds crazy, but that's what happened. I found it at the bed-and-breakfast my mom and I stayed at in Bruges. That's in Belgium. They have a legend about the glass there."

"Only it's not a legend," Kayla said. "It's real."

"I know where Bruges is." Friedrich looked at Kayla. "And you stayed there, too, at this bed-and-breakfast?"

"Yes, with my grandparents. I met Birdie there."

"And you've seen this glass before?"

"Yes. That's how I know it's real."

Birdie shot her a warning glance, but Kayla continued anyway. "You saw what happened, didn't you? How the storeroom shifted? It was full of food and supplies piled high. And the guard—"

"He was in costume." Friedrich rubbed his chin. "But I've not seen him here before."

"I'm sorry we disrupted the camp," Birdie said. "I won't bring the aventurine again."

"Oh, please." Kayla rolled her eyes. "He touched the damned thing so now he can see everything." She rounded on Friedrich. "How did the crates get into the storeroom?"

Birdie watched Friedrich closely. He seemed to wrestle with his thoughts, trying to fit what he knew and believed in with what he'd seen in the storeroom.

She understood how he felt. She hadn't wanted to believe either, as if believing in the aventurine meant admitting she'd lost her mind.

"I don't know. They could have been superimposed somehow, maybe with projectors."

"That guard," Kayla said, "wasn't a projection. And he wasn't in period costume. He was in period – period."

Friedrich considered her. "His sword was real."

Kayla moved closer to him. "If Birdie gives you the aventurine, I will show you how it works."

His eyes darted from Kayla to Birdie. He took a step back and hit the cool stone wall behind him.

Kayla slid in closer.

Friedrich ducked away from the wall and took two broad steps deeper into the keep. He held out his hand to keep Kayla from coming any nearer. "Birdie, it's up to you. You can end this now."

She considered her options. She doubted he would give up trying to figure out what had happened, despite appearing to give her a choice. "It's dangerous. We don't belong in that time and this was an armed fortress. You saw how the guard reacted when he saw us."

"Then you are telling me what Kayla says is true?" He narrowed his eyes. "Prove it."

She hesitated. "Okay. I will try to show you. Just once. Quickly. I can't exactly control the aventurine, so I'm not sure if it will work. But whether or not it does, I'm leaving camp and taking it back to the hotel."

Friedrich folded his arms. "Get on with it, then. The others are waiting."

Birdie retrieved the small piece of glass from her pocket.

The golden speckles were already swirling – the glass growing hot in her hand.

The crumbling walls shimmered.

CHAPTER EIGHT

The speckles in the aventurine swirled and glowed until the glass was almost too hot to hold. The Great Hall stretched and erupted with color as beams of sunlight shot through the stained glass windows.

"What is it doing?" Friedrich stared into Birdie's outstretched palm as the golden speckles flew together in the center of the glass. He brushed his finger across the surface. "What is that?"

"A shape. A clue, really. It looks like some kind of chest."

"A clue to what?"

"Um, we have bigger questions than that." Kayla's arms dropped to her sides. "Do you believe us now?"

The air had stopped shimmering, bringing the Great Hall into sharp focus. The once crumbling walls now stretched three stories higher, their unblemished surfaces soaring to a vaulted ceiling. Vivid lions and dragons glittered in the elaborate stained glass windows, and intricate tapestries graced every wall, lending a warmth to the space that Birdie would not have thought possible. It was colorful now, alive.

An enormous banquet table stretched roughly the length of the Great Hall, and heavy chairs with emerald cushions lined both sides. Beyond it, a large woman vigorously swept the tile floor. She wore an apron over a simple dress and a white kerchief over her hair.

Friedrich gaped at the scene before them. It was as if they'd stepped from a black-and-white photograph into a Technicolor movie.

Birdie rubbed her thumb across the surface of the warm aventurine. "Get us out of here," she whispered.

Friedrich set his hand over hers.

"What are you doing?" She tried to pull away, but he curled his fingers tight.

"We must stay. I must see this."

Kayla nudged her arm. "Birdie, we need to go!"

The glass cooled in her palm. She yanked again, but Friedrich's grip was so strong that her hand was losing circulation. She twisted toward Kayla. "It's not working. I—"

"What do you mean, it's not working?" Panic edged into Kayla's voice.

"I thought maybe if I rubbed it, we'd go back."

"Did that work before?"

"No, but Friedrich…" She jerked her hand, but he held tight.

"You don't know how it works?"

"You know I don't. You were in Bruges, you know we can't exactly control—"

"It is just as I imagined." Friedrich gazed at the Great Hall with wonder.

Birdie stopped tugging and wrinkled her brows at Kayla.

"Is he okay?" Kayla slanted her chin.

Birdie studied his awestruck face. "I'm not sure."

"It's just like the stories my mother told me." He stared at the tapestries on the walls. "Look at them – they show the harvest. And those portraits…" His voice faltered, and it took him a moment to continue. "Each member of the duke's family is there."

"Friedrich, we have to go." Birdie wrapped her other hand around his grip and attempted to pull him away. "We're going to get caught."

"There is the duke. And Princess Elisabeth. And there, beside her—"

The woman swiveled to clean a fresh area and saw them. Her reaction was immediate. She barreled toward them with the broom as if she planned to sweep them away with the dust and dirt. *"Sie! Dort! Aus! Aus!"*

Friedrich flinched and dropped his grip on Birdie's hand.

Kayla skittered backward on the tile. "What's she saying?"

"We must go." Friedrich seized their elbows with his long fingers and steered them toward the door. "Now!"

He shoved them through the entrance, which, to Birdie's dismay, no longer led outside. They were at the end of a lengthy corridor lined with gold and black banners emblazoned with coats of arms and flame-throwing dragons. Thick candles in heavy sconces lit the way to a massive door at the far end.

"This wasn't here before," Kayla said.

"No, it wasn't. Most of the keep was destroyed, remember?" Friedrich surveyed the corridor. "Hurry – this way!"

They sprinted to the door. Friedrich pulled the round iron handle and, as sunlight flooded the corridor, Birdie sent up quiet thanks that the door led outside rather than into another hall.

She followed Friedrich into the light and stopped short.

The courtyard, which had been barren except for tourists a few minutes before, was alive with people of all ages and persuasions dressed as if they were in the costumes they'd sorted that morning. The air was heavy with the fragrance of many things, some good – like baking bread – and others that were better to ignore. A thick layer of smoke clung to the sky, forming a haze and welcome cover to the worst of the smells.

Birdie pushed the aventurine into her pocket.

"We must hide." Friedrich kept his voice low. "Stay close to the wall. And stay down."

"Do you know where we're going?" Kayla said.

He scanned the courtyard. "I think so. This way."

They rounded a corner, and he disappeared through a slit in the stone wall. Birdie ducked in behind him and entered a narrow earthen tunnel. It was damp and cool compared to the hot sun outside. She hunched to clear the ceiling and squeezed against the dirt walls to avoid the torches that burned like beacons at each intersection.

She shivered. "Where does this lead?"

There was no need for Friedrich to answer – a moment later the tunnel ramped up and ended, dropping them back in the storeroom.

There was no sign of the camp or the other campers. The bearded guard sat on the rickety chair with his back to them, surrounded by crates and supplies. He held his sword at the ready, as if an enemy might pop up in front of him at any moment.

Friedrich put a finger to his lips and motioned back to the tunnel. They clustered there, watching the guard.

"What should we do?" Kayla whispered.

"Hide," Friedrich replied.

They held still in the gloomy tunnel, the only light coming from the flicker of a torch several yards away. Birdie scanned the web-like passageways that spiraled out, connecting the storeroom to the rest of the fortress. She was sure someone would come at any moment and catch them, hiding like mice.

It felt like forever before the guard moved, heaving himself from the chair and tipping it over on the way up. He bent to retrieve it, releasing a loud plume of gas as he did.

Kayla giggled.

Friedrich covered her mouth with his hand and leaned in close to her ear. "Shhh."

She stiffened, and he released her.

The guard checked his weapon then crossed to the stairs, which he mounted slowly, as if every joint in his body hurt. He pressed the door open, allowing daylight to gush into the storeroom before he disappeared outside. A heavy scraping sound signaled the placement of a wooden beam, and the door shook violently before they heard him move away.

Friedrich toppled out into the storeroom.

"Great, now we're locked in here." Kayla followed him and glared at the stairs.

"We can get out through the tunnels," Birdie said as she emerged. "We're not completely trapped."

"We will stay here." Friedrich seized the chair and set it upright. "I am not sure what is happening here, but I believe going back out there dressed like this is a bad idea. Especially you two."

"What's wrong with my outfit?" Kayla posed, her long legs crossed and her arms spread wide from her bare shoulders.

"Stop it, Kayla. You know he's right. We're in trouble here, and we need to get back to camp."

Kayla dropped her pose but not before winking at Friedrich, whose cheeks flushed red. "Besides, we're not really stuck, are we?" she said. "Camp should be right here."

"The room is the same." Friedrich turned in a slow circle. "But on the old maps, two tunnels emptied into the storeroom because of the water. Now there is only one."

Birdie couldn't tell if he was talking to them or to himself.

"What water?" Kayla asked.

"But it is the storeroom now, so that means it has to be at least the late 1400s."

"Friedrich? What are you talking about?" Kayla asked.

"The time period." He examined a sack leaning up against the wall. "It has to be at least the late 1400s because before that, this storeroom was part of the moat and there would have been two tunnels for the rainwater to flow through. If it were any earlier, we'd be swimming in here."

"A moat!" Kayla said. "You've got to be kidding me."

"No," Friedrich said. "I am not kidding you."

"Great. Well then, I guess things could be worse." She turned to Birdie. "How did you and Ben return to the present day in Bruges? Because rubbing the glass like it's Aladdin's lamp clearly isn't working."

Birdie thought about it. "Ben didn't make it back the one time, remember?"

"What?" Friedrich's eyebrows drew together.

"Well, he did eventually," Birdie reassured him. "It's complicated."

"When I was with you, there was a loud noise, something that kind of startled us back to the present," Kayla said.

"A taxi blew its horn. That happened twice." She turned to Friedrich. "The taxis in Bruges are ridiculous. They run people down."

He looked skeptical.

"And Louisa broke the connection when she smacked that lunch tray. It's like an auditory hammer smashed through the space-time continuum or something."

"So let's make a loud noise." Friedrich spied an iron crowbar several feet away. "That should work."

He retrieved the bar, held it high, and swung it hard, smacking a shield that hung from a thick rope on the wall.

Birdie clapped her hands over her ears as the sound reverberated through the storeroom, the noise deadening when it hit the stone walls.

Friedrich dropped the crowbar, which thumped against the hard dirt floor. He rubbed his arms.

"Are we back?" Kayla looked around.

Nothing had changed.

"Why didn't it work?" Friedrich demanded.

"I'm not sure." Birdie lowered her hands from her ears. "It was certainly loud enough."

"I thought you said it would work," he said.

Birdie rubbed her hands over her face and took a deep breath before she spoke. "If you wanted to get out of here, you should have kept your hands to yourself in the keep. I don't know if rubbing the hot aventurine would have worked because I didn't get the chance to try."

The wooden beam scraped against the door.

"Someone's coming!" Kayla crouched low. "Do something, would you?"

"It's the guard." Friedrich's voice trembled. "He's coming back."

"He must have heard us." Birdie surged toward the tunnel.

She was almost there when the scraping stopped. She peeked over her shoulder, expecting the guard to be staring back at her, but the door was still closed.

"Maybe he changed his mind?" Kayla said.

Then, from far away, a sharp noise broke through.

It sounded again, louder.

"What is that?" Kayla glanced around.

"No idea," Birdie said.

It sounded again and Louisa and the other campers shimmered into place, assembled at the long table as if nothing had happened at all.

"Louisa!" Friedrich cried. He bent forward and put his hands on his knees.

"What on earth?" She stood, handing Ryan the hammer and an iron spike. "Keep practicing."

Ryan took them from her but didn't move. He blinked hard. "How did you—"

"Birdie?" Sophia pushed her chair away from the table and stood.

And just like that, it was over.

They were in the modern-day storeroom, the leftover chips and sodas from lunch still sitting at one end of the table.

Silence spread as everyone stared at them.

Louisa broke it. "Where did you come from?"

"The tunnel." Kayla crossed the storeroom and slid into the chair next to Rich. "What are you working on?"

He stared at her, his lips parted.

Louisa gave Friedrich a hard look and said something to him in German.

His face flushed, and he looked down at his sneakers. "We have to tell her."

"Yes," Louisa said. "You do. Because I know you did not come through that tunnel."

Sophia approached Birdie. Sam got up and followed her. "I saw you," she whispered. "How did you do it?"

"We all saw you," Rich said from across the room.

"You just… appeared," Ryan said.

"It's the aventurine." Kayla spread her hands wide against the table. "I told you Birdie found a magic piece of glass in Bruges, but none of you believed me."

"I don't believe in magic." Sophia shot an annoyed look at Kayla. "It's a trick of some sort. An illusion. How did you do it?"

"Is it true, Birdie?" Sam asked. "Is Kayla telling the truth?"

Curiosity made Sophia's dark eyes sparkle. "Yes, an illusion. Can I see the glass?"

"That's not a good idea, Sophia," Birdie said.

"But if I see it, I'm sure I can figure out the trick. Or is that why you don't want me to see it?" She bit her bottom lip.

"I would like to see this so-called magical... what did you call it? Aventurine? I want to see it right now." Louisa held out her hand.

"Louisa," Friedrich began.

"Now. Or I'm sorry to say that I will be forced to call Birdie's parents and Kayla's grandparents to remove them from camp."

Birdie winced, and not just because Louisa assumed she had parents, plural.

She thought about her options, all of which stank.

If her mom had to abandon her research at Burg Eltz to pick her up, she'd never regain her trust. And if she gave Louisa the aventurine, she'd be one more person who knew the truth, who could see.

"I'll leave," she blurted. "I told Friedrich I'd take the aventurine home. There's no need to call my mom."

"Oh, no you don't." Friedrich straightened. "If you leave early, it will be because a parent picked you up."

"But—"

"Bring the aventurine here, Birdie," Louisa said.

She had to decide.

Louisa, though perfectly nice, was temporary, a blip, while her mom was permanent. The only permanent thing she had, really. She could live with Louisa learning the truth.

She didn't want to think about what would happen if she disappointed her mom again.

She pulled the piece of glass out of her pocket. The surface was cool, and the image of the golden chest held steady.

"Wait." Friedrich held up his hand. "Wait just a second." He rummaged in a box of camp supplies.

"What are you doing?" Louisa asked.

"Just give me a minute."

Birdie watched him search.

"Oh, for goodness' sake." Sam scooped the aventurine from her palm.

"No!" she cried.

"This is so cool." Sam turned it over in his hand. "Sophia, check out the sparkles!"

He passed it to her, and she studied it closely.

Birdie cradled her face in her palms.

"You sure did it now, Birdie," said Kayla, chuckling.

"Did what?" Raina came closer to peer over Sophia's shoulder. Sophia handed the glass to her for closer inspection, and, of course, she shared it with her brothers.

"What's it doing?" Ryan dropped it onto the wooden table. "It's getting hot."

"Give it—" Birdie began, but Louisa scooped it up.

"It is hot." She grabbed a petticoat from the costume pile to blunt the heat as she scrutinized it. She glanced up. "Birdie, what is this thing? Where did you get it?"

The storeroom shimmered.

"Not again," Kayla groaned.

CHAPTER NINE

The dull scrape of wood against wood echoed from the top of the stairs.

"What is happening?" Raina inched closer to Rich as crates, sacks, and barrels materialized around their stark classroom. "Birdie?"

"Shhh!" Friedrich sliced both hands through the air to silence her.

Birdie held her breath. There was nowhere to hide now, not for all of them. The guard would surely see them.

And then what?

A sliver of sunlight sliced through the room.

There was nothing left to do except wait for the guard to rumble down the stairs, take one look at them, and sound the alarm. They'd be captured, questioned, and held against their will.

A shadow passed through the opening, blocking the

sunlight as the door drifted shut.

Birdie gasped.

It was not the grizzled guard who'd slipped in, but a young woman in a black dress, her hair wrapped in a white scarf. She scurried down the stone steps in a rush of fabric, her gaze trained over her shoulder to ensure the heavy wooden doors stayed closed behind her.

She dipped into the shadows when she reached the storeroom floor, plastering her slight frame against the hard wall. She squeezed her eyes shut, her thin chest heaving in the cool, damp air.

Birdie glanced at the others, who had gone still.

The young woman regained her breath and opened her eyes, which grew wide at the sight of the stunned campers. She grasped her black skirts as if to flee, but then seemed to think better of it as hooves pounded the path above.

A guard – thinner and taller than the last, but with the same rose embroidered on his tunic – flung both doors wide as if they weighed nothing at all, thrust a torch into the storeroom, and waved it wildly.

He shouted as the golden light spilled over them.

"Nein!" Friedrich shouted back, pitching his voice a few octaves lower than normal.

Curiosity registered on the guard's face, and he squinted against the torchlight. He started down the steps as another regiment on horseback approached. He glanced over his shoulder at a passing guard, who yelled something that caused him to bound back up the stairs and outside.

The campers stood motionless as the doors drifted closed again, and remained that way until the clamor of the search party fell away.

Louisa cleared her throat. "Will someone please explain exactly what is going on?" She stepped forward and faced them. "Birdie—"

"*Dankeschön.*" The young woman's voice was barely audible from across the room. She slid down the wall to the dirt floor and covered her face with her hands. "*Danke.*"

"Is she saying thank you?" Birdie whispered to Louisa.

Louisa tilted her head as she considered the young woman. "She is."

"You're welcome." Rich pulled his attention away from the young woman and regarded the leather sacks and wooden barrels that lined the walls, the crates that teetered in towers toward the ceiling. He pointed to a pair of fiery torches illuminating the room and turned to Birdie. "What happened to this place? Was Kayla telling the truth? Did the glass do this?"

Ryan tugged on a piece of twine that held a sack closed. He peered inside, then up at his brother. "Food." A note of delight touched the word. "Cherries. Come see this." He rooted in the bag for one, tossed it into the air like a baseball, then popped it into his mouth.

Rich remained focused on Birdie. "Well?"

The others were silent, as if not sure what to pay attention to first – Rich and Birdie, the stockpile that filled the room, or the young woman, who still cowered by the stairs.

Birdie swallowed. "I'll explain everything. Just give me a minute."

"Start with her." Raina glared at the young woman.

"Who is she?"

"I will find out." Friedrich approached the young woman slowly, displaying his empty palms. When he was still several feet away, he paused and spoke to her in German, his voice soft.

She lifted her head and raised her chin defiantly. She wore no makeup, but her pale cheeks were flushed from running, her blue eyes bright and alive.

"What did he say to her?" Birdie asked.

"Shhh." Louisa shook her head. "Just wait."

"Can't you translate?"

Louisa seemed startled by the question. She looked at Birdie, then at the others who'd crowded in behind her. "Yes, yes, of course. I forgot that none of you—"

She shook her head again and translated. "He asked who she is."

Friedrich had moved closer to the young woman, who was still crouched low. She eyed him like a cornered kitten, unsure whether to flee or reveal its claws.

"You are safe here," Friedrich said, his hands open. "We will not harm you."

She peered around his legs at the others, as if trying to decide if she should trust this strange, spindly person and his ill-dressed companions.

When she finally spoke, the words came in a soft rush.

Louisa stepped forward to hear as she softly echoed the conversation in English for the others, who crowded behind her.

"I am Marielle." The young woman clasped her hands in her lap. "I'm in trouble. Horrible, horrible trouble. I fear for my life."

Friedrich folded himself down onto the dirt floor so they were nearly eye-to-eye. "What is this trouble? Surely it can't be that bad?"

Her face crumpled.

"Nein," Friedrich said hastily. "I'm sorry. Don't cry. Tell me what happened."

Marielle sucked in a deep breath. She shuddered and closed her eyes as she exhaled. When she reopened them, she seemed to have regained some of her dignity.

"I am lady's maid to Princess Elisabeth." She gathered a handful of her thick skirts and kneaded the material between her fingers.

"But," Birdie whispered beside Louisa, "that's who I play—"

Louisa placed a finger to her lips and Birdie fell silent.

Marielle seemed not to notice, to have almost forgotten the others were there, as her pleading eyes locked on Friedrich's.

"There has been a theft, a terrible theft from the keep. I did not do it. You must believe me. I swear I didn't do it. I've never seen what they search for!"

"I believe you." Friedrich glanced toward the top of the stairs, where the doors remained tightly shut. "But why do the guards think you're guilty? What happened?"

"But you must know!" She leaned forward. "The entire village has been preparing for the wedding. Princess Elisabeth is to be married in two days' time to the heir of one of the greatest fortresses on the Mosel River."

"Yes, of course." Friedrich spoke slowly. "The wedding."

"It is critical! The wedding must happen. The families have been warring for generations, and this marriage will bring peace to the lands between the Mosel and the Rhine once and for all."

"The wedding—" Friedrich's voice faltered, and he seemed lost in thought.

"But now – now the wedding cannot go forward. Everything is ruined!"

Friedrich refocused on Marielle. "Why? Why won't it happen?"

"Because the duke promised the prince – Prince Gunzelin – a significant dowry."

"Figures," Kayla whispered.

"Shhh!" the campers all said at once.

Marielle continued as if she hadn't heard them. "The dowry includes cloth, gold, silver, and weapons. But the duke has locked the most valuable item in a small wooden chest inside the trunk that protects the dowry."

Friedrich's eyes grew wide. "What is it?"

"Something Prince Gunzelin wants more than anything else. It's the only reason the families even considered the marriage."

"But what is it?"

Marielle leaned in closer, squeezing the fabric in her hands. "It's inside the chest. Locked away. You must understand. I overheard the princess talking to her father. She does not want to be married. She does not find Prince Gunzelin suitable. But her mother is gone and there is no one to argue against the marriage on her behalf. She tried so hard to dissuade her father from accepting the proposal, but he did not listen to her."

"Marielle." Friedrich's tone was strained. "What is in the chest?"

"The chess piece." She whispered the words, as if saying them aloud would bring more trouble to her door. "The knight on horseback, the last remaining piece from an ancient set. They say the man who possesses the knight will be forever blessed with wealth, privilege, and power. It was the promise of the knight that sealed the marriage proposal."

"A single chess piece?"

She nodded. "The knight on horseback, encrusted with jewels."

"And the knight will grant the prince all he seeks?"

"Prince Gunzelin seeks great wealth and power. The knight will bring him those things, and bestow them on all the generations who follow." Marielle glanced at the others before continuing. "But I don't believe the prince will stop there. The knight is just one piece. The other pieces vanished long ago. Some say they were buried in France, others say they were lost to the sea. The legend claims any man who possesses the complete set will rule the world!"

Friedrich was quiet for a moment as he took in what Marielle said. "And this theft?"

"The dowry." Marielle twisted her apron again. "The entire dowry is missing! Everything inside the trunk has disappeared. It is empty!"

"The cloth, the gold? The chest? Everything?"

"Stolen! Gone!" Marielle's eyes welled with tears. "And they think I took it!"

"But why?" Friedrich asked. "Why would they think that?"

"As lady's maid, I'm the only servant with access to the place where the dowry was locked away."

On the other side of the storeroom, Birdie wondered if it could be true, if this slip of a young servant could have done it, stolen everything from the trunk that held the dowry, and somehow spirited away the valuable chess piece. But where would she go with it? She'd be caught if she tried to sell it.

"We must help her," Louisa said.

"This is the best… history… camp… ever!" Sophia dropped into the guard's rickety chair and crossed her short legs.

They all stared at her.

"What?" she said.

"How do we know she didn't steal everything?" Raina placed her hands on her hips. "She could be making us accomplices to her crime."

Louisa translated for Marielle, although Birdie hoped she softened the question.

"I took nothing." Marielle wiped the tears from her cheeks and looked defiant. "I am not a thief. I am loyal to the princess. I have no need for fancy linens or silver, and the chess piece is useless to me. And even if I were a thief, which I am not, the chest that holds the chess piece is impossible to unlatch. It has a lock that only the duke knows how to open."

"So all those guards were searching for you?" Ryan dropped a handful of cherries back into a sack. "Wow."

"Yes," Friedrich replied, "they were searching for

82

Marielle. They must be frantic to find the dowry."

"What will they do when they find her?" Ryan crossed his arms.

"Torture the information from her."

"But she just said that she doesn't know anything."

"No matter," Friedrich replied.

"That's the way it worked back then, Ryan." Rich eyed Marielle. "They were pretty brutal."

"Well, it sure sucks to be her." Kayla strolled toward the stairs.

"Where are you going?" Sophia grinned. "This is just getting good."

"Kayla, you saw the image on the aventurine." Birdie shot a worried look at Sophia before she continued. "That can't be a coincidence. We can't just leave Marielle here to be tortured. Besides, you're bluffing. You know you can't go anywhere looking like that."

"Well, what do you suggest we do about it?" Kayla spun to face her. "For all we know, she really did steal the stupid dowry and stashed it away somewhere."

"Good question." Sophia twisted a strand of dark hair between her fingers. "Very good question." She considered her brother. "This is the first history camp with a mystery challenge. That steps it up a notch."

"Sophia, you're not getting this," Sam said.

She turned to Friedrich. "Tell us the goal of the game."

"I am afraid" – Friedrich offered his hand to Marielle as he stood – "that this is anything but a game."

CHAPTER TEN

"What do you mean, it's not a game?"

"Sophia, come on." Sam opened his hands wide. "Really?"

"Have you looked around?" Ryan motioned to the chair she was sitting on, the crates, Marielle.

"Do you remember what Kayla said?" Sam searched her face. "About the glass that Birdie found?"

Sophia's gaze darted to Birdie. "Yes, but it wasn't true. Birdie said it wasn't true."

"It was true, Sophia." Birdie's stomach sank. "I'm sorry I didn't tell you. I never should have brought the aventurine to camp. That's what the glass is called, aventurine, and sometimes, like now, it opens a window to the past. But I don't know how to control it."

"But then, where are we?" Sophia hugged her elbows to her body as she turned back to her brother.

"We're still at Burg Rheinfels," he said. "But we're not sure when."

"Approximately 1498." Friedrich stayed beside Marielle. "The marriage between Prince Gunzelin and Princess Elisabeth was extremely important and, as you know, it failed. Maybe we can right that wrong."

Raina inched closer to her brothers. "Birdie?"

"We'll find a way back, I'm sure." She tried to sound confident, but the words felt hollow. She pushed forward anyway. "We've always found a way back before. We just need to figure out—"

"How?" Kayla snapped. "We're all here. It's not like there's anyone left in the storeroom to bang on something."

"Is that what happened?" Louisa stepped forward. "You came back when I banged on the lunch tray?"

Birdie nodded. "And again when Ryan slammed the hammer down on that spike."

Angry voices rose beyond the doors at the top of the stairs.

"We can't stay here." Louisa glanced at the doors and then at Friedrich. "The search party will circle back when they don't find Marielle."

"I wish we had our costumes," Rich said. They were gone, along with the table they'd sorted them on. "We'll stick out like sore thumbs."

"I have this." Louisa held up the petticoat she'd used to cradle the aventurine. "But it won't do us much good."

"Oh my God." Raina stiffened. "We're going to die."

Friedrich ignored her. "It's too late to worry about costumes now. Our priority needs to be helping Marielle."

"No, our priority should be helping ourselves." Kayla folded her arms. "Do you hear the guards out there? I don't want to get decapitated by a battle axe or something."

"Or the guillotine!" Raina reached for the bun at the crown of her head. "They lopped people's heads off back then. I mean now. Oh my God!"

"Calm down. This is Germany, not France," Louisa said. "And no one is getting decapitated."

"Is there somewhere you can hide?" Birdie asked Marielle. "Somewhere we all can hide?"

Friedrich translated, and Marielle pointed toward the tunnel. "We must leave the walls and go to the forest. We can't stay in the fortress. It's not safe here for me, or for any of you as strangers. There's a cave in the forest where we can hide."

"The forest we saw this morning?" Rich asked.

Friedrich glanced up from Marielle. "The one behind the parking lot."

"It will be difficult," Marielle continued as Friedrich translated. "We must use the tunnels. They branch off underground. One will lead us beyond the fortress walls."

"Why should we all go?" Raina laid her hand on her chest. "I'd rather be in the storeroom than lost in a forest somewhere."

"We aren't safe here," Louisa said. "The only reason that guard didn't question us was because he was preoccupied with finding Marielle. We're strangers. And look at us. Besides, he'll be back."

"The tunnels might be guarded too," Rich said.

"I agree, but there is no other way," Friedrich said. "All

the guards are busy with the search."

"You don't think they'd search the tunnels?" Rich met his gaze. "That's the first place I'd look."

"I am certain they are searching them," Friedrich replied. "Of course they are." He quickly questioned Marielle, then turned back to the group. "She does not think the guards would waste time searching the tunnel to the forest because everyone knows it's blocked, and she could never get through it on her own."

"Um, why are we going into a tunnel that's blocked?" Kayla tilted her chin. "That makes no sense. And why is it blocked?"

"Superstition, probably," Louisa said. "The villagers believed the forests were haunted. It would make sense for them to block tunnels to keep evil spirits away."

"Or invading armies," Rich added.

"Excuse me for being Captain Obvious, but if it's blocked, then how will we get through it?" Kayla asked. "And, like Raina said, how do we know she's not the thief? She could be setting us up to take the blame."

"Marielle is not the thief." Friedrich glowered at Kayla. "We have no reason to doubt her. She needs our help, and this is the only way to save ourselves too. She can't escape on her own. Crates, barrels, and boulders block the tunnel."

"Boulders!" Raina threw her hands into the air. "I can't lift boulders!"

"She thinks we're strong enough to move them?" Rich glanced at Marielle, who stood watching them as they spoke, her gaze flitting to the top of the stairs at every approaching sound.

"If we all work together, yes," Friedrich said. "It will not be easy."

Marielle tugged his shirtsleeve and pointed to the tunnel. "We need to go now. Who's coming?"

Ryan's and Sam's hands shot up immediately.

"I'm in too," Rich said.

"And me." Louisa turned to Birdie. "You must come because you're the only one who knows how the aventurine works." She handed her the cooled glass, and Birdie slipped it into her pocket.

"I don't really—" she began, but the thunder of approaching hooves cut her off.

Marielle didn't bother to wait for the others. She darted toward the slit in the wall that concealed the tunnel entrance, her skirts swishing as she ran.

"Come!" Friedrich ushered them all toward the wall. "All campers must come."

"Great." Kayla lifted her right heel and dragged the strap of her sandal back into place. She repeated the action on her left heel and then fell in step behind Sophia, who'd entered the tunnel behind her brother.

"Are you sure this isn't part of camp?" Sophia pushed up next to him. "Some kind of challenge or quest they made up?"

"It's real, Sophia," Sam said.

"Wait until I tell my mother," Raina muttered.

CHAPTER ELEVEN

Birdie entered the tunnel last, behind Louisa and Rich, as the earthy perfume of weeping stone and hard-packed dirt filled her lungs. Sam plucked a torch from the wall and passed it up to Marielle to light the way, leaving Birdie in the shadows far behind its weakened glow.

As they traveled deeper underground, she wished she could double back and retrieve a torch of her own, but she didn't dare. As Rich and Friedrich had suspected, they were not alone in the tunnels. The search party's shouts drifted through the shafts, the deep voices booming as they drew closer, then fading as they scoured the maze of passageways.

Her back tingled as she strained to determine how close the guards were, certain that at any moment a hard, hot glove would strike out of the darkness and haul her away from the others.

She peered over her shoulder but saw only velvet

blackness closing in, pushing her along.

They were going more slowly than she'd have liked, hindered by the size of their group and the narrow cut of the walls. More than once she froze in place, holding her breath as the search party neared, sometimes so close she could feel the rumble of their footfalls in an adjacent tunnel.

The walking was difficult too. The ground was bumpy and pocked, and the height of the tunnel, which had been tall and airy near the storeroom, gradually shrank the further they traveled, as if the builders had grown tired of digging halfway through the job.

Birdie ducked as she followed the others down a short flight of spiral stairs, then banked right and hurried in silence deeper and deeper underground.

The low bay of a hound sounded somewhere far above, and the hair rose on the back of her neck. Up ahead, Rich dropped to his hands and knees to crawl through the passageway, which had diminished to nothing more than a long black chute in the earth.

She pushed forward in the dark, her shoulders brushing the walls, the ceiling forcing her lower. She squeezed her eyes shut as she squirmed into the tunnel behind the others, trying to forget the tons of dirt and stone above her.

Her breath came in short bursts, and her heart raced as she prayed the aventurine would hold, that it wouldn't trigger while they were deep beneath the fortress. She grew dizzy at the thought and opened her mouth wide to gain some air.

She had to keep moving, to push through, to get out.

She forced her mind to imagine a larger space – and

daylight – bright, beautiful daylight.

"Here!" Louisa's muffled voice reached her from several yards ahead. "We're here!"

Birdie crawled blindly, feeling her way through the base of wet clay that coated her elbows and caked between her fingers. She jumped when she felt someone touch her shoulders and cried out as Sophia helped her slip out of the hole and onto the hard-packed earth.

She stumbled forward and opened her eyes. The single torch illuminated a round chamber and the other campers, streaked with mud and breathing hard.

Friedrich motioned to Rich, and together they heaved crates and debris away from the last stretch of tunnel until a pinpoint of sunshine poked through. Encouraged, they moved faster, handing each crate off to the others, who stacked and shoved them against the curved walls and out of the way.

"Now what?" Rich crossed his arms and grimaced at a stack of boulders that stood between themselves and freedom.

"We need to move one of them." Louisa examined the pile. "But not all of them. If we push the top one out, we can climb out over the others."

Rich positioned himself against the stone like a football player preparing to shove a practice barrier. Friedrich lined up beside him.

"Ready?" Rich said.

Friedrich flexed his fingers.

"On the count of three."

When Rich reached three, they heaved their shoulders

against the boulder, grunting and straining as they pushed. The boulder didn't budge.

"Again," Rich said.

They lined up and tried again. Ryan squirmed between them and added his weight to the thrust. Still, no movement.

"That thing isn't going anywhere." Ryan ducked back into the chamber and rubbed his arms as Marielle dropped the torch and moved past the boys. She shoved at the stone herself, but her bony hands were no match for its weight. She spun to face them, her eyes pleading.

"If we could just get that one corner lifted." Louisa placed a gentle hand on Marielle's shoulder to move her aside. She pointed to a concave area on the bottom of the boulder where a bit of light filtered through. "If we lift it there, we could push it out the other side."

"Use this." Sam picked up the torch Marielle had abandoned. He snuffed it out against the wall and the chamber fell into darkness.

Birdie closed her eyes. She had to get out of there. She listened intently, waiting for the scrape of the torch's wooden handle against the heavy stone.

Instead, rustling rose behind her from deep inside the tunnel. Birdie's eyes flew open, and she froze in the center of the chamber.

"What is that?" Raina crouched low.

"Hurry!" Kayla cried, swiveling to peer behind her as the sound grew louder. "Someone's coming!" She seized a crate and shoved it at the tunnel entrance, but it was too wide for the hole.

Rich snatched the torch from Sam's outstretched hands

and shoved the end into the crevice beneath the boulder. He rocked the handle up and down, back and forth, until he'd wedged it under the stone.

"You ready?" he yelled to the others, who'd clustered behind him. "This wood won't hold for long. As soon as I lift, you'll all need to push."

The noise in the tunnel intensified.

"Do it!" Kayla shouted.

Louisa, Sophia, and the boys placed their hands on the stone. "One, two, three!"

Rich groaned as he leaned on the torch with all his weight. The boulder lifted barely an inch, but it was enough. The others channeled all of their force against it, and just as the torch handle splintered, the boulder tumbled out to the forest floor.

A shaft of sunlight shot into the chamber.

"Yes!" Louisa cheered.

"Oh, thank God." Kayla dashed toward the opening and freedom. She was nearly there when the shrill screech of attack drowned their whoops of joy.

"Bats!" Raina screamed. She covered her head and dropped to the ground.

Hundreds of bats streamed through the room, forming an undulating black mass of flapping wings.

Birdie sprawled flat on the floor and covered her head with her hands. The ripple of flight reverberated overhead, and she wondered fleetingly if it would ever end, if this would be the way she would go, discovered dead on the floor of an ancient chamber, her heart arrested by the sheer terror of it all.

The swarm seemed to go on forever as the squealing bats passed through the chamber and out into the forest beyond. When the last of them careened through the hole, the swath of sunlight once again brightened the space.

Birdie sensed the light but was reluctant to open her eyes, to witness the aftermath of the attack.

"Holy crap." It was Ryan. At least Ryan was still alive.

She opened one eye and surveyed the scene.

Raina was flat on the floor, her eyes squeezed shut. She was sobbing – huge, loud, body-shuddering sobs.

The others were gazing at the chamber, shell-shocked.

"Is… everyone okay?" Louisa swatted at her clothes as her knees shook. "Are you all okay?"

"What the hell were those bats doing?" Rich stared out into the forest. "It's not even dusk."

"They better not have rabies." Ryan rose to his feet. "Unbelievable."

At the sound of her brothers' voices, Raina opened her eyes, which were swollen with tears.

"I'm okay," Birdie said, more to herself than the others. She sat up and touched her hair. "Not sure why I bothered to brush it." She yanked the ponytail holder out once and for all.

Raina sob-hiccupped into a laugh, which made the others crack up too.

"Good." Louisa petted her braid, which was frayed, but still mostly intact. "Good. We are all okay. Now we must get Marielle to the cave."

"Too late," Ryan said. "She's gone."

"What?" Louisa said.

"Gone." Ryan raised his chin toward the place where the boulder had been. "She crawled out with the bats."

"You've got to be kidding me." Kayla rolled her eyes.

"I told you we couldn't trust her." Raina got to her feet.

Now that the shock of the bats was wearing off, Birdie remembered the aventurine. They weren't safe underground, especially if Marielle was no longer with them. "It doesn't matter. We still need to get out of here, fast."

"With pleasure." Kayla scrambled over the boulder and the others followed. Birdie almost cried out at the freedom of it.

Louisa was the last to leave. She hopped down and inhaled deeply. "The forest. We made it."

Marielle hadn't waited for them. She was dashing down a narrow path in the dense woods toward the valley floor. Birdie could just make out the flow of her black skirts as she ran between the trees.

"Marielle!" Friedrich set out after her and the others fell into step behind him.

"Wait!" Kayla yelled, and they slowed. From far below and centuries away, the eerie moan of a barge's horn coursed through her words. "Just hold on. Do we really need to trudge all the way down there?"

CHAPTER TWELVE

"Where did she go?" Rich drew up quickly as the trees arced and shimmered around them. A patch of soft earth near his feet crumbled away, and he jumped back. Louisa didn't stop in time and plowed into him.

"Whoa." He wrapped an arm around her shoulders to steady her.

She glanced toward the edge of the cliff and cuddled into him. "Thanks."

"A better question is, where did we go?" Sam said.

After the forest had shifted around them, they'd been left on a strip of ground that was little more than a catwalk, halfway up the mountain overlooking the valley. A series of switchbacks ran up and down the mountainside.

"Wait a minute." Sam peered over his shoulder. Where the boulder should have been resting on the ground, a tangle of leafy vines and dark brown tree roots camouflaged a narrow crevice in the cliff face. "That's it." He edged closer. "That's the tunnel." He brushed away the foliage to reveal the crack in the rock.

"That was the tunnel." Ryan reached Sam and seized a long vine. He pulled it away and pointed to a tight stack of rock and sediment.

"The entrance was here." Sam ran his hand over it. "You can tell. But it's so compacted that we'd need a backhoe to restore it."

"Good luck with that," Kayla said under her breath as she contemplated the drop to the valley floor.

Sophia followed Kayla's gaze down the hillside. "What about Marielle?"

"Oh, who cares?" Raina threw her hands into the air as she spun on Sophia. "Marielle is on her own, as far as I'm concerned."

"Hey." Rich dropped his arm from Louisa's shoulder. "There's no reason to be nasty to Sophia. It's not her fault."

"You know what? You're right." Raina pointed to Birdie. "It's her fault."

"Hey!" Rich took a step toward her.

"It's okay." Birdie held up her palm. "She's right. We wouldn't be here if I hadn't brought the aventurine to camp. I'm sorry about all of this. I'd take it back if I could."

"Well, we're in it together now, aren't we?" Rich said. "So be nice, Raina."

She folded her arms across her chest and glared at her brother. "We could have been crushed. So I don't exactly feel like being nice."

Kayla turned to Friedrich. "Do you know where we are?"

"Of course." He pointed to a spot far above them. "You do too. We stood up there this morning. That's the parking lot."

"How do we get back up there? I'm no rock climber."

Birdie eyed her filthy sandals but said nothing.

"We can't climb it. We need to get to a trail." Louisa scanned the woods. "Trails crisscross the forest. One will lead us up to the main road, then we can follow the fortification wall back down to the fortress gate."

"Are you sure we won't get lost?" Kayla eyed the switchbacks.

"We're sure."

Kayla didn't look convinced.

"We know the trails because we come up here sometimes," Louisa explained.

"You and Friedrich?" Raina curled her nose.

"No." Louisa waved the words away a little too quickly. "With my friends." She looked at Friedrich. "Uh, what I mean is—"

"Teenagers hang out in these woods," Friedrich said. "They meet up here sometimes."

"Why?" Kayla picked a long vine out from under her sandal strap as Raina slapped at a mosquito that had landed on her thigh.

"We hang out." Louisa shrugged. "Sometimes we bring drinks."

Kayla's face lit up. "Really?"

"Is no one else wondering what the heck is going on and where Marielle went?" Ryan asked. "Because I am."

"We don't have time to worry about that." Friedrich

stared at the valley floor where Marielle had disappeared. There was no sign of her now, no sign that she'd ever existed. He checked his watch, then began surveying the surrounding brush. "Louisa is correct – we need to find the trail that leads to the road. If we're not back by the time camp ends, they'll start looking for us."

"Who's they?" Ryan asked.

"Your parents," Louisa said. "And Frau Hamel."

"We're walking home, or to the hotel, or the train station, whatever," Raina said.

"It's a bed-and-breakfast," Ryan said.

"Yes, but we're not." Sophia brushed dirt from her arms. "And our parents will be like maniacs if they come to get us and we're nowhere to be found. I got lost at the park once and they called the police and the fire department."

"You were three, Sophia," Sam said.

"Still—"

"Here." Louisa tramped over a clump of woody weeds and pulled a branch aside. "I can make out the edge of the trail. We'll need to jump to reach it, but I think we can make it."

"So, again," Ryan called to the others after he'd leapt across to the trail. He was the last one to jump, and zigzagged behind them up the switchbacks toward the road. "We trudged all the way out here through a tunnel that doesn't exist to help a girl who's gone missing and no one thinks it's weird?"

"Oh, it's weird alright," Rich called back to him. "But I'm guessing Marielle is hiding in the cave by now. Friedrich said she knew the way."

"So that's it?" Ryan stopped. They'd reached the end of the last switchback and stood at the bottom of a ruined staircase that sliced straight up a crevice in the ancient rock. At least a hundred crumbling stone stairs led to the top.

"That's the road." Louisa pointed to the top of the stairs. She was in the lead, breathing hard from the climb, and she stopped to face him. "What do you propose we do?"

"I'm with Ryan." Sam glanced at the large watch face on Friedrich's wrist. "Why did we come all the way out here just to turn around? It's not that late. We have two hours until camp ends. Why rush back?"

"Uh, mosquitoes." Raina brushed another one from her bare leg.

Sam ignored her. "I mean, what about the cave? You said it still exists. Do you know where it is?"

Friedrich and Louisa were silent.

"They know," Raina said. "Look at their faces."

"So let's go check it out," Sam said. "It seems silly to go back to the storeroom after coming this far."

"He has a point," Rich said. "And I'd kind of like to see a cave that old."

"It's not that exciting," Louisa said.

Rich shrugged. "Neither is the storeroom."

"It's Friedrich's decision." Louisa faced him. "As head counselor."

Friedrich took his time thinking about it. He checked his watch, then considered each of the campers. "Okay. But we all must go. We cannot split up. Frau Hamel will get suspicious if she sees only some of us going to the

100

storeroom."

"Great," Kayla said. "Let's hope someone left some beer."

"We will stay together?" Friedrich repeated, and they nodded. "But we must be back by fifteen – I mean three-thirty – before your parents arrive."

"Then we better start hiking," Louisa said as Friedrich pushed past Ryan and reclaimed the path down the mountain.

"Watch out for that." Rich stepped over a curl of fresh animal dung that steamed in the middle of the path.

"Guess we aren't the only ones here," Sam said.

Birdie passed through a cobweb and stopped to brush the sticky tendrils from her face and bare arms. "We're the only ones here today. At least the only ones this tall on this trail."

They followed the switchbacks down the mountainside for several more minutes, sheltered from the sun by the towering trees. Cool, damp air blanketed the woods as they descended, and the scent of rain and decaying leaves grew stronger.

Friedrich took a sharp left and ducked onto another trail that led deeper into the woods. It was not as steep and hugged a hill where pine trees grew thick. Birdie inhaled the fresh air.

"This is much better than the storeroom." Sophia stepped up beside her.

Raina pushed past them. "Are we almost there?"

Friedrich halted on the trail. "Yes."

If your itinerary allows, explore the German countryside by car. You'll be rewarded with beautiful vistas of immaculately tended farmland, forests, and rivers. Explore a castle hidden in a wooded glen, or a cave deep in the forest where legends of dragons and fairy creatures thrive. —Marty McEntire, *Europe for Americans Travel Guide*

CHAPTER THIRTEEN

Foliage cleverly concealed the entrance to the ancient cave, rendering it nearly invisible to the casual hiker. Friedrich was not a casual hiker, however, and as they watched, he selected a thick limb and pushed it to the side, instantly creating an opening into the blackness beyond.

He turned to them. "Who is first?"

Leaves rustled and birds called back and forth.

Friedrich held the limb, waiting.

Louisa chuckled.

Ryan eyed the opening skeptically. "Did anyone bring a flashlight?"

Birdie wasn't sure what she'd been expecting, but a narrow hole behind a tree limb had not been it. It reminded her of the tunnels, and that was enough to give her pause.

"You are like small children." Friedrich ducked under the limb into the darkness. He reemerged a few seconds later toting a black duffel bag. He unzipped it and handed them each a flashlight.

"I guess you really do come here a lot." Birdie eyed the bag as she took a light.

For the first time since she met him, Friedrich smiled at her. "Yes."

He clicked on his light and shined it into the opening as he held the branch back again. "Now, who is first?"

This time Ryan stepped up and Sam and Rich followed close behind, clicking on their flashlights as they ducked inside.

"I don't know." Raina peered into the dark opening. "Is it safe?"

"Only one way to find out." Birdie brushed the foliage aside and stepped in behind the boys.

To her relief, the cave was open, airy, and almost festive from the dancing lights of the many flashlights. The cavernous chamber appeared well used, with a blackened fire pit surrounded by flat-topped stones. Water seeped down the limestone walls in several places, pooling on the floor.

Sophia turned in a circle to study the chamber. "What is this place?"

"It is nothing. Teenagers from Sankt Goar and the other villages hike here to hang out. It is normal in Germany," Louisa said.

"This is where Marielle hid." Rich ran a hand over the cave wall. "Do you think it looks the same now as it did then?"

"Yes," Friedrich said. "It is the only cave at Burg Rheinfels. If there were others, I would have heard about them – or discovered them myself."

"How deep does it go?" Sophia wandered a few yards away.

"Fifty meters?" Friedrich said.

Rich did a mental calculation. "That's what? Almost a hundred and fifty feet. Pretty deep."

"What's back there?" Sophia shined her flashlight into a broad, twisted passageway at the far end of the chamber.

"The cave has a series of rooms connected by those passageways." Louisa crossed to Sophia. "Follow me. I'll show you."

They hiked deeper into the connecting chambers, and the air grew so cool and damp it clung to Birdie's bare arms and left the taste of a penny on her tongue.

"We don't go back this far very often," Friedrich said as they moved through another chamber, this one smaller than the first.

"Why not?" Birdie asked.

"The smell. It is not so bad today, but sometimes animals leave droppings here and the walls absorb the odor."

Birdie washed the light from her flashlight over the floor. "What kind of animals?"

"Small ones." He paused, searching for the words. "Foxes and raccoons. Many raccoons."

"The raccoons find potato chips or other scraps that were left behind," Louisa added. "But it doesn't seem like anyone's been back here for a while, so the raccoons probably lost interest."

They passed through a short, twisted passage that led to a chamber not much larger than Birdie's bedroom at home.

She'd never felt so far away from that bedroom as she did right now.

"The main rooms end here," Friedrich said.

Sophia stepped up to the stone wall and ran a hand over its surface. She made her way around the room, examining the curves of the wall as she went.

"What are you doing?" Sam asked.

"Investigating. The walls are mostly smooth in this chamber, except for here." She rubbed a section where faint ridges formed a rough shape.

"It looks like some kind of ancient carving." Sam trained his light at the shape.

Sophia shifted a few steps to the left. "And here. There's a slash in the stone. You can feel cold air flowing up from it."

"What's back there?" Rich asked.

"There are many other sections of the cave," Friedrich said. "We do not have the proper equipment to explore them."

"So Marielle came here," Rich said. "I wonder if she made it."

Friedrich glanced at Birdie and then back at Rich. "There is a way to see."

"That's what I was thinking too," Rich said.

"You have the glass?" Friedrich asked.

Birdie's shoulders sagged. The aventurine was cool in her pocket and she wanted it to stay that way. "We completed our quest. Marielle escaped. Besides, we had a hard time getting back earlier today. The aventurine only works when it wants to, and even if I could control it, I can't guarantee we'd be back in time to meet our parents."

Friedrich dug under the collar of his shirt. "I thought about that."

He tugged a nylon cord and displayed a silver whistle that dangled from its end. "You said that a loud noise from the present brought you back."

"Like the cruise ship's horn," Rich said. "That's what broke the spell back in the woods."

"Yes, that's right." Birdie looked from Rich to Friedrich. "Although I'm not sure 'spell' is the right word."

"And when I tried to make a loud noise back in the storeroom, it failed – Louisa had to use something in the present to draw us back," Friedrich said.

She didn't like where this was heading.

"So I will take a piece of the present with us and we can make the loud noise."

"Do you think that will work?" Kayla asked Birdie as she eyed the whistle.

"I have no idea." But as much as it killed her, she had to admit that bringing a whistle was kind of brilliant. Why hadn't she thought of that?

"You mean you had that whistle the whole time?" Raina slouched against the wall. "Why didn't you use it before?"

"In the tunnels?" Friedrich smirked.

Raina considered his question. "Okay, so maybe that would have been bad."

"It looks like there used to be steps here." Sophia was still exploring the chamber and knelt to examine the crevice in the wall. "But they're all caved in."

"Caved in?" Sam knelt beside her to get a better look. He glanced over his shoulder at Friedrich. "Are you sure it's safe in here?"

"Very safe." Friedrich threaded the whistle back under his shirt. "Now and back then." He pointed to a steel shaft that was embedded in the wall a few feet from where Sam was kneeling. "The townspeople reinforced the cave so they could use it for storage during the war."

"No way. Did the Nazis keep bombs in here?" Ryan asked.

"Ryan!" Rich batted at his head.

Friedrich sighed. "There were no bombs in here."

"It was artwork, mostly," Louisa said. "Paintings, statues, things that were irreplaceable if Sankt Goar was destroyed in an air raid."

"What's an air raid?" Raina asked.

"Seriously?" Rich turned to his sister. "You don't know?"

Raina shrugged.

"It was war. World War II. The Germans bombed their enemies, and the Allies – England, France, and eventually the Americans – bombed the Germans. Many towns were destroyed."

"It is a dark chapter," Louisa said.

"So, the people from Sankt Goar hid their paintings in this cave?" Sam asked.

Louisa nodded. "It was normal. There are underground mines and caves all over Germany where town treasures were hidden."

"Also, stolen art." Rich checked Friedrich's reaction before continuing. "The Germans stole art from families and other countries and hid it in the caves and mines."

"This is true." Friedrich glanced at the steel shaft. "As

Louisa said, it was a dark period of our history. But in this cave, there were only the town's treasures. The artwork and also historical documents and archives. Some of the items you saw in the museum were kept here."

"So would that stuff have been here for Marielle to find?" Raina asked.

Rich wiped his hand over his face and shook his head. "No, Raina. Napoleon destroyed the fortress long before World War II. And Marielle would have lived centuries earlier, in the late 1400s."

"You know I'm no good at history."

"You could at least try to get the right century."

"It's time." Friedrich looked hard at Birdie.

She hesitated. The whistle was a good idea, but it might not work. They could get stuck in the past. But if they went back, they'd know for sure if Marielle escaped.

She looked at the others. "You're sure you all want to try this again?"

They gazed back at her expectantly.

"Okay then. I'll try." She retrieved the aventurine from her pocket and unwrapped the soft cloth that protected it. As soon as she did, she felt it grow warm in her hand, and the room shimmered. "It looks like we're supposed to be here."

"Is it happening?" Raina grabbed Rich's arm.

The cave grew brighter as iron sconces embedded in the limestone walls cast a warm glow. It was still a cave, but rather than a barren chamber, it was stacked high with wooden casks and smelled deeply of wine. The carving on the wall came alive with colorful paints.

Raina yelped as a torch fired to life above her head. "You

almost caught my hair on fire!"

Sophia stepped away from the wall. "Oh, my gosh. Look!"

On the opposite end of the chamber, Marielle hovered between two towers of casks.

And she was not alone.

CHAPTER FOURTEEN

"Halt!"

The young guard drew his sword as he leaped in front of Marielle. His hair was blond beneath his helmet, and thick leather gloves protected his hands. His gaze darted from person to person as his initial surprise shifted to curiosity.

Marielle peeked at them from behind his rose-embroidered uniform. She seemed comfortable with the guard, standing close, and not bothering to cover her braids with the long white scarf she clasped in her hands. Birdie was sure it had unraveled during their journey through the tunnels or her escape through the woods.

Friedrich raised his hands and said something in German.

"Friedrich's telling him we mean no harm," Louisa whispered, then continued to translate.

"They are friends." Marielle placed a hand on the young

man's shoulder. "They helped me get beyond the walls." She faced them, her face smudged with dirt, and her eyes bright. "This is Peter. He is helping me too."

Peter sheathed his sword. "Then you know of this terrible lie."

Friedrich lowered his hands. "We do. We accompanied Marielle through the tunnels and cleared the way for her escape."

"She escaped, but she is not free. She cannot leave this cave. If they find her…" He glanced over his shoulder, as if reassuring himself that she was still there. He turned back to Friedrich. "You must find the chest and bring it to me. That is the only way she will be truly free."

"Why can't he go get the chest?" Kayla said. "He's obviously a guard. No one would suspect him. They'd take one look at us and toss us in the brig."

"Dungeon," Ryan said.

"Whatever. The point is, why should we do anything? We already helped her get away. The rest is on her."

Kayla had a point, Birdie thought, although she didn't say it. She opened her fist and looked at the aventurine. The image of the chest held tight. Helping Marielle escape had not been the end of the mission. Something was still lost, and they were expected to find it. "Does he have any idea where it could be?"

"Seriously?" Kayla said. "Birdie. Do you have a death wish?"

She showed her the image on the aventurine.

"Oh for Pete's sake!" Kayla tilted her head toward the ceiling. "It didn't change when she escaped? I thought we

112

were done!"

Friedrich ignored Kayla as he translated Birdie's question.

Peter bobbed his head as he listened. "Across the Rhine. The chest is there. I'm sure of it. The villagers took it as revenge."

"Revenge for what?" Birdie asked.

"Against me." Peter stared at the floor. "I am the reason they will kill Marielle."

"What did you do?" Kayla asked. "And, again, if you caused this problem, shouldn't you be the one to go find the stupid chest?" She opened her hands to the others. "I'm not being ridiculous here, am I?"

Friedrich translated again, but Sam cut in. "He said it's across the Rhine. So we'd have to cross the river to get it back. Does he have a specific location?"

Friedrich translated that instead.

Peter shook his head. "The Rhine is under heavy guard on both sides. It is nearly impossible to cross without getting caught. They will put an arrow through your skull."

"Sounding better all the time!" Kayla said.

"If he asked us to get it, then there must be a way," Birdie said. "Ask him—"

The clang of metal striking stone rose from one of the outer chambers.

"Who followed you here?" Marielle demanded.

Louisa's voice grew panicked as she translated. "Friedrich?"

"It is not possible," he began. "How could—"

Peter spirited Marielle behind a tower of casks.

"We need to hide. Now!" Louisa spun in a circle, desperate to conceal them. Raina dropped low behind a barrel, as the others shifted behind whatever was close by.

Deep voices echoed in the passageway. *"Rottmeister, hier!"*

Six guards spilled into the chamber, helmets askew and heavy weapons drawn.

The bearded one they'd called Rottmeister shouted, and to Birdie's horror, they all charged forward, voices thundering as they lifted their swords and battle axes.

Raina screamed.

And then, an even sharper noise filled the air.

A whistle.

An eardrum-shattering whistle.

Friedrich blew it long and loud, again and again, even after the golden light was gone, and the scent of old, damp earth replaced the fruity musk of spilled wine and fermenting grapes.

Rich touched Friedrich's arm. "We're back, man. We're back."

Friedrich stopped blowing the whistle, his eyes wild. With trembling hands, he tucked it into his shirt.

Sophia dropped to her hands and knees on the cold floor.

Birdie knelt beside her. "Are you okay?"

No one said anything for a long moment, and then Ryan clapped his hands. "We ditched 'em! Great call with the whistle, dude!" He slapped Friedrich on the back, hard enough to make him skip forward to keep from falling.

"Is everybody okay?" Louisa had regained her voice as she counted heads to make sure they were all there.

"Yes. We're fine. Sort of." Sophia stood, leaning on

Birdie's arm to steady herself. "But what are we going to do? How will we find that chest now?"

"Are you serious?" Kayla asked. "Did you hear what Peter said? The part about putting an arrow through our skulls if we crossed the river? No thanks. I'm done with that stupid glass."

"Oh, you're done with it now?" Birdie felt the rage building inside her. "Really? You're done with it. That's rich. You're the one who kept asking me about it. You're the one who showed Friedrich. Don't tell me you're done with it. You started it!"

"I started it!" Kayla put her hands on her hips. "You're the one who brought it here!"

Friedrich glanced at his watch and spoke before Birdie could reply. "Kayla is right. Put that cursed piece of glass back in your pocket. We need to get back to camp."

"Yeah, Birdie, put it away," Kayla sneered.

"Shut up, Kayla. You and I are done." She unclenched her fist. The aventurine was cool now except for the warmth from her own hand, and the chest on its surface held firm. She rubbed it, but nothing happened.

"Come on," Sophia said softly. "Forget about Kayla. There's nothing else we can do here."

They made their way back through the twisted passageways and chambers and out into the thick pines, retracing their steps in silence until they reached the switchbacks. They pushed on, climbing the steep, crumbling stone staircase to the place where it emptied onto the sidewalk that separated the fortification wall from the main road.

Stepping onto the sidewalk felt like rejoining civilization, and the effect was jarring. The air was fresh, with no smoky haze rising from the fortress. The timeless humidity of the forest dissipated into the chalkiness of the sidewalk and the warm, dry breeze.

A car zoomed by on its way down the hill to Sankt Goar.

They rested, catching their breath, until the car disappeared beyond a curve in the road.

"This way." Louisa motioned toward the main gate. "It's all downhill from here."

"Wait." Birdie faced them. "You all need to promise me you won't say anything to anyone about what you saw today. Not even your parents."

"Oh, so now you want us to cover for you." Kayla folded her arms.

Birdie stared at the others.

Raina shrugged. "They wouldn't believe us, anyway."

Ryan snorted in agreement.

"Friedrich and I certainly won't say anything," Louisa said. "Not if we want to keep our jobs."

"Fine." Kayla released her arms. "Whatever. I won't say anything. Just leave the aventurine at your hotel tomorrow, would you? Before you get us all trapped in the Middle Ages. I'm flying back to America in three days, and I don't want that stupid piece of glass to screw it up."

Sophia linked her elbow with Sam's. "We won't say anything either, but if she doesn't bring the glass, how will we know what happened to Marielle?"

"Who cares?" Kayla said.

"I do."

"So do I, Sophia," Rich said. "We're in this now, like it or not."

CHAPTER FIFTEEN

Frau Hamel remained rooted to her stool in the ticket kiosk as the campers made their way past, twice, in quick succession. She narrowed her eyes as they jogged to the storeroom to gather their things, and again a few minutes later as they returned to the parking lot. Birdie felt the heat of her gaze each time she measured them up, this strange semi-annual crop of American tourists intent on invading Burg Rheinfels.

Did they look different from the others? They were teenagers – but odd ones – too quiet, too lost in thought. Had Frau Hamel ever measured a group so silent at the end of a day at camp?

But then, what was left to say?

Birdie lingered on the curb in the bright sunlight with the others, waiting for their parents as day-trippers descended on the fortress – completely modern day-trippers – intent on snapping shareable photos and buying souvenirs at the gift shop. It was as if the past few hours hadn't happened, as if they'd been a dream.

The morning, after all, had been so ordinary.

But if Frau Hamel or the other tourists looked closely, they'd see dirt clinging to their clothes and determination in their eyes, the only clues that something had gone awry that afternoon. They'd faced actual danger in the tunnels and the cave, and she sent up a silent thank you that Friedrich's whistle had worked.

"See you tomorrow." Sophia ducked into the back seat of her parents' rental car behind Sam. "At breakfast?"

"Sure, sounds good."

The Hennesseys were making their way to the main gate. Ryan tapped Rich on the shoulder, then sprinted back. "Hey, are you guys doing the sleepover tomorrow? I was going to see if I could skip it, but now—"

"Probably. I think my mom expects me to."

"No way out of it." Kayla tented her hand over her eyes and watched a small, sagging car approach the curb. "My grandparents already paid."

"Okay. See you tomorrow then." He sprinted back to rejoin his siblings.

"Later, Birdie." Kayla opened the car door.

"Did you say Birdie?" Helga leaned a fleshy arm through the passenger window, a wide smile brightening her face. "I wondered if you might be here! Look, Harry! It's Birdie Blessing!"

"Hello." Birdie bent a little and waved at Harry, with his unmistakable bushy white mustache, in the driver's seat.

He gave her a wink as Helga asked, "Where are you staying?"

"Just down in town. In Sankt Goar."

"We're a couple of towns down from here. Tell your mother we said hello!"

"Will do." She straightened as Harry stepped on the gas.

Her mom arrived a few minutes later, and Birdie exhaled as she slid into the front seat.

"How was camp?" Mrs. Blessing contemplated a group of leather-clad motorcycle riders ambling toward Frau Hamel.

Now there was a question. She buckled in. "Okay, I guess."

"Hmm... just okay?" She shoved the stick shift into gear and eased away from the curb. "You can tell me all about it at dinner. Herr Mueller arranged a bike rental for us, and I thought we could ride to Bacharach and eat at one of Marty's recommended restaurants."

Bacharach. That was where the Hennesseys were staying. "How far is that?"

"Not too far. Six miles or so?"

Birdie settled deeper into the bucket seat, glad to be off her feet, to be leaving the ruins.

Her mom slid a glance her way. "Does that sound okay?"

Birdie shrugged. A bike ride felt like a foreign concept. It seemed so... normal.

As they drove through the main gate, she peered up the sidewalk to the spot where the trailhead met the road. Marielle was somewhere in that forest, deep in another time, hiding from the guards. She prayed they hadn't found her.

"Unless you're too tired." Her mom had continued talking. "But I thought we could check out some of the other castles along the Rhine. Herr Mueller said we can see them from the bike trail that runs along the river. We can take our sketchbooks and, oh, wait, whoa—" She slowed as they approached an underpass and pointed to a sign with two cars on it. "That means the other car goes first. I learned that the hard way earlier today. Let's just say I'm glad I don't understand German very well."

They waited until a black BMW zoomed out of the underpass, then inched through and down the hill to the public parking lot.

"I can walk to camp tomorrow." Birdie closed the car door and pointed to the hulking ruin on the cliff above them. "There's a trail, and a few of the other kids are walking."

Her mom eyed her over the roof of the car. "Are you sure? I figured I'd have to twist your arm to go back."

"Yeah, I'm sure. Unless you're saying I don't have to go to camp at all."

She laughed and closed the door. It sounded good to hear her laugh – a real laugh, not the least bit touched by sorrow. "No, I'm not saying that. You're going."

They wandered down the main street, which was called Heerstrasse, on the way to the hotel. A few tourists shuffled in and out of shops and cafés near the small town square, while others posed beneath a whimsical statue of two boys who dangled beehives high above their heads.

"So what about the bike ride?" her mom asked as they skirted around the statue to avoid photo bombing an elderly couple.

"Yeah, okay. But I want to get cleaned up first. We got pretty dirty exploring the ruin." Between the tunnels, the cave, the bats, and the underbrush, her skin was crawling. When they reached the hotel, she washed up and changed her clothes while her mom completed the arrangements for the bikes. She adjusted her bangs over her bruise, which had turned the yellowish green color that meant it would soon fade away.

That meant there was only one thing left to take care of.

She plucked her shorts from the floor and dug around in the pocket. The aventurine was cool, the golden chest shining like it belonged there. No one would suspect the image shifted and changed at will. She found the soft cloth from Bruges, wrapped the glass, and stowed it deep in her roller suitcase, zippered into the compartment that held her extra socks and underwear.

She exhaled as the closet door clicked shut. She needed to figure out what to do with the aventurine, she knew that. But there were no simple answers. She could tell her mom, but who knew if she'd believe her? She wouldn't believe it herself if she hadn't seen its power with her own eyes.

She could ditch it – throw it in the river – but there were no guarantees that another person wouldn't find it, that it wouldn't wash up on shore and cause just as much havoc for someone else – someone else who would use it for their own gain.

She sighed. There were no simple answers. She swapped her jacket for her sketchbook and pencils and slung her pack over her shoulder. She glanced at the closet door to make sure it was closed and left the room.

CHAPTER SIXTEEN

Hotel Flussufer was larger than the bed-and-breakfast in Bruges, but unlike any hotel Birdie had ever stayed in, with just five rooms on each floor. A sweeping staircase connected the floors, with a double landing near the bottom that led to the breakfast room on one side and a back door on the other. Herr Mueller had given them a code for the back door and a stern warning against using the front door after hours. He had a family, too, he said, and evening was their private time.

As promised, they found two blue bikes perched on kickstands by the front stoop, helmets dangling from the handlebars. The late-June day was bright even as it approached dinnertime and, to her surprise, Birdie felt refreshed and ready for the ride. "Which way?" She straddled the bike and glanced up and down the river. Burg Rheinfels loomed at the top of the hill to their left.

"Right. To the south."

The bike path that snaked between the Rhine River and the main road was wide enough for two bikes to ride side-by-side, as long as they fell back to single file when bikers or hikers approached from the other direction.

As they pedaled toward Bacharach, they passed a flotilla of small boats moored at the dock and bobbing in the current, and a campground with a colorful OPEN flag fluttering in the breeze. As they rounded another bend, the river sprawled wide and the view opened up, revealing a parade of castles in varying stages of disrepair upon the cliffs.

"Here, let's pull over." Mrs. Blessing steered toward a lookout point. They parked their bikes and leaned against the metal railing overlooking the river. They studied the castles in silence for several minutes before Birdie's mom spoke.

"So how bad was camp? Are you still mad at me for sending you?"

Birdie swallowed. Staying mad felt useless after everything that had happened. "Kayla was there."

Her mom faced her. "Kayla? From t'Bruges Huis?"

Birdie laughed. "I'm pretty sure that's the same look I had on my face when she walked in." She told her mom about Kayla and the other campers, and how they'd explored the fortress in the morning and been given roles for the festival.

"That sounds fun."

"I wouldn't jump right to fun. But there are some okay kids there."

As they watched the river flow past, a breeze kicked up

off the water. Birdie adjusted her bangs. "What about you? What are you doing tomorrow?"

"Well, I did a lot of sketching at Burg Eltz today and talked to a few people who work there. It has an interesting history. Anyway, I met a man who builds furniture like the pieces in the castle. He uses old woodworking techniques and fabricates his own materials. He's going to take me to his workshop."

"He's going to do what?" Birdie turned away from the view and gave her mom a hard stare.

"Take me to his workshop?" Her mom reached out to squeeze her hand.

"Where?"

"Not too far from Burg Eltz. It's in the countryside near there."

"Are you sure that's safe? I mean, going off with some strange German guy?"

Mrs. Blessing looked like that hadn't occurred to her. "Oh, Birdie, I think so. He seems harmless and the family who owns Burg Eltz introduced me to him. And it will be really cool. I might hire him to help me make some pieces for my accessory line."

Her mom had sure come a long way from the woman who could barely leave the house a few months ago.

"But his workshop is about an hour away, so you walking to camp will help."

"Yeah, sure, no problem. So you'll be there all day?"

"If I'm lucky. But I'll try to get back in time for the festival. What role did you say you're playing?"

"A servant."

"That I would pay money to see." Her mom wrapped her arm around Birdie's shoulders and gave her a little hug as they turned toward the bikes. "Come on, we'd better go if we're going to make our dinner reservation."

They continued along the river until they reached Bacharach, which turned out to be a village of half-timbered houses, charming cobblestone lanes, and the remains of a town wall, lookout towers and all. They rode through an archway under a tower and parked their bikes in front of the restaurant. Birdie twisted the key on her bike's built-in lock and then dropped it in her pocket.

The restaurant was full of tourists and locals and, unlike the breakfast room, very lively. They ordered savory pork cutlets and crispy fries at a table overlooking the Rhine.

Birdie hadn't realized how hungry she was until the waiter set the plate of hot food before her. She half-listened as her mom talked about the engravings on a four-poster bed frame and the antiques she'd sketched, enjoying the gentleness of her voice more than the words themselves. She thought about sharing the details of her own day, about the aventurine and the magic and the guards, but she didn't.

Her mom was happy. Genuinely happy and interested in something that took her mind off the past. Her mom needed this trip, this place, and she would not spoil it for her. She could handle the aventurine and camp and Marielle on her own.

It would be fine.

After dinner, they walked their bikes to the river's edge and settled onto a bench to sketch a ruined castle that rose tall across the river.

Birdie turned the pages in her sketchbook, passing the drawing of Henri she'd done in Bruges and one of a barroom she'd sketched on the long drive from Belgium to Germany. Another turn revealed a blank sheet of cream-colored vellum. She set a dark pencil against its textured surface and drew. She intended to sketch the castle, but Marielle took shape before her.

Each stroke of color added the details she remembered – the heavy fabric of her dark dress, the white scarf that covered her hair, the small scar near the bridge of her nose, and the worn boots that showed their shine beneath a layer of dirt and dust.

She caught the fear in Marielle's blue eyes when the young woman had first met Birdie and the others. She emerged on the paper small and mouse-like, easy to overlook and unlikely to be missed in the everyday hustle of the fortress if she were to disappear.

But fire lit those eyes too. And anger. She'd been wrongly accused, and now everything – including her coveted position in the household – was at risk.

Birdie lifted the pencil from the paper and stared out across the river.

She pictured Marielle and Peter in the cave, cowering behind the barrels of wine. They'd been alone, trapped, and in terrible danger. There had to be a way to help them, to find the chest and return it to the princess's father in time for the wedding.

Princess Elisabeth, Louisa had said.

Locating the chest would be tricky, though. Burg Rheinfels wasn't like Bruges, a port city where strangers came and went all the time and no one thought anything of it. The fortress was more like a small town where people knew one another and would notice an odd group of young people with strange haircuts and mannerisms, their costumes not quite right.

Mrs. Blessing sighed with satisfaction and gently closed her sketchbook. "That was fun."

Birdie made a few more marks with her pencil.

"Are you done?" Her mom glanced at Birdie's drawing. "Who's that?"

"It's me. As a servant."

Notice how other tourists cruise through, snapping hundreds of pictures with abandon, on a mission to get to the next thing. Don't be that tourist. Leave the camera in your bag and explore. Take time to really see the place you came to visit. —Marty McEntire, *Europe for Americans Travel Guide*

CHAPTER SEVENTEEN

The ride back to Sankt Goar from Bacharach passed quickly. There were fewer bikers and hikers this late in the day, and Birdie and her mom cruised by the campground and the lookout point without needing to slow or let others get through. When they reached the hotel, Herr Mueller was busy folding cloth napkins at the front desk.

"Ah, the beautiful Blessings! Did you enjoy the bike ride?"

"Yes, thank you for arranging the bikes." Mrs. Blessing handed Herr Mueller the keys to their bike locks. "It was great. Lovely weather too."

"Ah, yes, that is good. I will see you at breakfast tomorrow." He turned away to hang the keys on the pegboard behind the reception desk.

Mrs. Blessing led Birdie toward the stairs. "I'd like to get some more work done tonight, and I need to make a list of questions for the craftsman. I don't want to forget to ask him anything tomorrow. Could you read or draw for a while?"

"Do you mind if I hang out down here?" She motioned to Sam and Sophia, who were tucked into a seating area near the breakfast room, deep in conversation. "I see a couple of kids from camp by the fireplace."

Her mom sized up Sam and Sophia. "Sure. I guess that's okay. Just don't be too late." She headed up the stairs.

Birdie started toward them but hesitated.

What was she doing? Who knew how they'd react to seeing her outside of camp, especially after everything that had happened during the afternoon?

Sam and Sophia looked up, recognition flashing across their faces.

She swallowed and finished crossing the lobby. "Hey."

"Hey, Birdie." Sam motioned to an empty seat. "Just the person we wanted to see."

Her shoulders relaxed as she slid into the cushy chair across from them.

"We've been researching Burg Rheinfels." Sophia pointed to a laptop and a bedraggled book on the coffee table. "I found a website with stories about the Rhine River and Sam picked up this book from the little library upstairs in the hall." She closed the cover. "It's called *Legends of the Rhine River*."

"Did you find anything?"

Sam crossed his sneaker over his knee, his dark eyes sparkling with amusement. "I'll say we found something. Did you know, for instance, that there were once fire-breathing dragons that guarded the river's treasures in a cave?"

Birdie grinned and shook her head.

"Well, there were. The dragons were here at the same time the giants roamed the shores of the river. And not just giants, mind you, there were goblins too. Evil goblins who stole the treasure from the dragons' caves."

Birdie lifted her brows. "Evil goblins?"

Sam laughed. "Yep."

Sophia rolled her eyes. "I saw those stories, too, but I was more interested in a legend I found. It's about a princess who was jilted at the altar when her dowry went missing."

Birdie's smile faded. "Wait. What? You seriously found a legend that said that?"

Sophia couldn't hide the excitement in her voice. "I did. And it mentioned a chess piece too."

"No way. What happened to it?"

"No one knows. They never found the dowry."

Birdie let that information sink in. If the dowry was still missing, then the chest was too. That meant – unless Marielle ran from Burg Rheinfels and Sankt Goar for good – the young woman's fate was sealed. From the look in Sophia's eyes, she'd understood that too.

"Now we have to go look for it." Sam uncrossed his legs and leaned in. "It'll be like a real-life treasure hunt. Who knows? Maybe those goblins took it somewhere for revenge and hid it."

"I found a legend about that too." Sophia picked up the laptop.

"About goblins?" Birdie asked.

Sophia shook her head. "Not about fairy tale creatures. Sam, really, stop with all that nonsense or Birdie will think you actually believe it. I found a legend about real people.

Real living people who wanted revenge."

Birdie and Sam exchanged glances. "We're listening," he said.

"Okay. So it goes like this. There was a village across the river. There still is, actually, but it was different back then. Back then, the people in that village despised the people in Sankt Goar."

"Why?" Birdie asked.

"There doesn't seem to be a good reason. Just a lot of rumors, superstitions, and misunderstandings. It was the Middle Ages, remember."

"It could have been a disagreement about who could collect the tolls," Sam said.

"Maybe. So anyway, one night, the men from that village launched a sneak attack against Sankt Goar to steal wine and silver and anything else they could get their hands on. They wore chainmail and helmets and waited upstream in a cove until dark. Then they set off in skiffs across the water. The Rhine was a broad, wild, untamed river then, so they had to wait until the weather was calm and the night had no moon.

"They pushed through the water, using the current to their advantage. But they didn't know Sankt Goar had stationed sentries on the town wall. That night, the sentries were two baker boys who had to stand watch until their shift began at dawn at the bakery."

"That must have been awful," Sam said. "Up all night and then off to work."

"Well, they were awake when it mattered. The boys heard the splash of water rushing over the oars as the skiffs neared. One of them ran to tell the elders what was happening. Within minutes, the whole town was awake."

"Everyone?" Sam tilted his chin.

Sophia shrugged. "It's a small village. So anyway, as luck would have it, one townsman was a beekeeper who kept his hives at the foot of the town wall, where they were less likely to be disturbed. It also happened to be where the men from across the river thought they were least likely to get caught. So they propped their ladders against the walls and scaled them, rung by rung. They'd almost reached the top of the wall, and then—" Sophia jumped up and imitated the swoosh of the hives coming down onto the men's heads. "The baker boys thrust the beehives down onto the tips of their pointy helmets!"

"Well, you can just imagine what happened." She reclaimed her chair. "The beehives burst open, bees, honey, and all. The men slid back down the ladders and ran, screaming, all the way back to the river where they jumped in to escape the swarm. Needless to say, they were completely humiliated and vowed to get revenge on the people of Sankt Goar."

Birdie remembered the statue in the square. She leaned in closer. "And they got that revenge by stealing the princess's dowry?"

"Could be, because the timing seems right and, after the wedding was called off, the town across the river prospered and Sankt Goar struggled."

"It does kind of match the story that Peter told us." Sam rubbed his chin.

"But he said that they wanted revenge against him, not

the town," Birdie said.

Sam stopped rubbing. "Maybe he's one of the baker boys."

"Oh Sam, I hadn't thought of that. But it would make complete sense!" Sophia slapped her knees. "After the baker boys thwarted the invaders, the duke's family made them personal guards at the fortress. It was a prominent position and Peter would have surely known Marielle."

"So maybe the thieves really did hide the chest somewhere on the other riverbank," Sam said.

"That's awesome research, Sophia. Did you find anything else?"

She pulled her phone from her pocket. "Just an illustration of the chest and the chess piece."

Birdie sat back against the chair. "You're kidding."

Sophia rotated the phone to face them. The black-and-white illustration was small, and she had to zoom in to make the details big enough to see. "This is the chest."

Birdie studied the fine lines from each mark the woodworker had made. "Where did you find this?"

"On a museum's website. It's in Cologne. They've put a lot of their collection online so people can visit them virtually."

"What does the description say?"

Sophia zoomed in on the words. "Lost Jewel Chest. Rhine River. Late 1400s."

She zoomed back out so they could see the image.

"So that's the chest," Sam said. "It's kind of small."

"It probably is fairly small," Sophia said. "This was a special piece – like a safe – that they could hide inside the larger cedar-lined trunk that held everything else."

"The details are amazing." Birdie studied the image on the screen. "Even in this sketch. The carvings are so perfect."

Sophia pulled up a second illustration.

"The chess piece," Sam said. "A knight. Is that from the same museum?"

Sophia nodded. "They found the two illustrations together."

The figure showed an armored man atop a horse that reared up on its hind legs. Even in the black-and-white illustration, Birdie could tell the piece was laden with jewels and gemstones.

"So the chest and the knight were real." Sam leaned back in his seat. "Marielle was telling us the truth."

"Very real," Sophia said. "Or at least real enough for someone to take the time to document in these drawings."

The bell on the front door chimed, and they all jumped. They turned in time to see an older man and woman shuffle in, lugging heavy suitcases behind them, their faces red from exertion.

"Finally!" The woman leaned heavily against the suitcase handle.

"I thought we'd never make it," the man puffed. "Remind me to give that damned Marty McEntire a piece of my mind if I ever meet him. Dragging us out here to the middle of nowhere. And for what?" He gestured around the lobby with a chubby hand.

"Let's get checked in and find someplace to eat," the woman said. "Assuming there is some place to eat way out here."

Herr Mueller appeared behind the front desk and greeted them in German.

"Expression-zee-English?" the man bellowed.

Birdie covered her mouth to hide her grin.

"This place is really off the beaten path, isn't it?" The woman didn't seem to care if Herr Mueller could understand her or not. "Please tell me there is a restaurant here?"

Herr Mueller switched to English, his voice patient and kind. "Yes, ma'am, there are many." He calmly pulled the town map from the pile he kept under the counter and spread it out. He pointed to a place on the map. "This is a pizza—"

"Pizza!" The woman threw her hands into the air. "I thought this was Germany."

"We should go for a walk." Sam nodded toward the couple.

"It is kind of nice outside," Birdie said.

"I could use some fresh air." Sophia snapped the laptop closed. "I'll text Mom and Dad and let them know. You should tell your mom too. Sam, run this laptop and book up to our room, will you?"

"Which way?" Sophia asked several minutes later as they stepped down onto the empty sidewalk in front of the hotel. The bikes were already gone, probably stored in the shed she'd seen in the backyard from the window in her room.

Birdie pointed to the bike path. "Let's go that way. There's a lot to see. My mom and I rode bikes out that way for dinner."

The sun remained bright despite the hour, and the main road was quiet. They crossed it and started down the path. Historic markers lined the route, pointing out interesting sites along the way. Birdie hadn't noticed them when they'd cruised through on their bikes, but on foot they were hard to miss.

"Where did everybody go?" Sam glanced up and down the trail as they read a marker detailing the history of shipping on the Rhine. "This place is deserted."

As if on cue, the sorrowful whistle of a train floated down from the station a few blocks above them.

"I think this is more of a day trip kind of place," Birdie said. "That's how it was when we were in Bruges, anyway. As soon as the tour groups pulled out, it got quiet."

"We were in London before we came here." Sophia tugged a hair-tie from her wrist and looped it around her dark hair to stop it from blowing into her face. "It was never quiet there. Are you going to London?"

Birdie thought about it. She had to make a better effort to remember their itinerary. "That may be our last stop at the end of the summer."

"You'll love it. There's a ton to do, and it moves so fast." Sophia looked around. "Kind of the opposite of here."

"I don't know, Sophia." Sam leaned against the railing overlooking the river. "I kind of like having the place to ourselves. London was cool, but Sankt Goar has its charms too. Where else do they have dragons, giants, and goblins?"

CHAPTER EIGHTEEN

They strolled along the bike trail, in no rush to get anywhere in particular or to return to the hotel lobby. They paused at each of the historical markers, which oscillated between ancient legends and more utilitarian descriptions of modern maritime commerce.

"I wondered where this one would be." Sophia stopped in front of a wrought iron post. "I knew there had to be a marker for the Loreley."

Birdie read the description aloud. "The Song of the Loreley. The beautiful siren who drew sailors to their deaths on the rocks."

"The spot where the Loreley was supposed to lure her victims must be nearby." Sophia tented her hand over her forehead and peered across the Rhine, but tall hedges and a decorative fence partially blocked her view. "That campground's in the way though."

"My mom said there's a little café there that's open to the public."

"Want to check it out? I have some euros." Sam patted the front pocket of his shorts, then led them to the campground entrance as a striking view of the river and cliffs emerged. "This is prime real estate, here."

The well-kept campground hugged the bank of the river, with travel trailers parked side-by-side in long rows. The trailers were tiny compared to the ones at home, and there wasn't a pickup truck in sight. There were cars, though, and they must have been powerful enough to pull them.

The café was in a two-story building with a wide porch and window boxes overflowing with purple petunias. It sat at the heart of the campground, near the tennis courts and a playground. Inside, they found a spotless counter and a few empty tables.

A blond-haired woman who was a little older than Birdie's mom eyed them with a curiosity that bordered on suspicion. She spoke to them in clipped English, apparently having sized them up and determined that they were not local, campers, or even German. "We are closing. I have only drinks. The kitchen is closed." She gestured to a tall cooler near the end of the counter.

"That's all we were hoping for. Three sodas." Sam flashed a bright smile, which she did not return. She rang up the order while Birdie and Sophia grabbed the bottles from the cooler.

"Let's sit outside. There are more chairs there." He turned back to the woman and tipped his small glass bottle in a gesture of goodbye. "Danke."

"*Bitte.* You must recycle the bottles."

As they settled into a trio of heavy deck chairs arranged in a circle near the porch railing, Birdie heard the click of the café door locking behind them. She glanced over her shoulder in time to see the lights flicker out and the woman's shadow disappear into the back room.

"This is cool." Sophia propped her sneakers up on the railing. "I'm glad we decided to go out." A refreshing breeze swirled off the river, and the only noise was the endless rush of water flowing past.

Despite its lovely vantage point, they were the only ones on the porch. A few campers milled about, some sitting in folding chairs near the riverside, others working around their trailers. They took no notice of the three of them up on the porch.

Across the Rhine, a rocky bluff rose from the water, tree roots marbling the stone like veins, too stubborn to let go. Nearby, rows and rows of grapevines marched to the summit of a steep hill. Sophia took out her phone and snapped a picture.

"How do you think they harvest those grapes without tumbling down the hill and over the bluff?" Sam considered the slope. "That soil must be really special. Why grow them there otherwise?"

"Louisa said this area is known for its wine," Birdie said.

"Mom and Dad seem to like it," Sophia said. "Did you see how many bottles they brought back to the room?"

Sam twisted in his chair. "Yeah, it's a good thing we rented a car. Can you imagine trying to lug all that onto a train?"

"Do you think that's the Loreley?" Sophia nodded toward the mountain of rock that rose along the curve of the river. "The sign for it was out front and it kind of looks like the rock Louisa pointed out to us this morning."

"Maybe?" Birdie studied the formation. "I think so. But there are so many curves in this river. I'm not sure why that one got so famous. I guess because the sailors couldn't navigate it."

"We could ask one of them." Sam gestured to the campers. "I'm sure they all know the story by heart if they set up camp here."

"It doesn't look very scary, does it?" Sophia tilted her head as she considered the bluff across the river. "But those villagers were sure scared of it back in the day."

"It's what's hidden below." Birdie watched the water lap against the shoreline. "The danger you can't see. That's what scared them and led them to make up all the stories. In their minds, there was no other explanation. The deaths had to be caused by an evil magic."

"I wonder if everyone believed the stories, even back then," Sam said. "Couldn't it be that a handful of people told the stories to keep everyone else scared? To keep the children away from the dangerous bluffs and to warn the sailors of the strong current?"

Birdie thought about that. "Good point. That makes more sense than everyone blindly believing."

Sam's eyes lit as an idea came to him. "Maybe they made sure everyone was scared so they could hide something and be sure no one would ever find it. Maybe even play up a story about an evil mermaid to keep people away?"

"She was a siren, not a mermaid," Sophia corrected.

"She was a figment of their imaginations," Sam said.

"It's an interesting theory." Birdie sipped her soda. "It would be a great way to make sure people stayed away."

Sam shrugged. "Yeah. But still. Look at that slope. You'd be a fool to want to climb it anyway."

They sat in silence for a while, pondering the gorge and the flow of the wide river, until a loud clatter coming from behind the café building drew their attention.

"What on earth is that?" Sophia twisted in her chair as a teenager pushing a cart piled with dirty laundry rounded the corner. "Friedrich?"

Birdie sucked in a breath.

Friedrich pulled up short, his eyes narrowing at the three of them on the porch, bottles in hand and feet propped up like they owned the place.

He'd changed into a pair of simple denim shorts and a tight-fitting T-shirt with the campground's logo ironed on the front. He'd swapped his expensive sneakers for a pair of well-worn sandals.

"What are you doing here?" Sam asked.

"I… I live here." Color crept into his cheeks. "Well, not really live… we have a house—"

"You live at a campground?" Sam raised his eyebrows.

Friedrich straightened as if suddenly remembering he was their head counselor. "In the summers, yes. I live here with my mother. She manages the campground. I help now and then."

They stared at each other.

Birdie cleared her throat and lowered her feet to the floor. "Uh, that's a lot of laundry."

He stared down at the cart as if he'd forgotten it was there. "It is from the rentals. Some people rent trailers rather than bring their own."

"It's close to the fortress," Sam offered. "The campground, I mean."

Friedrich peered over his shoulder to the hulking ruin that was visible even from this far down the trail.

"I bet you meet a lot of interesting people," Sophia added.

"Yes, of course." He turned back to them. "But... what are you doing here?" He pushed the cart to the side of the porch and folded his arms across his chest.

"Taking in the view." Sam tilted his soda bottle toward Friedrich. "This is a great little café."

"You can sit with us if you want to." Sophia motioned to an empty chair beside her.

"I have work to do. I must help my mother get ready for the weekend. It gets very busy here on the weekends."

Another awkward silence fell over them.

"Is that the Loreley?" Birdie pointed across the river.

"It is." Friedrich glanced at the bluff. "This is about the best view you can get."

"Do you think the villagers who took Elisabeth's dowry might have hidden the chest somewhere on that rock?" Sophia's voice was guarded, as if she wasn't sure she should say what was coming next. "We've been talking about it and it seems like that would make sense, you know, for them to hide it somewhere everyone was afraid to go."

Friedrich shrugged. "It's possible. There are trails there now, but back then, it was less accessible."

"Especially if everyone was afraid of the Loreley," Birdie said. "Everyone would have stayed away."

"How do you get over there?" Sam asked.

"There is a ferry." Friedrich checked his watch. "It stopped running an hour ago."

"Have you ever been over there?" Sophia asked.

"Of course. No one is afraid of that stupid rock anymore, not even the boat captains."

"We should go check it out tomorrow." Sam leaned in, elbows on his knees.

Friedrich reached for the cart. "We cannot leave the grounds during camp."

"Aren't you at least a little curious?" Sophia said. "I mean, about Marielle and the chest? What if they really did hide it over there?"

"What if it's still hidden over there?" Sam opened his hands wide.

"There are many legends." Friedrich sighed as if just thinking about them all exhausted him. "There are so many legends about this place. Some are based on history, but they are fantastical. To go over there, it would be – what do you say in English? Chasing wild gooses. Besides…" He stared hard at the bluff across the river.

"Besides what?" Birdie asked.

"Never mind." He turned back to them. "I need to work. And you need to leave. The café is closed."

"So then, you're not curious?" Sophia repeated.

Friedrich met her eyes but didn't answer right away.

"Well?" Sam asked.

Friedrich grabbed the metal handle and shoved the cart hard in front of him, sending it several feet down the path. He followed it, muttering as he went.

"What did he say?" Sophia asked.

Birdie stared after him. "He said, 'More than you could know.'"

CHAPTER NINETEEN

The next morning dawned bright, the warm sun splashing through the butter-yellow curtains of the hotel room. Mrs. Blessing cranked a window open to let in some fresh air while Birdie showered and dressed in the bathroom. When they were ready, they went downstairs and picked up bananas and granola bars from the buffet in the lobby.

"Guten Morgen," Birdie's mom said to Herr Mueller as he rushed by with a full pot of coffee.

"Coffee, Mrs. Blessing? To go?"

Birdie's mom held up a paper cup with steam rising from under the lid. "I found some at the buffet. Thank you, though. You are very kind."

"Do you have an umbrella? Chance of storms again today," he called over his shoulder.

"Yes, in the car. Danke!"

Herr Mueller nodded and was off again, serving the

other guests in the restaurant. Birdie noticed the couple who checked in the night before, appearing calmer and more collected as they heaped food onto their plates at the buffet. Sam and Sophia were there, too, shoehorned into a table near the window with their parents and looking perfectly miserable.

"Are those your friends? Do you want to wait and walk with them?"

"No. Their parents are driving them to the fortress. I'll see them up there. We can go."

Mrs. Blessing checked her phone. "Okay, good. We're right on time."

They retraced their route from the previous morning, following the broad sidewalk down Heerstrasse to the parking lot. With fairer weather and better spirits, Birdie saw the village in a new light and smiled as they passed a string of souvenir shops with cuckoo clocks and beer steins in the windows.

She liked Sankt Goar, she decided. It was compact, with only a few roads that looped up the hillside, and there was little traffic this early in the morning. As they passed a short side street, a group of children with matching T-shirts and daypacks trailed behind two teachers. They wandered down the middle of the road and didn't seem at all concerned that a car might appear to ruin their outing.

They passed a group of senior citizens enjoying the morning sun at an outdoor café and Birdie smiled at them. Unlike Bruges, Sankt Goar was a town first, with ordinary people living in the half-timbered houses that lined the roads, and a tourist destination second.

When they reached the small gas station at the far end of Heerstrasse, she hugged her mom goodbye and watched her cross the empty street to reclaim the rental car from the parking lot. A few blocks above them, the train whistle moaned.

"Good luck with the old guy!" Birdie called to her.

Her mother half-turned, the highlights in her hair sparkling in the morning sun. "Thanks. See you at the festival!"

The festival.

Right.

Birdie glanced at Burg Rheinfels rising high upon the hill.

From down here, it looked like an impossible climb, but she knew from Herr Mueller's map that there was a trailhead just a few blocks away at the youth hostel. She slung her pack onto her shoulders, rescuing her dark hair from beneath the heavy straps, and started toward the trailhead, passing the gas station and making a straight climb up the road toward the railroad tracks. As she crossed them, she could make out a flashing red light on the train that had just rumbled through.

A few yards beyond the tracks, she turned toward the hostel and saw the Hennesseys starting across the parking lot.

"Hey!" She cupped her hands around her mouth. "Wait up!"

Raina tapped her brothers on their shoulders. They were all wearing jeans and sneakers, just like she was, probably to fight off the chill of the storeroom.

They stopped to let her catch up.

"If it isn't shimmer girl." Raina's hair was in a ballerina bun again. "I thought you got a ride to camp."

"Be nice, Raina," Rich said.

"I told my mom I'd walk today." Birdie tried to ignore the dig. Shimmer girl? Really? "We have to walk halfway here to get to our car, anyway. Are you guys staying at the hostel?"

"My mom would never stay at a hostel," Raina said.

"No." Rich shot Raina an irritated look. "We're at a bed-and-breakfast in Bacharach. We took the train to Sankt Goar this morning."

"Right. You said that yesterday. How long did that take?"

"Ten minutes?" Rich bent slightly to hold open a crooked garden gate at the edge of the parking lot as they all passed through. Beyond it, they climbed a narrow path bordered by several long-neglected flowerbeds.

"My mom and I rode our bikes to Bacharach for dinner last night. It's a cute little town."

"Emphasis on little," Raina said.

The sun was bright and the breeze from the river was cool as they climbed the hillside trail, which veered up into a scraggly patch of trees. Birdie's shoulders were weighed down by her pack, stuffed full with a set of pajamas, a change of clothes, her toothbrush, deodorant, and a tube of toothpaste.

The one thing it didn't hold was the aventurine. She'd left it tucked in the suitcase, far away from Burg Rheinfels and the other campers. If Sam and Sophia wanted to talk Friedrich into taking the ferry across the river to search for the long-lost chest, that was fine, but they wouldn't do it with the aventurine along for the ride. Yesterday proved too dangerous and unpredictable, and she wouldn't put anyone in harm's way again. She'd been careless, and they'd almost all paid the price.

The events of the day before hung unspoken in the air as they hiked up the trail, and she could sense the siblings trying to think of a way to broach the subject.

Ryan finally came out with it. "So, what's the story with that stone?" They'd made it halfway up the hill and paused to catch their breath. "I'm still shaking my head about it. Part of me wants to believe it was a big setup, that Friedrich and Louisa planned the whole thing. But it seemed so real."

"It's technically glass, not stone. Although it looks like a river stone to me."

"Where did you say you found it?" Rich seemed even taller this morning, standing a few feet above her on the trail. His hair was windblown from the walk and, for the first time, Birdie noticed a splash of freckles on his cheeks. She glanced at Ryan and Raina and saw they had them too.

"In Bruges. That's where we stayed in Belgium. It's where I met Kayla. She and her grandparents were staying at the same bed-and-breakfast as my mom and me."

"Did weird stuff happen there, too?" Ryan asked. "Like what happened yesterday? Is that how Kayla knew you had the stone – oh wait, I mean glass? What's it called again?"

"Aventurine. And yes, weird stuff happened. We – my friend Ben and I – found a rare book that belonged to a boy who lived there."

"And?" Ryan bounced on his toes. Birdie couldn't tell if he was excited or just trying to stretch his feet.

"And, that boy – his name was Henri – was not from our

time. The aventurine opened a window to the past somehow, just like it did yesterday. We used it to help return the book to him."

"What do you mean, opened a window to the past?" Rich asked. "How?"

"It worked the same way it did yesterday. There was a legend in Bruges about the aventurine – that it came from Venice and had mystical powers. Although no one thought it was real. But then I found the glass and, well, all I can say is Ben and I were definitely in some other time when we helped Henri."

"Is that how you got that enormous bruise on your head?" Raina's lips twisted as her eyes locked on Birdie's forehead.

She smoothed her bangs over the spot. It had faded to yellow overnight, with a few ugly shades of green still mixed in for good measure.

"Nice, Raina." Rich shook his head. "Why do you have to be like that?" He met Birdie's eyes and she could tell he was searching for the truth there. "So that's what happened yesterday? We all traveled back in time? It wasn't some hoax that you cooked up with Louisa and Friedrich to juice up the camp? Maybe with projectors and actors?"

"I wish. But no, it wasn't a hoax, at least not on my part. The girl we met yesterday – Marielle – was from the past as far as I can tell and she needed our help to escape from the guards."

"So we helped her," Ryan said.

"Yes."

"And that's it?"

"Probably. Maybe? Once we helped Henri, everything went back to normal."

"But did we really help Marielle? The chest is still missing," Rich said. "We ditched her in a cave with armed guards, don't forget."

"Sam and Sophia were wondering the same thing last night. They did some research and discovered that there really was a Princess Elisabeth whose dowry disappeared."

"You're kidding," Ryan said.

"Oh, for Pete's sake, what a load of BS." Raina pushed past Rich and tramped up the trail. "I think Friedrich set it up so that girl and the guard dressed up like we will be tonight and then led us on the stupid quest."

"What's your problem this morning?" Rich asked her. "Did you wake up on the wrong side of bed or what?"

"Or maybe the wrong side of the Atlantic?" Ryan snickered.

Raina kept going, climbing faster and not bothering to answer her brothers. Birdie stepped behind Rich on the trail, jogging a little to keep up.

The subject dropped, and Birdie was grateful that the grade kept them breathing too hard to carry on the conversation.

The morning was too beautiful for an argument, anyway. At the end of each switchback, she let her gaze linger on the view that stretched below them, the broad river winding through the gorge. She took a mental picture of it, hoping to preserve the memory for a while before spending the rest of the morning cooped up in the underground storeroom.

CHAPTER TWENTY

Birdie and the Hennesseys reached camp winded from the final trudge up the curved sidewalk that connected the trailhead to the fortress gate. Frau Hamel sat erect at her post in the ticket kiosk, sporting a purple Burg Rheinfels polo and black pants. She frowned as she watched them pass.

"Back to the dungeon," Raina grumbled as they reached the open storeroom doors and descended the stone steps.

Friedrich and Louisa were already there, heads bent behind the stacks of costumes at the end of the long table. They were poring over the clipboard, and Birdie wondered if they expected more campers. She slid into the chair beside Louisa and saw that it wasn't the attendance sheet tacked to the clipboard, but two roughly drawn maps of the fortress grounds.

"Friedrich drew these last night." Louisa tapped the map

at the top of the page. "This is Burg Rheinfels today, or what's left of it, anyway, and this is our best guess of how it looked when Marielle was here."

Rich rested his hands on the back of their chairs and peered over their shoulders. "Not bad." He reached into the back pocket of his jeans, unfolded a piece of notebook paper, and spread it flat next to the maps that Friedrich had drawn. "Almost as good as mine."

Louisa smiled up at him. "Close."

Raina rolled her eyes and pulled out a chair at the far end of the table.

"I used a picture of the map in the museum as a starting point. It was drawn about two hundred years before Marielle's time, so I imagined what would have changed in the intervening years. I wasn't sure about the moat. It looks like it flowed right through this storeroom."

"It's hard to say," Louisa said. "The storeroom was definitely part of the moat at some point, but then it was drained. Or it dried up."

"It was dry yesterday – that's how I knew roughly what time period we traveled back to." Friedrich glanced from his map to Rich's and back again. "We must assume it was the late 1400s or early 1500s."

Birdie leaned in to get a better look at the drawings. "When the aventurine sent us back in Bruges, we thought we were in about 1500 too. The town was past its high point and trying to hold on."

"So, why do we need a map?" Ryan plopped down across from Birdie just as Sam and Sophia trotted down the stairs.

Louisa glanced at Friedrich. "You might as well tell them

what we were talking about."

He pushed his chair away from the table and stood tall to address them. "If we decide to help Marielle find the missing chest, we will need to plan a route."

"Wait a minute." Birdie opened her hands on the table. "I thought you called it a wild goose chase last night."

Raina perked up. "You guys hung out last night?"

"We all did." Sam sat down next to Birdie. "We ran into Friedrich at the—"

Friedrich cleared his throat.

"Er, in town," Sam finished.

Birdie ignored them. "Why the change of heart, Friedrich?"

Sam faced her. "Who cares why? Don't you think it would be cool to find the chest?"

"Or we could stay here all day." Ryan motioned to the storeroom. "That sounds fun. Not."

Birdie shook her head. "It's too dangerous to go to Marielle. We don't belong there. The guards found us, remember?"

Sophia squeezed between Friedrich and Louisa and picked up Rich's map. "I agree with Birdie about it being dangerous to go back. Maybe there's a way to avoid that."

"How?" Friedrich asked.

"Well, according to the legend, they never found the chest, right?"

"Correct."

"That means it could still be here somewhere – hidden or buried in the present – at Burg Rheinfels or across the river."

Raina snorted. "You honestly think you'll find a wooden

chest some villager hid like five hundred years ago? You're crazy."

"I'm not crazy. And you shouldn't say that." Sophia glared at Raina before continuing. "Anyway, it might be worth exploring across the river before we decide to put ourselves in danger again."

"Okay, so let's say we cross the river and find the chest," Sam countered. "We'd have to take it back to Marielle, anyway."

"We would," Sophia agreed. "You're right. But we wouldn't have to wander all over the fortress to do it. We could get to the cave and give it to her there."

Ryan rocked back in his chair. "Assuming she didn't get tagged by those guards."

Raina slapped the table. "You know this is all a trick, right?"

"I wish it were a trick." Louisa sat up straighter in her chair. "We have to do something. I found news about Marielle. That's why we're here with these maps."

"What kind of news?" Sophia asked.

"Bad news. They executed her."

Sophia stepped back. "How? I saw nothing about that in my research."

"I read it this morning. On a website about Rhine legends. The whole story was right there. The website was in German, so maybe it didn't come up for you?" Louisa shuffled the papers in front of her. "Anyway, Marielle wasn't mentioned at all in the original stories. They must have decided she was innocent and her name wasn't significant enough to include in the legend."

Sophia collapsed into the chair next to her brother. "What happened to her?"

"They convicted her of being a thief, even though the chest was never found, and of something far worse."

"What could be worse than a thief?" Ryan asked. "A murderer?"

Understanding dawned on Rich's face. "A witch. They thought she was a witch."

"Exactly." Louisa leaned forward. "The legend said Marielle summoned a ghost army in the cave and the guards had to vanquish it."

"There were no ghosts in the cave," Ryan scoffed. "We were there. We would have seen them."

Rich turned to his brother. "They were talking about us. We must have looked like ghosts to them."

Sophia met Louisa's eyes. "What did they do to Marielle?"

"Burned her at the stake, along with Peter, who, until then, had been a village hero."

Rich raked his hands through his hair. "We changed history. They weren't supposed to die."

Sophia sucked in a breath. "I read about the village heroes."

"That means Peter really was one of the boys who saved Sankt Goar with the beehives." Birdie turned to Louisa. "There's a statue of him and the other boy – Nikolaus – in town."

Louisa shook her head. "The statue is missing. I looked for it on my way here today. It's gone."

"Gone?" Birdie thought back to her walk across Sankt

Goar that morning. She'd been so busy watching the villagers she hadn't noticed the missing statue.

Movement on the stairs startled them all.

"Hey, campers." Kayla crossed the storeroom. For the first time since Birdie met her, she was wearing sneakers with her shorts. "Let's get this party started."

"You're late." Friedrich pointed to his watch.

Kayla shrugged. "So sue me."

"Anyway," Louisa continued, "it's more important than ever that we find the chest. Marielle and Peter were not the only ones who died. They killed their families, too, to make sure the evil line didn't continue."

"Whoa," Ryan said. "That's wicked."

"Very," Sophia agreed.

"It's more than wicked." Rich rounded the table and sat down next to Ryan. "If they both ceased to exist, and their families are gone, too, then there could be all kinds of things that change, including whole families that never existed. Friedrich and Louisa could have friends who descended from those people and when they go back to school, it will be like they never lived."

"Because, without Marielle and Peter and their families, they never did," Sophia said.

The room fell silent.

"Sophia's right," Rich finally said. "We should cross the river and see if we find anything. If we do, we can bring it back here and return it without being seen."

Friedrich snatched the clipboard. "We must consider how to do this. We may not leave the fortress during camp hours. And we must be ready for the festival tonight. They expect us to train this afternoon for our positions."

"Then we'll have to work fast." Sophia flattened her hands against the table. "And get past that lady at the ticket kiosk without raising her suspicions."

"That's true – Frau Hamel will be watching." Louisa glanced at Friedrich.

Birdie shivered. "She's always watching."

"Yes, and she was watching us. She stopped me this morning to ask why we ran past from outside the gate yesterday," Friedrich said.

"What did you tell her?" Rich asked.

"I said we hiked in the woods to see how big the fortress was."

"Did she believe you?"

"I am not sure."

"We could take a tunnel." Louisa pointed to Rich's map. "There's still one under this pitch hole. We may have to crawl again, but we can get out of the fortress without being seen."

Birdie swallowed.

"Where does it come out?" Sophia squinted at the map.

"Here, below the fortifications. We'll be halfway down the mountain."

"I noticed a door in the hillside on the trail from town this morning," Rich said. "I figured it was a gardening shed."

"No, that's it." Louisa tapped the map. "That's where the tunnel exits the fortress."

"So, let's say that works and we get out of the fortress without Frau Hamel seeing us. We still need to cross the river," Sam said.

"I considered that." Louisa turned to Friedrich. "What do you say, head counselor?"

"If we get caught they will fire us both."

"I'll risk it."

Friedrich gritted his teeth. "We will take the ferry. But if we get caught it is on your head." He glared at Birdie. "And for the record, I do think going across the river is a wild goose chase."

"Then why are we going?"

"Because it's our only idea." He wagged his index finger at her. "But leave that glass here. We cannot be on the other side of the river and go back to Marielle's time. It would be a death sentence."

"Don't worry. I didn't bring it."

Kayla started. "What do you mean you didn't bring it?"

"After what happened yesterday? You really want to take that risk again?"

"Never mind the aventurine." Louisa scooped up the maps. "We can't worry about it right now. We have a plan that doesn't require it. We don't have much time. Grab a flashlight. Is everyone in?"

Each of the campers nodded, except for Raina, who hugged her arms to her chest.

"Come on, Raina." Rich met her gaze from the other end of the table. "It won't be that bad."

"And we'll be outside instead of cooped up in this musty storeroom all morning," Ryan added.

She released her arms and shoved away from the table. "Fine. I'm in."

They reached the end of the sloped tunnel quickly, sliding several feet down a rocky incline to the door. Louisa hoisted the wooden beam that held it closed, then shoved it open on creaky hinges. They ducked through the doorway one by one, spilling out into the sunshine and fresh air far below the fortification wall. Friedrich wedged a broken hunk of ancient brick into the doorjamb to ensure it stayed open for their return.

They followed the path Birdie and the Hennesseys had taken less than an hour before, past the overgrown gardens, through the small gate to the hostel, across the train tracks, and down to the public parking lot. Her mom's car was long gone, replaced by idling tour buses.

"You may be disappointed," Louisa warned as the boatmen threw heavy ropes to lash the ferry to the dock. "The Loreley is a tourist trap. They built a visitor's center on the bluff and put a small statue down by the water."

Friedrich checked his watch. "We have exactly two hours. The ferry takes fifteen minutes each way. That leaves an hour and a half to search."

Birdie followed Louisa aboard, catching her sea legs as she swayed down a narrow walkway that bordered the inside cabin. She jostled past a group from a tour bus, then lined up with the other campers along the railing, watching the river slosh beneath the square hull as the boat lumbered away from the dock. Heavy rocking punctuated the ferry's slow pace as it cut through the choppy current, pausing for minutes at a time to let barges continue their trip to the North Sea.

Sam tilted his head at Raina. "Are you okay? You look a little green."

"Are you going to puke?" Ryan eyed his sister with amusement.

Louisa grabbed a paper bag from a holder near the door to the inside cabin and shoved it into Raina's hands. "Here. Breathe into this. And if you have to, puke into it instead of onto the floor."

"Or onto us." Kayla curled her nose at the younger girl.

Raina wrapped the bag around her lips and closed her eyes as it expanded and collapsed with her breath.

Across the river, Burg Rheinfels loomed like a battered giant, a sentinel above the constant activity on the water. Tiny Sankt Goar hugged the riverbank below it.

As they pulled up to the dock on the opposite bank, Rich patted his sister on the shoulder. "Come on. It's time to get off."

Raina opened her eyes and followed him. She breathed into the bag until they'd all disembarked and moved beyond the dock, their feet steady on dry land, except for the latent sway of the boat in their bones.

"Okay, that's enough." Louisa swatted at the bag. "You'll hyperventilate. Just hold onto it for the return trip."

When Raina lowered the bag, she looked far less green.

"Okay, where to?" Kayla peered up a flight of steep steps that led straight up the bluff.

Raina followed Kayla's gaze. Her eyes narrowed as she considered the long flight of steps. "Does anyone want to see the statue instead?"

"This isn't a sightseeing trip." Louisa started up the stairs.

"We're here to search for the chest."

Raina groaned.

Louisa turned around and faced the group. "We can visit the statue if we have time before the ferry returns, but for now, we better focus on what we came to do. These stairs lead to the visitor's center, but we're not going there. We'll turn off onto an old trail that goes to the top of the bluff, and then lose the trail altogether. My grandfather told me a story about an abandoned village up there. That's where we should start."

The name Loreley derives from the Old German words for "murmuring" and "rock." The enormous bluff looks indestructible, jutting out from a sharp bend in the river that is, even now, impossible for sailors to see around. Today there are signaling lights to warn boats of oncoming traffic, but in the long sweep of history that is a new invention.
—Marty McEntire, *Europe for Americans Travel Guide*

CHAPTER TWENTY-ONE

They climbed straight uphill for several minutes, relief coming only when Louisa cut off onto an overgrown path that hopscotched along the top of the bluff. There were no trees to speak of and, as dark clouds gathered in the distance, Birdie felt exposed on the rock.

Her legs ached from all the climbing she'd done over the past two days, and the pain reminded her of Sam's observation about the vineyards the night before. There were field hands who climbed every day during the harvest, bracing themselves on the angled earth as they gathered the grapes. Their legs had to be made of steel, and hers decidedly were not.

They marched in a single file along the path, and Birdie wondered if they'd make it to the abandoned village before the time came to return to the ferry.

Raina must have had the same thought. "How much further?"

Thunder rumbled in reply.

Sophia eyed the sky nervously. "Is it supposed to rain?"

"Why are you asking me?" Raina whipped around and threw her arms wide.

"I, uh, wasn't." Sophia stopped short, then understanding dawned on her face. "Oh, I get it. Because your name is Raina. People must always ask you about the weather."

"You think?"

Kayla pushed past them. "Which way?"

Louisa pointed to a section of the path that was wild with weeds. It crested before cutting steeply to the water.

Raina raised her eyebrows at Sophia, then followed Kayla, whose loose blond hair rippled in the strengthening wind and flowed out behind her like a flag. She was the only one in shorts, and angry red scratches marked where the brambles had raked her calves.

Another crack of thunder, much closer this time, made the rocky earth beneath their feet vibrate.

"Not good." Sam tapped Louisa's shoulder. "Where's this village?"

She turned to answer as the air snapped again and the dark clouds opened. Sheets of rain pelted from the sky and turned the ground slick, soaking them through in an instant.

"This way!" Louisa yelled over the deluge as she ran to the crest. She'd barely reached it when the wet earth gave way beneath her sneakers. She slid several feet down a muddy rock face, grasping for anything that might slow her descent. When she finally caught herself, she stood on shaking legs and looked up.

Rich, who had slid down after her, barely had time to

slow before he plowed into her. He grabbed her by the waist and held tight, keeping them both from tumbling over a rocky ledge.

"Again?" Ryan raised his eyebrows.

Up on the crest, Birdie was not amused. She tried to push the thought away, but her mind kept returning to another day, to another wicked thunderstorm, when her dad and Jonah had still been alive. She'd been young, six or seven, and they'd been at the lake. She hadn't cared about the storm, and when the rest of the family dashed back to the safety of the house, she'd stayed at the water's edge. She'd been mesmerized by the ripple of the wind on the water, billowing millions of tiny waves away from the shoreline rather than sending them in. It was as if the entire lake had changed direction before her eyes and the water beckoned her to follow.

Her mother had screamed her name. She'd heard her as if in a dream, the urgency muted as it traveled a great distance.

The ripples were beautiful.

Another rumble of thunder had torn through the sky that day and, as it did, she'd been swept away not by the water, but by her father's powerful arms as he spirited her back to the cottage. A flurry of emotions had slid across his scruffy face – fear, relief, love, and then anger at her stupidity.

"Never, ever, stay out in a storm like that again, do you hear me?" He'd rattled her shoulders to ensure she was listening. She'd cried then, and he'd pulled her into a hard hug, his dark shirt drenched from the pounding rain.

Birdie's nose tingled at the memory. Her father was not

here to save her now.

No. He would never save her again.

She squared her shoulders against the wind and fought back against the memory. She would not freeze, and she would not cry – she would save herself.

Far below, the river swirled and raged, its frothy tips grasping at the rocky shoreline, striking it with such force that she thought it might collapse in the rushing water.

On the ledge between the river and where Birdie stood, Louisa disengaged herself from Rich's grasp and pointed down the muddy hillside toward a pile of rubble. "That's it!" she called up to the others. "We must get down to the cellars in the old village!"

Raina crouched low. "No way! It's a mudslide! We'll die."

"Oh, for goodness sakes. You won't die." Kayla went first, sliding through the mud toward Louisa and Rich. When she reached them she stood tall, as if daring the lightning to strike her.

Birdie turned to the others, still undecided whether to follow.

Sam gestured to his sister. "Come on, Sophia. We need to get into a cellar."

She stared down the muddy slide, shaking her head. "Sam, please don't go down there!"

He glanced at her, then over his shoulder at Ryan, who was now sliding down the hill to join his brother. "You stay if you want but I'm going!"

"Sam!"

Beside Birdie, Friedrich stepped back.

"You're not going?" she asked.

"No. The storm is too dangerous. If we slip, we'll hit the rocks." He turned away and started back down the trail they'd just come up.

"Where are you going?" Raina cried after him.

"To the dock," he called over his shoulder. Thunder rumbled and a flash of lightning brightened the river upstream. "You should come too. All of you."

Sophia watched Sam slide further toward the abandoned village. "I'm not leaving."

Birdie felt the fear in her trembling voice. "I'll stay with Sophia. You two go. We'll meet you down there."

Friedrich muttered something in German as Raina scampered to catch up to him, slipping twice before she reached him.

"Birdie!" The cry of the river almost drowned Kayla's voice. She'd made it halfway to the village. A steep section of rock lay before her, slick with mud. "Coming?"

Sam cupped his hands around his mouth. "Sophia?"

"No!" Sophia clasped Birdie's arm as they watched Sam and the others slip the rest of the way to the cellars, grasping at roots and rocks as they went, skirting the ledge.

"They'll be okay," Birdie whispered, but it was more of a prayer than a statement.

As the others reached the rubble of the abandoned village, Kayla stopped and stared out over the river, as if she'd heard something. She crouched low.

"What is she doing?" Sophia dug her fingers into Birdie's arm.

Kayla paused for a moment longer, then dropped to her hands and knees and crawled to the very edge of the outcropping. She steadied herself on the bluff and then slowly stood, head high and chin out, her wind-whipped hair flying madly.

Far below, the low horn of a barge sounded once, then again, its deep tone haunting in the storm.

"Kayla!" Birdie cried, but her words were lost to the rain.

From the edge of the village ruins, Louisa bent and screamed to Kayla, who shook off whatever had drawn her to the ledge. She gazed one last time at the swirling water far below, then continued her descent toward Louisa.

Thunder cracked, and a bolt of lightning shot toward a small island in the river.

"We can't stay out here." Birdie turned in a slow circle in search of shelter and saw a rocky overhang several yards away. She pointed to it. "Maybe we can take cover there."

Sophia nodded and followed Birdie as she carefully picked her way toward it.

"It's getting worse," Sophia said as they ducked beneath the overhang.

As Birdie scrambled back against the rocks, something behind her gave way. She smoothed a section of moss away from the stone wall, revealing a stone-lined ramp. She yanked her flashlight from her pocket. "It looks like an old stone shed."

Sophia's gaze darted from the wild river below to the lightning flashing nearby. "Let's get in it."

They crawled onto the ramp, and Birdie swept the beam of her flashlight through the dark.

Something huge scurried across the floor.

"OUT!" She scrambled backwards up the ramp. "Out!

Sophia, go! Go!"

She didn't have to tell her twice. They sprinted back to the crest of the hill. Birdie lost her footing as she glanced over her shoulder to make sure the creature hadn't followed them. She fell hard on her knee, but quickly scrambled back to her feet.

"Which way?" Sophia cried over the pounding rain.

Birdie glanced at the path Friedrich and Raina had taken, then pointed in the opposite direction.

"You want to go down to the ruined village?" Sophia's eyes grew wide. "The others barely made it!"

"I'd rather be with them than a wild animal. Or Friedrich."

Sophia stared at her blankly for a few seconds, then she brushed her hand across her forehead to sweep away the raindrops. "You have a point."

CHAPTER TWENTY-TWO

The route to the cellars was as treacherous as it appeared from the top of the path and – as she slid several feet down the muddy incline – Birdie wondered if following the others had been a good idea after all. Where the sodden ground wasn't as slick as ice, it threatened to suck her sneakers into the mud.

They'd made it to level ground and almost reached the rubble where Louisa and Kayla had disappeared from sight when Sophia tapped Birdie on the shoulder. "I'm sorry."

"For what?"

"It was my idea to cross the river. I realize now how dumb I was."

Birdie laughed as she lifted her gaze to the gray sky and let out a sharp breath. "Oh, Sophia. You can't blame yourself. We all wanted to come. Anything was better than sitting in that storeroom having Friedrich teach us how to be villagers. And Sam's been pushing to come over here since we met Marielle. Besides, even with the storm, this is still better than camp."

"Is it? I'm not so sure. At least we'd be dry if we'd stayed at the fortress."

"Seriously. Don't worry about it. No one would be here at all if it wasn't for me." She ducked through a narrow opening in the rubble, only to find the others climbing toward them.

"There you are." Sam's T-shirt clung to his skin. "I figured you'd follow us."

Sophia folded her arms and glared down at him.

"What's back there?" Birdie rose to her tiptoes to see around them. "A cellar?"

"A whole lot of nothing." Kayla's bare legs were caked with mud. "An empty room with a puddle in the middle."

"A pool," Sam corrected. "At least three feet deep."

"Whatever. There was nothing in it, and that's the point."

"We saw one thing." Sam crept closer to Sophia.

She continued to glare at him, her dark eyes narrowing until the tug of curiosity got the best of her. "Fine. What did you see?"

"Ourselves." Sam bit back a smile. "The pool was perfectly still. It reflected us."

"Oh, big whoop." Kayla gathered her wet hair and wrung it out, the water splattering as it hit the steps. She secured it with a ponytail holder from her wrist. "I've got a mirror in my room that'd show the same thing." She gazed beyond Birdie and Sophia. "Where's Friedrich?"

"Gone." Birdie said.

"What do you mean, gone?" Louisa raised an eyebrow.

"He said the storm was too dangerous, and he left."

"He left? Unbelievable. He is gone?"

"He went to the dock."

Kayla smirked. "Some prince he turned out to be."

"His response was reasonable, to be honest," Sophia said. "And smarter than the rest of us combined. We had no business being on that path in this storm."

Rich met Birdie's eye. "Is Raina with him?"

She nodded. "She left with him."

"So, bottom line, this was a big fat waste of time." Kayla scooted past Birdie and Sophia. "I'm going to the dock before I miss the next ferry."

"Hold on a minute," Sophia said. "You said there was a pool of water? Is it just from the rain? Like a puddle that collected?"

Sam glanced over his shoulder and then back at his sister. "Kayla said it was, but I'm not so sure. It looked to me like someone dug it on purpose."

"What purpose?" Kayla paused near the entrance. "It's a ruin, Sam."

He took a deep breath. "I understand that, Kayla."

"I wanted to go in," Ryan added. "But Rich said not to bother."

Birdie turned to Sophia. "What are you thinking?"

Sophia brushed the mud from her wet jeans. "Sometimes things hide in pools of water."

"You're saying the chest could be in the water?" Sam asked. "After all these years?"

"I don't know. But it's a possibility, and we came all the

way over here, so it feels like we should check it out. We can spare a couple of minutes before we go back down to the ferry."

"I'll go for a swim if you will," Ryan said to Sam, a grin spreading across his face.

"Let's do it," Sam said. "Anybody else?"

"I want to see the pool," Birdie agreed. "But I'm not going in the water."

"Sure." Rich considered his little brother. "I'll go back in there. We were so worried about the storm we could have missed something."

"Forget it." Kayla ducked through the opening. "I'm with Fred."

Birdie and Sophia watched her go, then followed the others down a short staircase into the cellar's inky darkness.

"Hold on." Louisa clicked on her flashlight. "There."

Birdie gazed into the pool. She'd expected an oversized puddle, but this – she had not expected this. "It's beautiful."

The water was still, black as coal along the edges and emerald green in the center. It glowed in the beam of Louisa's flashlight.

Birdie peered into the water. Her face stared back in wonder, as if the reflection was as curious about her as she was about the pool itself. It was disorienting to see herself so clearly, so alive, in the dark water. She closed her eyes to wash the feeling away, but when she opened them her reflection remained.

Beside her, Sam stripped down to his boxers.

Sophia gaped at him. "What are you doing?"

"I don't need my pants getting any more soaked than

they already are. You can wring them out if you want to."

She scrunched her nose and let the jeans rest where he dropped them.

Sam waded into the water, and Birdie's reflection shimmered and broke. It dissolved into the pool and disappeared.

"That was so weird." She rubbed the goosebumps on her arms. "My reflection just vanished."

Sam slipped the rest of the way in, his head and shoulders bobbing above the surface. "The bottom's rocky. And it's deep."

"Don't swallow any of the water," Sophia warned.

"Hadn't planned to." He began a calculated exploration of the pool, serpentining along the sides. Ryan stripped down to his boxers and joined him, and together they dove toward the bottom as Louisa's light pierced the dark water.

Ryan surfaced several seconds later and shook the water from his light brown hair like a wet dog. "I didn't feel anything along the bottom. I opened my eyes but I couldn't see anything. It's pitch black down there."

Sam's dark head popped above the surface. "Empty."

"Well," Sophia sighed, "it was a long shot. We knew that all along."

The boys splashed out of the pool, the heavy water undulating around them before resettling.

"Why is it here?" Rich hung close to Louisa. "Have you ever seen anything like it before?"

She shook her head. "It is not normal."

"It must be spring-fed." Sam brushed the water from his legs and reclaimed his jeans. "Otherwise, that water would be stagnant and gross."

"Why is the center so green?" Birdie asked.

"I don't know, but it reminds me of that legend." Sam struggled to tug his jeans over his wet skin. "The one we read about last night? I could totally see a dragon hanging out in here."

Thunder clapped outside, and they all jumped.

Louisa made her way to the opening and peered at the darkening sky. "We'll have to wait it out. Hopefully, the storm passes quickly."

"The last one did," Rich said. "We'll be fine. Worse case, we have to take a later ferry."

"Not an option." Louisa rejoined them. "Unless we want to get caught."

"You don't think Friedrich would cover for us?" Sam asked.

"I do not," Louisa replied.

"He covered for us this morning, when Frau Hamel asked him why we came back from outside the gate."

"This is different. We've abandoned the grounds, and we'll be late for our training sessions for the festival."

Birdie circled the room as she listened, running her palms along the smooth stone walls. "It's like a grotto," she said, more to herself than to anyone else.

"A what-o?" Ryan asked.

Birdie was alone near the far end of the pool, deep in shadow, while the glow of Louisa's flashlight cast an eerie illumination on everyone else.

"A grotto. It's like a cave where mermaids live."

"Nope, no mermaids." Ryan skimmed his hands down his

bare legs to flick off the last drops of water before pulling on his jeans.

Louisa shuddered. "That is a good thing."

"Why?" Ryan asked.

"Because they are evil creatures, at least here in the Rhine Valley."

"Evil how?"

"They lure you with their sweet songs and beautiful faces." Louisa stared at her reflection in the pool. "And then they morph into frightening creatures that trap you under the water."

"Sirens," Sophia explained. "Like the Loreley."

"And you drown," Louisa finished.

"Great." Ryan sat down on the dirt floor and stared into the water. "I'll keep that in mind before I jump into any more pools."

"So now what?" Sam asked. "There's no old wooden chest here, no chess piece. This cellar looks like it's been picked over."

"Is there anywhere else we can search?" Sophia asked Louisa.

She shook her head. "Not that I know about."

Rich leaned against the wall. "Peter said it was here because the villagers stole it."

"I doubt he was lying to us," Birdie said. "He seemed to really think that's what happened, that the villagers from this side of the river took it. And it matches up with the legend Sophia found."

"If the chest was ever here, it must have been hidden somewhere people wouldn't have looked," Rich said.

"They feared the Loreley, so they would've avoided the bluff," Sophia said. "But Friedrich said no one is afraid of this place anymore, and the trails prove it. Something would have turned up before now."

Silence filled the chamber. Even the thunder ceased to rumble.

"It could be anywhere," Rich said. "Or nowhere. They could have blown it up with the rest of this village, or melted the chess piece down for metal during the wars."

In the distance, a horn blasted.

"That's the ferry leaving the other side of the river." Louisa walked back to the opening and peered out. "The rain has slowed down. We can make it if we hurry."

CHAPTER TWENTY-THREE

When they arrived back at Burg Rheinfels, Friedrich crossed the storeroom and addressed them from the end of the long table. "We lost a lot of time, and we have much to accomplish to prepare for the festival and pageant. Therefore, we are breaking you into teams. I will take team one and Louisa will take team two."

It was the first time he'd spoken since chastising them as they'd sprinted onto the dock and waved down the boatmen, who'd been busy unlashing the ferry. It had been a cold, windy trip across the Rhine, followed by a long, wet hike up to the fortress. By the time they emerged from the tunnel, Birdie was chilled to the bone. They'd taken turns changing into the dry clothes they'd packed to wear the next day, then scattering their wet things along the backs of the extra chairs. Only Friedrich looked crisp instead of rumpled.

No one objected to his pronouncement as they collected

181

their lunch trays and huddled at one end of the long table to eat. Birdie was too tired, too lost in her own thoughts to care much about which team she ended up on or how she'd learn her role. They were back at camp, where they were supposed to be, but none of it seemed to matter.

"Okay, my team," Friedrich said. "Follow me."

Birdie shoved her chair away from the table and followed Sophia, Sam, and Raina out into the warm sunshine that had blossomed in the wake of the storms. The fortress was abuzz with workers erecting wooden stalls and scaffolding as they transformed the battered ruin into a colorful medieval walled town.

As they made their way across the grounds to the courtyard, Sophia scuffed her sneakers on the path. "I really wish the chest had been over there."

"Me too. We all did. Well, except for Raina." She glanced over at her to make sure she wasn't listening then leaned closer to Sophia. "Besides, I'm not ready to give up yet."

"What do you mean?"

"I don't know exactly. Maybe there's another way to save Marielle? Something we're missing?"

They paused as two wiry workers rushed past with boxes that overflowed with toy swords.

"Do you still think we can save her without using the aventurine?" Sophia began walking again. "I know you said it'd be too dangerous, but the more I think about it, the less likely it seems we'll find anything now that they hid so long ago."

Birdie sighed, loudly enough that a worker at a beer stand glanced up. He took one look at Friedrich marching ahead of them and gave her a chin-up kind of smile. She smiled back, but her heart wasn't in it.

"We might make things worse," she said. "I don't have a good answer, to be honest. I'm hoping someone will come up with an idea that doesn't get us all killed too."

"I hope you're right. The whole thing is just dreadful." Sophia placed her hand over her heart. "I mean, she died. *Died*. Because of us."

They'd reached the courtyard, which had been transformed from a windswept wasteland into a tournament field encircled by stalls selling all manner of medieval wares.

Friedrich pointed to a stall with a wood-fired oven. "Sam, you are to meet with the baker, Herr Becker. He will tell you what to do. You must help him figure out how to get more sales. Hiding him out back would be a good start."

"Better customer service. Got it." Sam shuffled off toward the bakery.

"Raina, you are to learn a traditional dance and perform with a troupe from Sankt Goar." He pushed her toward a group of teenage girls and boys who were crossing the field. "Join them now."

"What about me?" Sophia asked.

"I will take you to meet Frau Cheval. She runs the stables."

"So that leaves me. The servant. Should I have been on Louisa's team?"

"Yes, that leaves you. We must get Sophia settled and then we will take care of your position."

Like the rest of the temporary festival structures, the stables were a makeshift collection of wooden stalls set up in the open air behind the former keep. Six horses – three white and three black – grazed in the tall weeds.

Frau Cheval was a tiny round woman with a friendly face who greeted Sophia with a strong German accent and a genuine smile. She wrapped her arm around her shoulders and took her into the fold as if she were a long-lost daughter.

"Now me?" Birdie glanced at Friedrich.

"Soon," he replied without meeting her eyes.

She followed him as he circled back to Sam and Raina, making sure they were where they were supposed to be and imparting strict instructions as if he were their boss instead of their camp counselor. It was only after they'd returned to the stables and he was confident that Sophia had settled in with Frau Cheval that he turned his attention to Birdie.

"Where is the aventurine?"

"What?" She'd expected to be bombarded with a long list of servant instructions, and his question took her by surprise. "I… I told you I didn't bring it."

"I thought perhaps you were lying." His eyes were hard.

"No, I wasn't." She took a step back.

Friedrich closed the gap. "You must get it. You are staying at Hotel Flussufer, correct?"

"Correct, but – wait, how did you know where—"

"I will drive you there." His body seemed to almost vibrate with energy, as if he felt more alive in that moment than he had in ages.

Birdie hugged herself and shied away. "But you said we can't leave—"

"Nice try. "I brought a car today. It will take only ten minutes to get there and back. No one will know we're gone."

Birdie stilled in the sunlight. Workers skirted them on the path, too busy moving medieval props into place to care about two campers in their way.

She struggled to make sense of Friedrich's sudden demand. He'd deserted them at the Loreley and was disinterested in hearing what happened when they returned to the ferry. Now he wanted her to get the aventurine?

"I thought you agreed it was better if we didn't use it again."

"Not on that side of the river," he said. "That would have been a suicide mission."

"But—"

"It will be fine."

"I won't do it." Her voice rose as she unfolded her arms and stood tall.

Friedrich leaned in close. He spoke slowly and clearly, his accent nearly eliminated from the carefully formed words. "Go get the glass, or I will tell your mother you stole an antique from the museum."

Her mouth dropped open.

He straightened. "Now, we go." He started down the path.

Birdie didn't move. "Why? Where is this coming from? What do you want to do with it?"

"I will do nothing with it." A corner of his thin mouth lifted. "You will."

Her eyes narrowed. "Okay, what am I going to do with it?"

"Take us to the cave so I can question Marielle. I must

make sure she returns the chest to Elisabeth's father so the wedding proceeds."

"The wedding? Who cares about the stupid wedding? What about Marielle's life?"

Friedrich shrugged. "They may spare her life if she returns the chest."

"But Marielle doesn't know where it is."

"She knows more than she says. I am sure of it. I will question her, and then we will find the chest so she can return it to Elisabeth's father."

"Friedrich, the guards obviously captured her, so it would be extraordinarily stupid for us to go back to that cave right now. We could get caught."

"It is a risk I will take."

"But why? Why put everyone in danger like that?"

"Not all. Just you. And me, of course. You said you want to find the chest."

"I want to save Marielle, but in a way that keeps us alive. She told us everything she knew, and she was wrong. What else would she tell you, assuming we even find her in the cave? She may already be dead for all we know."

"We were fools to believe anything could still exist on the Loreley."

"You didn't seem to think it was so foolish when you agreed to cross on the ferry. Make up your mind. Maybe it was a wild goose chase, but I have zero interest in going on this new wild goose chase you've cooked up."

Anger flared in his pupils. The fortress hummed with activity around them, yet it felt as if they were the only ones there.

"I have a plan," he hissed, his patience fraying. "That is all you need to know. My plan requires you to get the aventurine and take me to the cave so I can question Marielle."

"Okay, you have a plan. Great," Birdie said. "Let's hear the rest of it."

"No."

"Why not?"

He glared at her. "Do you want to save Marielle?"

"I thought you didn't care about Marielle."

He stepped closer. "We must return the chest. The wedding must take place. We can fix everything."

"I guess I'm not understanding what else needs to be fixed," Birdie said. "Or why it needs to be fixed right now without including Louisa and everyone else? Our goal is to save Marielle."

Friedrich fell silent as he surveyed the activity around them.

"Well?"

He returned his attention to her. "I will tell you. But you must agree to get the aventurine."

She didn't respond.

"The princess? Elisabeth? She was my ancestor."

Birdie's eyes narrowed. "She was—"

"My ancestor. A member of my family."

She almost laughed. "Are you sure?"

"I am sure. My mother has told stories of the failed marriage all my life. Now, with your help, I can make it right." He reached for her hand. "We must go."

Birdie pulled away before he could touch her. "That

seems, um, unlikely, Friedrich. How do you know it's true? And why didn't you say something earlier?"

"It is no one's business." He wrapped his hot hand around her elbow and, gripping hard, guided her to a fortification wall near the back of the fortress. "Enough questions."

Her mind raced. She considered yelling, alerting the workers scurrying around them. But what would it accomplish? Nothing, except to make her mom pick her up early, for stealing.

That couldn't happen.

She had to figure a way out of this. If only she could get back to the others.

A pair of workers barreled toward them in a golf cart weighed down with supplies, forcing Friedrich and Birdie from the path.

That gave her an idea. "What about your job? You can't just ghost them, especially today when everyone is so busy. I wouldn't want you to get into trouble."

"I will not get in trouble." He motioned toward an opening in the wall. "Go through there. It is a shortcut to the parking lot. Ladies first."

"I—"

"Now, Birdie."

She dug her heels into the sandy path. There had to be a way to keep from leaving. "What do you think will happen if we go back to the cave?"

"I told you, I have a plan."

"Share it with me. This isn't a game. What if we get stuck? The aventurine held us in the past longer than before."

He patted his polo. "I will use the whistle."

"Wait." Her eyes grew bright. "Here's a better idea. Let's share your plan with everyone else first. They may be able to help. And I'll make you a deal. If everyone else is on board, I'll go get the aventurine."

"I am not concerned about the others," he growled. "This is not their business!"

"It's not?"

"Don't you understand? My family would have ruled all the land between the rivers if Elisabeth had married the right man."

Birdie felt the shock wash over her face. "Oh, wow, okay." She checked to see if any of the workers had heard him, but no one was paying attention.

She locked her knees so he couldn't pull her any further. "Friedrich. Are you serious right now? That was centuries ago. How do you know what would have happened? If Elisabeth had married a different man, you might not have been born."

"I am descended from Elisabeth's sister."

"I doubt it matters," Birdie said. "There's been so much change, so much history, so much war – none of this family's power still exists. This place is literally in ruins!"

"You will not go?"

"We can't use the aventurine again unless we're absolutely positive we can save Marielle."

"You said that. And I told you I do not care about Marielle other than making sure she returns the chest. I must go back because I must talk to Elisabeth."

"The princess?"

"Yes, the princess. Don't you listen?" He released his grip as he threw his hands into the air. "I must make Elisabeth understand why this marriage is so important."

"But…" She tried to process the warped idea that Friedrich thought he could become, what? A prince? A duke? He seemed willing to ignore all of history – never mind that there was no way he could just mosey up to a medieval princess – to see if it would work.

"But what?"

She steadied her voice. "It seems like a long shot. What makes you so sure Marielle knows where the chest is? Peter didn't lie to us yesterday. He believed it was across the river."

"She knows something that she has not told us. I am sure of it. And if she returns the chess piece, she may be saved."

"And Princess Elisabeth? How would you get close enough to talk to her?"

He glared at Birdie for several moments. When he finally spoke, it was through gritted teeth. "What if I agree to talk to the others first?"

She hadn't expected that.

"That is what you want, correct? To include the others?"

She nodded.

"Okay. But we cannot stand here any longer. We must go now to get the glass. There will be no other time when we will not be missed."

"What are you saying?"

"I am saying… I will include the others. I will share my plan with them and with you."

"And your plan is about making Elisabeth marry the

prince?"

Friedrich nodded.

"And we will tell the others before we use the aventurine?"

He nodded again.

"Swear it."

"I swear it." Friedrich stared into her eyes but she couldn't read him, couldn't say for sure if he was telling the truth.

She had to decide.

"Okay." She poked at his chest. "But I will only do this if the ultimate goal is to save Marielle. We can't be concerned with whether you become a real-life prince in this fantasy you've dreamt up for yourself."

His eyes flashed again, but his voice remained calm. "We are agreed."

He bowed, and Birdie slipped through the opening to the parking lot.

CHAPTER TWENTY-FOUR

The hotel was quiet in the middle of the day, and Birdie used the back-door code to slip inside and retrieve the aventurine. Herr Mueller was absent, and the cleaning crew was busy on a lower floor.

True to his word, Friedrich was steering his small car back up the hill toward Burg Rheinfels less than ten minutes after they'd left the parking lot. But when they reached the main gate, he didn't turn in.

"You missed it." Birdie twisted to stare out the window as he sped past the entrance and continued up the hill. He slowed several yards ahead and maneuvered the car off the road.

"Why are we parking here?"

He turned in the driver's seat to face her. "We are going to the cave."

She closed her eyes and leaned into the headrest. Why

had she trusted him? Every instinct had told her not to, and she'd gone with him anyway. Now they were alone and she had the aventurine.

He tapped her knee. "Tell me. If we go to the past, will the others go too?"

Birdie opened her eyes and glared at him. "You seriously want to go back now?"

"Answer the question."

"We're not prepared. We should at least put our costumes on and tell everyone else. You swore we'd include them. Besides, what if the guards are still in the cave? You're not thinking this through."

"I brought the whistle. Now, tell me. I must know if the others will also go back."

"Why?"

He released a frustrated breath and threw his car door open. "Why are you so difficult? Come now."

Birdie opened her door and stepped onto the sidewalk. He'd parked next to the trailhead, which she now realized was hidden from the road. The slender opening between the rock faces was nearly imperceptible beneath a heavy layer of vegetation. If they hadn't disturbed it yesterday, she wouldn't know the trail was there at all.

"The others will wonder where we are. We should go back."

"We will be fast. Follow me." He passed between the rocks and bounded down the stairs.

Birdie hesitated, and he was halfway down before he realized she was still on the sidewalk. "Come now!" he bellowed.

She considered her options.

And then, she ran.

She flew down the sidewalk as Friedrich roared in German. Seconds later, his footfalls pounded fast behind her. "Birdie Blessing! Stop!"

She ran harder, barely slowing as she slipped through the main gate.

Frau Hamel whipped around as Birdie dashed past the ticket kiosk. Kayla was crammed next to her in the small booth, her back to the window.

Birdie slowed to a jog and then a walk as Friedrich caught up and fell into step beside her.

"Why did you do that?" he demanded between gasps for air.

She hurried down the storeroom stairs. She prayed Louisa and her team would be there, but it was empty. "Better get your car. People will wonder why it's parked there."

"Birdie—"

She stopped short and spun to face him, hands on her hips. "Look, you're a camp counselor and not my boss, and not actually a prince, okay? I barely know you and I think it's weird that you're being so sneaky. I am not going back to the cave with you. Marielle is dead because of us. We could be next. Now, stop messing around. Where am I supposed to be?"

Friedrich's jaw slackened.

She raised her eyebrows at him, waiting, her own anger flaring. He'd played her for a fool and she'd fallen for it. But no more. And she could tell he knew it.

"Es tut mir leid," he mumbled, his shoulders slumping. "Sorry, Birdie."

She narrowed her eyes. Too easy. And she was in no mood to forgive and forget.

When she didn't respond to his apology, he strode over to the table and, after shuffling through several piles of clothing, pulled out a long black dress, several skirts, and a white scarf.

"Here, servant." He held the costume pieces out to her. "These are your clothes. You will look like Marielle."

She plucked the costume from his outstretched hands warily, ready for him to snap again at any moment. "Where am I stationed?"

He started toward the steps. "Follow me."

Once again, she didn't move.

"What now?" A bead of sweat skimmed his sharp cheekbone. "I said I am sorry. What else do you want?"

"You didn't say the magic word."

He snarled. "Follow me, *bitte*. Please." Then he mumbled something in German that Birdie didn't understand.

"Where are we going?"

"To the keep. That is where you will be stationed until the pageant. It's also where Louisa should be, posing for photos with the children. You are to manage the line for her."

She walked beside him to the tournament field, not trusting him to walk behind her and not liking the visual of tagging along after him like a puppy.

He stayed silent and did not press the issue of the aventurine again. It was as if the past fifteen minutes had

195

occurred in some alternate reality, like they were in some kind of weird do-over. But no matter how quiet he was, she wouldn't forget what happened or how easily he'd turned on her.

When they reached the keep, Friedrich introduced her to an older servant woman.

"I will see you at the pageant." He met her gaze before he passed through the doorway. "Then we will speak."

Birdie was aware of the aventurine deep in the front pocket of her jeans, and of the curious gaze of the older woman upon them both.

She flashed her best dance class smile. "See you there!"

CHAPTER TWENTY-FIVE

The next few hours passed quickly as Birdie trained for her role as Louisa's lady's maid. There was much to learn about how the pageant would unfold, how she should act, and why her role was important. She changed into the dress without too much difficulty, but wrapping her hair in the long white scarf proved a challenge that required three experienced costumers to get right. By the time they finished, she did indeed look just like Marielle.

She waited for a chance to tell Louisa what had happened, to let her know about Friedrich and the aventurine, to share his claim that he was somehow related to Elisabeth, but the chance didn't come. Louisa was training in a different part of the fortress, and as more reenactors arrived and fell into position, the events of the morning fell further away.

By the time the festival began, one hundred volunteers

had descended upon Burg Rheinfels, bringing the fortress to life with an energy and vibrancy that Birdie could not have dreamed possible. The musicians alone, with their stringed lutes, harp-like lyres, and simple flutes, filled the air with joyful melodies that made her heart lift.

She was positioned in front of the keep, where she could see the maneuvers of a regiment of costumed guards stationed along the remaining fortification walls. Sellers of various goods lined the walkways and the tournament field, calling to passersby in multiple languages. Young girls in flowing dresses wandered the lanes with baskets of flowers for sale, and the scent of fresh-baked pastries and roasted nuts permeated the air. Within the crumbled remnants of the apothecary, a wild-haired man in period clothes sold herbs and tonics. Behind him, plumes of fragrant smoke rose from the kitchens, where large hunks of meat were being smoked.

Birdie read and reread the English translation of the event script, but it was difficult to focus on the words when there were so many interesting things she wished she could explore. She longed to taste the sugar-laden pastries and play the old-fashioned games of chance that were causing children to call out in delight.

She focused on the long strip of paper in her hand. All the announcements and activities would be in German, and she needed to understand what was happening to avoid messing up.

The rustling of fabric announced Louisa's arrival. "I'm so nervous, Birdie. I didn't know there would be so many people. My mother told me this was a big festival, but I didn't realize how big."

Birdie glanced over her shoulder and couldn't help but smile. Louisa looked one hundred percent the part, her thick braids pinned elegantly high on her head. She wore a rich green gown that made her look as lovely as any movie princess. "You'll be great. Don't worry."

"I'm glad you'll be there with me." Louisa squeezed her hand quickly before taking her position in front. "Catch me if I fall off the horse, okay?"

They greeted guests and stayed in character as they waited for the pageant to begin. Louisa grinned as she hugged little girls who wanted nothing more than to have their picture taken with the princess. Birdie held her place behind Louisa and helped her manage the photo line when it grew unwieldy.

The grounds were thick with people as the time drew near for the pageant to begin. Every so often, on the other side of the tournament field, Ryan struck the huge hammer to iron, and the sound reverberated like a drumbeat over the murmur of the crowd. Several stalls down, Sam, dressed in baker's whites, waved thin loaves of freshly baked bread at passersby.

When the signal came for the pageant to begin, Birdie hurried the last few children through the photo line, then gathered her heavy skirts and followed Louisa into the ruined keep, which was serving as a staging area. She lifted her gaze to the broad blue sky, remembering the walls and windows that soared above them the day before, the colorful tapestries that created a beautiful retreat for the ruling family.

There was no such air of serenity today. A stout woman with a clipboard shouted orders to various groups, first in German and then in English. Birdie and Louisa lined up behind two guards wielding twenty-foot-tall banners in black and gold. Sophia arrived with Frau Cheval, leading a regal white horse adorned with ribbons. She wore a long-sleeved shirt, quilted vest, heavy britches, and knee-high boots. She'd tucked her dark hair beneath a boy's cap.

"You look great," Birdie said.

Sophia smiled. "So do you." Frau Cheval tapped her shoulder and motioned to the door. "See you out there!"

Two soldiers hoisted Louisa onto Sophia's horse, where she teetered in a sidesaddle in her elaborate gown. Birdie waited beside her, careful to avoid the massive hooves.

From beyond the keep, trumpets blared.

The massive wooden doors at the end of the ruined keep drifted open and groups of reenactors paraded onto the tournament field as the musicians played a song that seemed handpicked for the summer day. A regiment of guards marched in formation, followed by a cadre of acrobats and jesters. Each group met appreciative applause from the crowd.

The woman with the clipboard pointed at Louisa.

She clutched the saddle. "This is it."

The guards holding the black-and-gold banners marched through the doors, and Louisa's horse followed them obediently, well trained for its role. Birdie stayed beside them, ready to catch Louisa if she slipped from its back.

They entered the sunny tournament field to the cheers of both the waiting crowd and the rest of the reenactors, who'd arranged themselves in a colorful circle of honor. By the volume of the cheers, Birdie knew Louisa was the star of the show.

A trumpeter bounded onto the stage to deliver a proclamation in German to formally introduce the princess.

Birdie held her chin high, feeling the weight of the scarf wrapped around her hair, and stared forward. Her role, which fell closer to prop than actor, required little more than that.

At the opposite end of the tournament field, a second set of trumpets blared as four guards toting long red banners led Friedrich onto the field. He was draped in chainmail and a dark cloak and astride a black horse, waving a sword in an attempt to appear princely.

Birdie wrinkled her nose at the sight of him, but caught herself before anyone could notice. He appeared to be enjoying his role a bit too much.

More booming announcements followed, and boos bubbled up from the crowd. Louisa's trumpeter spoke again, and a cheer replaced the boos. Soldiers from both groups made a show of a contest with swords and lances. They continued their battle to much fanfare until the trumpets sounded again.

The crowd shifted to face the low-slung stage, where Raina and the local troupe moved into position. Raina was lovely in her traditional costume and, as much as she hated to admit it, Birdie thought she did a beautiful job with the routine, especially considering she'd only learned it that afternoon.

As the dancers continued, Birdie scanned the crowd for

Kayla and Rich but came up empty. She figured Kayla was still in the ticket booth with Frau Hamel, and Rich was indistinguishable among the legion of costumed guards. She shifted her gaze to the stalls, where Sam and Ryan stood watching the dancers.

Her eyes grew wide as a prickle of heat tingled against her thigh. Deep beneath her skirts, in the pocket of her jeans, the aventurine was growing warm.

She glanced up at Louisa, still sidesaddle on the horse and watching the dancers with rapt attention, her hands clasped at her chest as if she'd never seen anything so beautiful before.

Birdie's heart raced as the music rose and fell and the dancers moved faster and faster upon the stage. There was nothing she could do. She couldn't lift her skirts high in the middle of the pageant. And even if she retrieved the aventurine—

She laid her hand where the heat radiated through her black skirt and closed her eyes, willing it to cool down. Maybe, just this once, it would work.

Above her, Louisa gasped.

Birdie's eyes flew open.

Barely there, shimmering in front of them, was Marielle. She was lashed to a sturdy piece of wood in the middle of the tournament field. She was no longer dressed as a lady's maid, but in a plain brown sack, her blond hair loose and waving down her back.

Firewood rested beneath her.

"Birdie," Louisa squeaked. "Do you see?"

Before she could respond, Marielle saw them too. *"Hilf*

mir!" she screamed, the words cutting through the centuries. *"Sie musst ihn retten!"*

"What is she saying?"

"She needs our help." Louisa's knuckles turned white as she clutched the reins. "And so does Peter. She wants us to save him."

A few yards away, Peter was on his knees, secured in wooden stocks, his head and hands hanging low as he awaited his fate. Birdie had seen him only once before, in the cave, where he'd been so brave and strong, willing to stand up to all of them to save Marielle. Her heart sank as she saw him now, completely bowed.

Marielle screamed to them again, pleading.

Louisa lifted the reins. From the corner of her eye, Birdie saw Sam step out from the baker's stall and start toward the center of the tournament field. Up on stage, Raina slowed and missed a step as the music reached its crescendo. Friedrich began to dismount.

And then, the trumpets blew.

Long and loud.

And Marielle and Peter were gone.

CHAPTER TWENTY-SIX

Birdie felt lightheaded as the aventurine stopped radiating heat against her leg and cooled in her pocket. The crowd fell silent, anticipating whatever was to happen next, unaware of the heart-wrenching scene the campers had just endured.

The trumpeter made an announcement, but no one moved.

Birdie wasn't sure she could. She was rooted to the ground, certain her knees would buckle if she tried to take a step.

It was Friedrich who recovered first, shaking off the shock of seeing Marielle and Peter and climbing back into his saddle. He adjusted his cape and, as he did, Birdie noticed a red falcon, its wings spread wide, embroidered across the back.

Friedrich lifted his bony chin, and his handlers led his horse toward Louisa. They progressed slowly, building suspense for the crowd, who looked riveted by the story unfolding before them.

Friedrich met Birdie's gaze for several seconds, his eyes unreadable, and she wondered if he was sending some kind of message. If so, she had no clue what it was.

He shifted his focus to Louisa and spoke to her in German, projecting his voice for all to hear. Birdie knew from the script that this was the proposal.

Atop the regal white horse, Louisa was shaking. She paused for longer than they'd practiced, gripped the horse's reins as if they would grant her strength, and fell into character.

There was nothing else she could do. The audience was waiting.

Louisa tossed her head back and guffawed at the proposal, then shook her head emphatically. She said a few cutting words, and the crowd joined her laughter.

Friedrich played his role well, his expression shifting from shock at Louisa's rejection to anger at his humiliation, with practiced expertise. He drew his sword high, and a gasp rippled through the crowd. Louisa's guard closed ranks around her, shuffling Birdie off to the side.

And then, Rich appeared, galloping onto the tournament field on a larger horse than the one Friedrich rode, wielding a longer sword, and calling out a series of threatening lines from the script to send Friedrich and his guard packing. Rich was dressed like a knight rather than a guard, and Louisa's cheeks grew rosy as she watched him perform.

Birdie was impressed by how well Rich pronounced the German words, at least to her untrained ear. While she was wrangling kids for photos, he must have been promoted and given his lines to practice. His tone was low and menacing, and even if she hadn't read the translation, she'd know that Friedrich was no longer welcome at the fortress.

Friedrich reared back on his horse and thrust his sword through two of Louisa's golden banners, shredding them. The crowd booed. He galloped toward the exit and, turning in a spray of dust, warned them all he would return. He charged off the field, his guard at his heels.

The crowd cheered his departure.

Rich raised his sword in triumph and approached Louisa. He winked at her as he bowed deeply in his saddle, then rode off after Friedrich. Louisa clasped her hands to her heart and stared after him in wistful admiration.

The crowd loved it.

With the proposal thwarted, Birdie helped Louisa dismount and then followed her to wooden bleachers that had been set up across the field from the stage. She filed into the row behind Louisa and watched in silence as Sophia led the white horse away and a series of performers took the stage.

"You have the aventurine," Louisa said without turning around.

"I do. I wanted to tell you, but—"

Sophia returned and scooted in behind her on the bleachers. She leaned in close. "Why did you lie to us?"

"I didn't. I swear."

"You have the aventurine," Louisa said. "You just admitted it."

"Yes, but—"

"But you told us you left it at the hotel," Sophia said.

"I did leave it at the hotel."

"Then how did you get it?" Louisa smiled and waved at the next performer.

"I wanted to tell you earlier, but there was no time. Friedrich made me get it."

Louisa turned around, breaking character completely, her eyes filled with disbelief.

"When we split into teams? He got everyone else settled and then drove me to Sankt Goar."

"Alone? Why on earth did you go with him?" Sophia asked.

Birdie was silent.

"Birdie?" Louisa said. "Answer the question."

"It's stupid."

"It couldn't have been that stupid." Sophia rested her elbows on the rough knees of her stable britches. "You went with him, didn't you?"

"He said he'd tell my mom I stole something from the museum."

"He did not." Louisa scowled.

"Oh, that's bad," Sophia said.

"Yes, he did. Do you think I'd go off with him in his car otherwise?"

"I believe you." Louisa turned back to face the stage. "I just cannot believe him."

"That's not all. He tried to make me go to the cave with him."

"He did what?" Louisa pivoted to stare at her again.

"I didn't do it. I ran back to the fortress when he started

down the trail. He chased me, but he didn't dare make a scene in front of Frau Hamel."

"That doesn't make any sense." Sophia swiveled her hand and Louisa faced the stage again. "Why would he do that? He knows we're all trying to figure this out. Why go on his own and drag you with him?"

"He said that Elisabeth – the princess Louisa is playing – is his ancestor. He seems to think that if she married Prince Gunzelin – the prince he plays, not the guy she really married – that his life would be different. He says he's descended from Elisabeth's sister."

"That's ridiculous," Louisa said.

"That's what I told him. But it didn't matter. He wants to talk to her and make sure the chess piece gets returned to her father so the wedding goes through."

"I'm going to kill him." Louisa gritted her teeth as she smiled and waved to the crowd. "He was so worried about leaving camp for the ferry and then he pulls this?"

The trumpets sounded again and the crowd shifted its attention away from the stage. Friedrich returned to the tournament field with his guard. Louisa's guard, with Rich at the lead, faced off against them.

"We must pay attention." Louisa didn't turn around. "The crowd will watch to see how we react."

The joust progressed as planned, with a few near misses and a dramatic failure by Friedrich's team in the end. Louisa jumped up and cheered at the result.

She was still clapping wildly at Friedrich's loss when Sophia tugged Birdie's sleeve. "Oh, my gosh. I figured it out."

"Figured what out?" Birdie was also clapping, glad to see Friedrich get his comeuppance, even if it was all staged.

Louisa reclaimed her seat and leaned back, smiling.

"It's you!" Sophia tapped Louisa's shoulder.

"What's me?"

"Not you – you, the princess you."

Louisa twisted on the bleacher and raised her eyebrows.

"The princess – Elisabeth, you – doesn't want to marry the prince – Friedrich."

As she spoke, Friedrich and his team left the field, heads hung low.

"Correct."

"What if the dowry wasn't stolen at all? What if the princess hid it somewhere as insurance in case her rejection didn't work?"

"What do you mean, if her rejection didn't work?" Birdie asked. "Do you mean if she told him no, but it didn't matter?"

Sophia nodded.

"Because she had no power over such things." Louisa's eyes lit with understanding. "She had to do what her father wanted her to do or risk exile."

"Exactly." Sophia leaned closer. "In the pageant, you say no and Friedrich gets lost. That's a modern version of the story, but it's not what happened in real life. In real life, no one would've cared that she didn't like him. She would have to marry him, no matter what. It wasn't until someone let it slip that the dowry was missing that he rejected her."

"She got rid of the dowry herself?" Louisa said.

"There's a strong possibility. She probably never

imagined they'd accuse her lady's maid of the theft."

"But where would Elisabeth have hidden it?" Birdie asked. "And how?"

"Good questions." Sophia glanced from Birdie to Louisa. "But one thing's for sure. She wouldn't have taken it across the river. She wouldn't dare cross into enemy territory."

"She must have had help," Louisa said. "She was never alone."

"Almost never," Sophia corrected. "They left her alone with Marielle."

"So you think Marielle was in on it?" Birdie didn't want to believe it. That would mean Friedrich had been right that she knew more than she was letting on. She shook her head in disbelief. "But why would Elisabeth let her be murdered if she was helping her?"

"She wasn't supposed to die, remember?" Louisa said. "She wasn't even supposed to be accused of anything. If she was in on it, I don't think she knew she was in on it."

"What do you mean?" Birdie asked.

"I doubt Marielle knew anything. If she did, she wouldn't have run to Peter and put him in danger too."

"Good point," Sophia said.

"Elisabeth could have done something, though, right?" Birdie said. "To stop the execution?"

Louisa shook her head. "I doubt it. Not if they were accusing Marielle of witchcraft. They would say the princess was under a spell or something."

"So Marielle died for her." Sophia sat back on the bleacher. "A loyal servant to the end."

"So what do we do now?" Louisa asked.

"I think we're supposed to save her," Birdie said.

"But how?"

The bleachers had emptied, and the crowd was thinning. Near the stage, Mrs. Hennessey had cornered her children and was talking to them animatedly.

"I need to return to the keep." Louisa stood. "I'll meet you in the storeroom."

Birdie noticed her mom standing with Harry and Helga on the other side of the field. "I'll see you there. I want to say hi to my mom."

"Me too." Sophia nodded toward Sam, who'd already met up with their parents. "I won't be long."

"We should go back to the cave," Rich said an hour later. "It's the only logical place to look."

They'd regrouped in the storeroom and Sophia had shared her latest theory. They were still in costume, crowded around one end of the long table, noshing on leftover apricot strudel that Sam brought from the bakery.

Friedrich stood apart, brooding in his dark cape near the tunnel entrance.

Their parents and the other tourists had shuffled from the fortress shortly after the pageant ended. Birdie had wished she could have told her mom everything and left with her, but she'd been so proud of the performance that Birdie couldn't bring herself to cause her any worry. So she'd simply given her a hug goodbye and come back to the storeroom to join the others.

The sounds of hammers and drills beyond the open doors signaled the dismantling had already begun.

"You want to go back to the cave?" Raina stared at her brother. "But it's almost dark. What if we get lost in the woods, or worse?" She shot Birdie a dirty look. "Besides, what if we find the stupid chest? Then what? Doesn't that mess things up even more? The princess would have to marry" – she poked her thumb back toward Friedrich – "him."

"All we know for sure is the timeline shifted and Marielle, Peter, and their families died because of it." Rich looked at the other campers. "That's why we need to find the chest and return it to Elisabeth's father so he can order Marielle to be released."

"You know, maybe Elisabeth was supposed to marry the prince and Marielle was supposed to die." Kayla flopped into a chair. "Did you ever think of that? Maybe we didn't change history, maybe we fixed it."

"No," Birdie said. "I don't believe that. And even if she was supposed to die, it can't be because of us. I think we stayed in the past longer than we were supposed to – we were only there to help Marielle escape, but then we followed her to the cave."

"We owe it to Marielle to try to save her," Sophia added.

"I agree." Rich glanced at Louisa, who was standing beside him. "So, how do we get to the cave? This place is crawling with workers and the tunnel to the forest is collapsed."

"We wait. We cannot go now. Frau Hamel will lock the doors in one hour. We wait until then."

"We wait until we're locked in." Raina rolled her eyes. "That makes total sense."

"Just trust me," Louisa said. "If anyone needs to use the toilet, I suggest you do it now while the door is still open."

"We should get out of these stupid costumes too." Kayla held up the ends of her heavy skirts. Even in the ticket booth, she'd been required to be in period dress.

"Bad idea." Rich shook his head. "We should stay in them. I don't want to get caught in the past in street clothes."

"Easy for you to say. Try running in this get-up."

Louisa crossed the storeroom and rested her elbow on a stack of cots that had been delivered during the festival. "We don't want to get caught now, either, so we must do what we would have done if we were settling in for the night."

"We would have changed," Kayla grumbled.

"That means setting up these cots. Boys on one side of the storeroom and girls on the other. I'll get the projector set up." She pointed to a bulky black box on the table. A huge lens poked out the top. "We are supposed to watch movies tonight."

"What kind of movies?" Kayla reached over and picked up a battered DVD case. "*Robin Hood?*"

They worked together to set up the cots and organize their belongings. Some of the clothes they'd hung had dried. They'd nearly finished when Frau Hamel darkened the doorway at the top of the stairs. "All set, Friedrich?"

"All set." He moved to the center of the storeroom where she could see him.

"You are still in costume."

"Yes."

"Make sure none of the pieces goes missing." She took a

mental inventory of their costumes before continuing. "I have the pizzas." She stepped aside to let a deliveryman pass. He shoved several boxes on the table and made a quick retreat.

"Good night then." Frau Hamel nodded to Friedrich. She backed out of the doorway and let each of the heavy wooden doors swing closed. The storeroom grew dark as the latch outside slid shut.

"Okay, now what?" Sam asked.

"Now we wait," Louisa said. "Eat the pizza. Friedrich, do you have the flashlights?"

He lined the flashlights up on a cot as the rest of them grabbed slices of pizza and sat down.

"So, what exactly are we looking for in the cave?" Kayla asked. "Marielle?"

"The chest." Raina picked at her crust. "The stupid wooden chest. Haven't you been paying attention at all?"

"Watch it, sister," Kayla said.

"And the chess piece," Sam said.

"Which is in the chest," Raina said. "Duh."

Birdie set her pizza down. "Actually, we're looking for a dragon."

CHAPTER TWENTY-SEVEN

They shifted in their chairs to stare at Birdie as she dug under her skirts and pulled the aventurine from the pocket of her jeans. She balanced it on her palm.

"A dragon."

Although she hadn't seen it happen, the image on the glass had changed during the pageant. The dragon reminded her of a child's drawing, blocky and edgy with a single flame shooting from its mouth.

"Like the one that protected the treasures of the river." Sam leaned in for a closer inspection.

"Exactly. Only I think this one may protect the dowry. Or at least the chest that was part of it. The legend says the dragon guards a treasure in a cave." She hesitated. "You all saw Marielle and Peter in the courtyard during the pageant, right?"

"I didn't see anything except Frau Hamel in the stupid

ticket booth." Kayla smiled at Friedrich. "Oh, and I met the boy Louisa marries. Very cute."

"We saw them," Sam said.

"When they appeared, the aventurine activated, but I couldn't pull it out without disrupting the pageant. When I finally looked at it, this was what it showed. I think its magic is tied to lost things. Important objects that end up in the wrong place or time or need to be returned to their rightful owners."

Sam straightened. "You told us earlier you didn't have the glass with you today."

"I didn't."

"Then how did it—"

"It was me. I made her get it." Friedrich was once again brooding by the tunnel. "This afternoon. I thought we might need it." He continued before anyone could question him. "Get ready. Take a flashlight but don't turn it on. We're going through the tunnel. There's a watchman on patrol so we can't use the lights until we get to the woods. Stay close and do not get lost. Does everyone understand?"

"But the tunnel is collapsed," Sophia said.

"There is another way."

Birdie slipped through the opening in the storeroom wall – calmly this time and not in a rush to escape. The clandestine sliver was concealed from the casual visitor, but a lifeline to the rest of the fortress. Electric sconces revealed a maze of passages, three of which they'd explored already – one from the courtyard the day before, one down to the trail that morning, and one – which was now caved in – to the forest. There were two more to explore, and Friedrich turned down one of them.

"Where does that one go?" Sam glanced at the passage they hadn't ventured down.

"To the kitchens," Louisa said. "Sometimes they hold fancy dinners in the storeroom and that's how the servers move back and forth to deliver the food."

"Cool."

The tunnel emptied a few yards away in an underground workroom in the museum office. Friedrich placed his finger to his lips, then punched a code into a numbered panel on the wall. He motioned for them to follow him through the darkened museum, which looked no more interesting in the emergency lighting than it had during the day. The pile of cannonballs and chunks of stone were just as boring, the large model of the original fortress just as lifeless, the ancient toy blocks bringing joy to no one.

They crouched out of sight as he checked the path for signs of the night watchman. A few moments later, he returned. "Follow me, single file, stay low."

Outside, the sun had set, leaving faint streaks of pink and yellow across the deepening blue night. A lone star shone in the sky.

Birdie's sneaker slid on the loose sandstone path and caught in the hem of her dress. She regained her footing, then knotted the fabric to keep it off the ground. She imagined they were quite a sight, wrapped in layers of costumes from the pageant.

They passed the apothecary, then hid in the brewery ruins for several nerve-racking minutes as the night watchman used his flashlight to check each of the remaining stalls. The workers had broken down many props, including the stage, but there was more to do when they returned in the morning.

They waited until the night watchman retreated toward the restrooms and then sprinted for the front gate.

"Be quick!" Louisa glanced up and down the main road. "Someone could come at any moment!"

They tucked close to the fortification wall and ran uphill to the trailhead. When they neared it, Friedrich took Birdie by the elbow and pulled her close.

"Hey!" She tried to peel his fingers away but he held on tight.

When they reached the two rocks, he clasped his other hand on Birdie's shoulder and pushed her through in front of him. When they reached the bottom of the stairs, Friedrich released her.

She rubbed her elbow. "Jerk."

Smug satisfaction glinted in his eyes.

Kayla wove through the group to stand beside her. "What's going on with you and Fred?"

"That jerk? He's been acting weird all day." She began to unravel the scarf that covered her high bun.

"Oh, Birdie, don't." Rich waved his hand to stop her. "If we get caught in the past, you'll want your head covered."

"It's hot. And to be honest, I'm hoping we don't end up in the past again."

"I know. But we're better off in our costumes."

Birdie sighed and lowered her hands. He was right, but he also didn't have to walk around with all that fabric weighing him down.

"We must go," Friedrich said. "We don't have all night."

"Well, technically——" Kayla began, but he shot her a look that cut her off. "Fine, Fred. The mosquitos are biting anyway."

The woods were darker and cooler than the fortress grounds had been, and after the run up the sidewalk to the trailhead, the air felt refreshing on Birdie's cheeks.

Friedrich moved at a fast clip, and when he reached the halfway point, he sped up.

"Friedrich!" Louisa called as the others slowed. "We must rest."

"Nein," he called back over his shoulder.

She glared at his back as she bent over, hands on her knees. "We need a rest. What's the big hurry?"

He loomed above them on a higher part of the trail, the breeze catching his dark cloak. He'd swapped the armor he'd worn under the cloak at the pageant for a leather guard uniform, and in the flashlight's glow, he had the aura of an evil prince.

"There's no rush," Louisa said softly. "Take a minute and catch your breath."

The greens of the pines and oaks blended into the falling darkness. It smelled fresh from the recent rain, and the ground was soft and giving beneath their feet. The only sounds, now that they'd stopped rustling their own costumes, were the soft whistle of their breath and the dance of the leaves above them.

"Why is he acting so weird?" Sophia kept her voice low so Friedrich couldn't hear.

"What are you talking about down there?"

"I am checking to make sure everyone has caught their breath. Yes?" Louisa straightened. "Okay, we must continue."

Friedrich waited until they reached him, then swept off toward the cave.

"You first, Birdie," he said when they reached the entrance.

She faced the others before she stepped inside. "Remember, we need to find a dragon. That's what comes next. If we don't find a dragon, we'll never find the chest."

"Dragons don't exist," Raina said.

She met her gaze. "I know. Neither do mermaids."

"Or Loreleys," Ryan said.

"Or goblins," Sam added.

"Go." Friedrich clicked on his light and ushered them all inside.

CHAPTER TWENTY-EIGHT

Their flashlights cast long shadows in the outermost chamber of the ancient cave, forming images that danced along the walls and ceiling as they passed, as though they were trapped in a flickering lantern.

When they reached the room where the guards had discovered them, Friedrich rounded on Birdie. "The glass?"

"But we just got here!" Raina's voice trembled as she moved closer to her brothers. "And Birdie said we might not have to go back at all."

Ryan snickered. "And you said this was all a load of crap."

Raina bowed her head. "I saw her too. On the tournament field. Screaming. She screamed at us. Her friend, the guard, Peter? He was there too."

"It's okay, Raina." Rich wrapped his arm around her shoulders. "We all saw them. That's why we're here."

"I… I know, but—"

"We have to make this right."

Raina lifted her chin and nodded.

"The aventurine, Birdie." Friedrich held out his hand. "Time is short. They will murder Marielle and Peter at dawn."

Rich stepped away from his sister. "How do you know?"

"It was normal," Louisa said, "to schedule executions at dawn."

"Put your hand down. I'm not giving it to you." Birdie hiked up her knotted skirts and reached into the pocket of her jeans for the glass. "It's still the dragon. That's what we need to find. The image has to be here somewhere."

"Make the glass take us back so we can find it," Friedrich demanded.

The aventurine remained cold in Birdie's palm. "I can't do that. If we go back at all, it'll be because we're in the right place. This must not be the right place."

"It worked here before," Friedrich said, the irritation clear in his voice. "Where else would it be?"

"I may know." Sophia stepped forward and circled the room, sweeping her light up and down the stone walls until she found the carving. She brushed a layer of dirt away and shined her flashlight on it.

"There you are." She ran her palm over the lines. "What are you hiding?"

"Is it a dragon?" Sam joined her as Friedrich closed the distance in one stride and loomed behind them both.

She used her puffy sleeve to brush more dirt away.

"Wow." Sam touched the wall where a faded dragon now

roared. "That's amazing. There's still some color in the flame."

Friedrich shoved them aside.

"Hey! Watch it!" Sam said as he regained his footing.

"The chest is behind here!" Friedrich dropped to his knees and scratched at the crevice in the wall.

"Friedrich!" Louisa yanked him up by the collar. "Get ahold of yourself."

Birdie narrowed her eyes at the dragon, which seemed to grow brighter. A prickle of heat pierced her palm and the chamber shimmered. The scent of spilled wine returned as barrels and crates crowded into the space. "It's happening! Be prepared for anything!"

She steadied herself between two barrels and crouched low, expecting to see the guards waiting for them, but they were alone. She shined her light on the dragon, which had transformed into a vividly painted work of art adorned with ash and natural colors.

"The dragon guards the treasure." Sam ran his fingers along the carving. "I bet there's another chamber behind here."

Louisa released Friedrich and made her way to an opening on the other side of the room. "This passage is collapsed in our time and you need special gear to climb down. I scaled it once with my friends, but it wasn't worth it. Stones and boulders block everything. But now—"

"Brilliant, Louisa!" Friedrich shot past her through the opening.

They stared after him in surprise.

Kayla raised her eyebrows. "Should we follow him?"

Louisa shrugged. "I guess?"

The passage led to an intersection where a series of interconnected chambers converged. Beyond them, the cave seemed to go on forever, with chambers and passageways spilling deeper and deeper underground.

In the distance, a light bobbed against a chamber wall, swung toward the passageway, then jerked wildly. It flickered up and down, then snuffed out as a shuffling sound rippled through the darkness, followed by a solid thump.

"What on earth was that?" Sophia said.

"Maybe Friedrich hit his head and dropped his flashlight," Kayla said. "He's kind of out of his mind at the moment."

"We'd better go see. Stay close." Rich moved toward the chamber, poised to fight. The others crammed behind him and Birdie could feel the heat from their bodies.

When they reached the chamber, Rich aimed his flashlight. "What the—"

Friedrich stood frozen in the center of a long chamber, cradling an intricately carved wooden chest.

"You found it!" Rich said.

Louisa moved into the chamber. "Where was it? Tell me it wasn't just sitting in here." She swept her light around the room and her breath caught. A young guard was sprawled on the hard stone floor behind Friedrich, his sword sheathed and helmet askew.

"Who on earth is that?" Louisa pointed to the boy.

"Did you hit him?" Birdie crossed the room and took a knee beside the injured guard, who couldn't have been more than twelve or thirteen. He stirred, and she helped him sit up. His head wobbled against her chest.

"Is it Peter?" Rich moved closer to help Birdie.

She slid the helmet's long metal sheath away from the boy's nose, revealing his pale face. "No. It's a different guard. He's much younger."

Panic rose in the boy's unfocused eyes. "It's okay." She patted his leg and turned to Louisa. "How do you say 'friend' in German?"

"Freund."

"Freund." Birdie smiled at the young guard. His muscles tensed, and she knew he would run if he were able.

"Open it." Kayla had crowded close to Friedrich and stared at the wooden chest.

"I… can't."

"Why not?" She reached for it, but he swung his arms away.

"It's locked."

"Shine a light on the latch," Birdie said, as Sophia moved closer to examine the chest.

It was a masterful piece of craftsmanship, with intricate scenes carved into the marbled wood. A magical forest lived on its surface, with trees and deer and water interwoven into the landscape. The wood shone with a high gloss, and an intricate latch secured the two halves.

"It's locked alright." Sophia ran her hand over the mechanism. "This might take a while."

"We don't have a while." Birdie shifted on the floor as the guard groaned in her arms. "This part of the cave is collapsed, remember? It's time to go. Now that Friedrich found the chest, I'm not sure how much longer we have."

"I thought you said we needed a loud noise to get back," Louisa said. "The cave is empty in our time. We should be safe."

"Yes, a loud noise seems to work, but sometimes the shimmer ends on its own."

Rich backed toward the passageway. "Birdie's right. We shouldn't risk it. Let's go where we know we'll be safe."

"What about him?" Ryan considered the guard, who was looking more frightened and confused by the minute.

"Leave him. He'll be fine," Rich said. "He's from here, remember?"

Birdie touched the guard tenderly on the shoulder and eased him back to the hard stone floor. When he landed, he closed his eyes. "He'll think he had a horrible dream."

Rich nodded. "Good call. Come on, everyone."

They picked up speed as they retreated to the intersection.

"Which way?" Raina pivoted in a circle and stared down each passage. "Which way leads out?"

"I'm not sure." Louisa turned. "They all look the same to me."

"We need to go!" Birdie said. "We cannot be down here if the aventurine stops working."

Ryan pointed down a passageway. "This way! We came this way."

"Are you sure?" Raina had gone rigid and Birdie wasn't sure she'd be able to move, no matter what Ryan said.

"I'm sure." He placed his hand on his sister's back and pushed her forward. "Go!"

She broke free and darted up the passageway.

"The glass is cooling off!" Birdie cried as they ran, the light from their flashlights bouncing against the walls. The stone floor shifted beneath her feet. "Run!"

But they were too slow.

The ground shifted again and Birdie's knees gave way. She tumbled several feet down onto the collapsed floor.

Raina screamed.

Then she screamed again.

"Raina!" Rich yelled from somewhere close behind Birdie. "Raina! Stop screaming!"

She choked off the next cry.

"You're okay." He shined his flashlight at her. "It looks like we're all okay."

They'd fallen together in a heap on the cave floor, which looked like it had collapsed centuries before.

Louisa got to her feet and brushed herself off. She steadied herself on the uneven floor as she pointed her flashlight toward the ceiling, then along the walls. The light revealed the truth: They were trapped in a narrow corridor on the wrong side of the passageway, several feet shy of the upper chamber.

Birdie's heart raced. This was what she'd feared. She had no control over the glass, no way to stop it from hurtling them through time and space. She sent up a silent thank you they'd at least made it through the intersection.

Everyone appeared slightly dazed, but they were alive. Boulders blocked the passageways behind them. A few more seconds of hesitation would have ended their lives. They'd have been gone, forever trapped. Who knew how long it would've been until someone found their bodies? They might never have been found.

"We must climb out." Louisa fitted her foot into a space on the wall and hauled herself up toward the opening. "We'll fit if we go one at a time."

She placed her sneakers with care, searching for handholds as she scaled the wall. Rich spotted her as she climbed into the chamber, and then Louisa reached back to offer Raina a hand.

Birdie shivered as she watched Rich boost Raina into the upper chamber.

She couldn't let this happen again. She needed to get rid of the aventurine.

To destroy it.

Permanently.

CHAPTER TWENTY-NINE

In the upper chamber, the dragon had faded, its colors once again translucent against the stone. Sophia sank into a cross-legged seat in the middle of the floor. Friedrich set the wooden chest in front of her, stepped back, and folded his arms.

Sophia ran her fingers over the elaborate carvings, feeling for hinges and openings as she sized up the latch. "Well, the good news is, the chest looks just like it did in the other chamber." She sniffed her fingers. "And it's well-oiled, which means someone's been maintaining it."

Birdie remembered the leather-bound book she and Ben found in Bruges. It seemed brand new at first, even though it was centuries old. "Do you think you can open it?"

Sophia removed her cap. Her long, dark hair had been twisted in a fancy knot beneath it for the pageant.

She hunched over the chest and got to work, sliding the

latch one way, tentatively, and then back into place.

She glanced up at them. "I can open it. I've read about this type of latch, but never saw one in real life before. Many, many books detail its inner workings. They usually include sketches or diagrams of the lock itself. Some of the illustrations are works of art. The theory behind the mechanism is—"

"Sophia." Sam's voice was gentle. "Just open the chest." He spread his hands wide. "Please."

She sighed. "Okay. But the theory behind this mechanism is particularly intriguing." She slid the latch again and twisted it, slowly, until an audible click signaled that something had shifted into place. "Exactly as I suspected."

She twisted the latch three more times, then slid it back into its original position. The lid floated open.

"You did it!" Sam knelt beside her. "Amazing!"

Friedrich snatched the chest from the floor and pointed his flashlight inside. "Nein!"

"What's wrong?" Louisa asked.

He tipped the chest forward. A miniature wooden block broke loose from the fur lining and rattled to the inner edge. "The chess piece is gone."

Kayla picked up the wooden block, which was twice the size of a die in a board game. She passed it to Ryan.

"What a complete, utter waste of time." Raina slumped against the wall. "I am so done with all of this. I'm tired. I'm thirsty. And I want out of this stupid leotard. Let's go back to the storeroom and get some sleep."

Friedrich dropped the chest in front of Sophia, who scrambled to catch it before it hit the ground.

"What are you doing?" She eased it to the floor. "This chest is beautiful. Even if it is empty. Look at the carvings. I can see why the chess piece was in it – it's a work of art all on its own."

"What happened to the other stuff?" Ryan studied the small wooden block. "I wonder if that guard back there took it?"

"Marielle told us there were other items in the dowry trunk," Louisa said. "Expensive cloth, gold, silver, but who knows what was in this smaller chest, if anything."

"The chest was locked." Friedrich didn't bother to hide his frustration. "The guard was attempting to pry it open when I found him. That's why I punched him."

"Whoever took the chess piece knew how to open this chest." Sophia studied the lock. "But I can't imagine many people knew how the latch worked. It's an unusual mechanism. The Chinese had them for a long time, but these locks didn't become popular in Europe until much later. And I mean much later. In fact, they didn't take off until settlers in the American frontier started recreating them. They got popular and people in Europe wanted them too. They would put the locks on trick boxes."

"How does she know all this?" Ryan asked Sam.

"President of the Puzzle Club, remember? I never dreamed it'd come in handy."

Sophia lowered her eyelids at him. "Very funny."

Sam looked sheepish. "She's also amazing at math, so it all makes sense."

"Anyway, someone must have brought this to the family from China," Sophia said. "I don't know why else it would be here."

"A ship may have bartered with it to pay a toll." Sam considered the intricate carvings. "A big toll."

"So, these trick boxes had special locks?" Birdie bent and touched the soft fur that lined the bottom of the chest.

"Yes. They have complicated locks like this one. Sometimes – a lot of times – they also include secret compartments—" Sophia's eyes grew wide. "Oh, Birdie. That's it!" She ripped up the edge of the fur lining. It gave way with a small puff of dust. "Look!"

The artist had carved the boxy outline of a dragon into the bottom of the chest.

"That's the dragon on the aventurine." Birdie gazed into the chest, then glanced up at the others. "It's an exact match. This is what we were supposed to find!"

Sophia raised the chest and bent her neck to peer underneath it. "There must be a secret compartment under the dragon." She shook the chest, but it didn't make a sound.

"Could the chess piece fit under there?" Birdie asked.

"That's where I'd hide it."

"How do you open the secret compartment?" Raina had been drifting toward the next chamber, but now she came back to stand with the others.

Sophia set the chest on the floor and squirmed flat on her belly to study it. "Sometimes, if you push in the right places, a hidden drawer pops open." She tried a few alternatives, but nothing happened.

"Enough of this!" Friedrich grabbed the chest and lifted it high above his head.

"No!" Rich jumped and rescued it from his hands. "You

can't smash it. Do you have any idea how old this is?"

Friedrich lunged for the chest, but Rich swung it away from him.

"No." Rich's jaw tightened. "Knock it off."

Friedrich gritted his teeth and backed away.

Rich brought the chest back around and scrutinized it. "There's definitely enough space under the dragon to hide something. Any other ideas, Sophia?"

She tented her fingers against her lips. "Let me think."

Raina peered inside the chest. "That's sure one weird dragon. It's so boxy. The person who carved it wasn't very good."

"It is weird, isn't it?" Rich ran his fingers over the indentation. "The rest of the chest is so intricate. You'd think the same person would have carved both the inside and the outside."

"Raina's right," Friedrich announced.

"What?" Raina jerked her head toward him. "Right about what?"

"We must get back to the storeroom before someone realizes we're missing." He stood apart from the others, seething. "It is bad enough we didn't find the chess piece. I do not want to lose my job too."

"Hold tight, Fred." Kayla stared at the rough-hewn dragon. "You know what that dragon reminds me of? Those puzzles you have when you're a little kid. The big blocky ones with handles on the pieces? They're super simple and fit into preformed spaces on the puzzle board."

"A puzzle board?" Sophia jumped up and brushed the dirt from her stable jacket. "That's it, Kayla. How many pieces would that dragon have if it were a puzzle?"

Kayla studied the outline. "Seven."

"You just solved it."

"Want to fill in the rest of us?" Sam looked up at her.

"It's a tangram. One of the oldest puzzle forms that exist. A tangram always has seven pieces that fit together to make a square and to make one other shape. Here, they fit together into a dragon."

Birdie stood to stand beside Kayla. They stared at the outline of the dragon.

"The tangram serves as a lock," Sophia explained. "If we find all seven pieces, I bet they'll trigger a secret mechanism under the dragon. You can't open the hidden compartment without them."

"But where are the rest of the pieces?" Raina asked.

"That's the million dollar, er, euro, question," Ryan said.

"My guess is Elisabeth hid them," Birdie said. "So that even if someone found the chest, they wouldn't discover the chess piece."

"She really didn't want to marry you, Fred," Kayla said.

"It's Friedrich," he snarled.

"If we want to save Marielle, we need to find the pieces," Rich said. "But they could be anywhere."

"And the princess hid them five hundred years ago," Ryan added. "Don't forget that detail."

"Why don't we just give the chest to Elisabeth's father and be done with it?" Raina suggested. "We hand over the stupid chest, he frees Marielle and her baker boyfriend, and everyone lives happily ever after."

"Except for Elisabeth," Kayla corrected. "She'd be forced

to marry Fred."

"She's a princess." Raina folded her arms. "I'm sure she'll be fine. Besides, she's the whole reason we're in this mess."

"Technically, it was her father who started the mess by trying to marry her off to him." Kayla poked her thumb back toward Friedrich.

"You all understand I am not Prince Gunzelin, correct?"

"One problem – we don't know for sure the chess piece is still inside." Rich studied the wooden chest. "For all we know, Elisabeth hid that somewhere else too. If we take an empty chest to her father, we'll all hang."

"Oh, for goodness' sakes, yes, the chess piece is the key." Friedrich stepped forward. "It is the only reason the prince wanted to marry Louisa at all."

"Hey!" Louisa smacked his arm.

"Any ideas where we should search?" Rich asked.

Sam circled Rich as he stared at the chest. "If I were Princess Elisabeth, and I had a heavy dowry trunk – and it was way back then – I bet I didn't have the trunk at all. It was probably in my father's chambers."

"True," Rich agreed.

Sam paced the chamber. "If she wanted the dowry, she'd be forced to steal the trunk from her father's rooms. Except the trunk was way too heavy to move on her own."

"Okay. Let's say that's true," Rich said. "Her best bet would have been to remove everything from the trunk, piece by piece, including this chest. But would she have known how to open it?"

"Possibly." Sophia ran her fingers over the lock. "Her

father may have shown her the chess piece at some point and shown off the lock because it's so unique."

"Let's say she gets ahold of the chest," Rich continued, "smuggles it out of her father's chambers, and then has to get rid of it somehow."

"She's like a prisoner, though." Louisa shifted closer to Rich. "She's not permitted to travel anywhere alone outside the keep."

"Right. She needs help," Rich agreed. "But no one would wittingly hide anything from the princess's dowry. That would be certain death."

Louisa's eyes lit up. "So she stages a robbery – she removes the cloth and the gold from the trunk and hides them somewhere, probably among her own things."

"And maybe she takes the puzzle pieces from the chest and gives them to someone to hide for her," Sophia said. "Someone like Marielle."

"But how did the chest end up in the cave?" Sam asked.

"I'm not sure." Sophia thought about it. "Maybe Elisabeth hid it in a handcart that went back and forth to this wine cellar? In a cask or something? She may have been able to manage it without raising too much suspicion."

"Especially if Marielle accompanied her," Louisa said.

"But why are the guards so sure Marielle is the thief?" Sam asked.

"Because she had access to the keep," Rich explained.

"That may not be the only reason," Sophia said. "Once Elisabeth's father realized the dowry was missing, he would have told the guards what to look for, including the pieces to the tangram. What if that's the reason they suspected her?

What if they saw her with them?"

"We need to find the pieces to the tangram." Rich stared down at the dragon.

"We have one." Ryan held up the small wooden block. "That's a start."

"Let me see that again," Birdie said. Ryan handed her the block, and she turned it over in her hand. "I know where the other ones are."

CHAPTER THIRTY

The woods echoed with the song of the night as they hiked the switchbacks and climbed the crumbling stairs to the sidewalk beyond. No one spoke, choosing instead to concentrate on their footing in the dim circles of light cast by their flashlights. Beyond their glow, the forest was cloaked in darkness.

They crossed the tournament field and arrived at the museum door without being spotted by the night watchman. Friedrich held the door as they passed through, peering nervously up and down the sandstone path. As he latched the door, Birdie wandered to a glass case in the center of the gallery.

"What are you doing?" Friedrich hissed. "We must go."

"I knew it." She placed the small wooden block on top of the case.

Sophia stepped up behind her and peered inside. "They're

the same!" She turned to the others. "Toy blocks. You can see the parts of the dragon!"

"There are only two." Birdie sighed. "We need six."

"That's two more than we had a minute ago," Sophia said.

Friedrich knelt at the end of the glass case, ran his hand under it and, with a nod, clicked a button underneath. When he did, the end popped open. "Grab the pieces."

Birdie picked up the two small blocks.

"Don't forget this one." Sophia scooped the third one from the top of the case.

"Okay, go." Friedrich stood. "I will close the case and rearm the museum as soon as you are all in the tunnel."

It was a short walk back to the storeroom, and when they arrived, everyone except Raina gathered around the table. Sam grabbed a slice of cold pizza from the box and settled into one of the creaky chairs.

Rich set the chest on the table and turned to Sophia. "Let's see if they fit."

Sophia unlocked the outer mechanism, and the lid floated open, revealing the piece of fur that covered the outline of the tangram. Birdie handed her the pieces.

Sophia fit them into the puzzle indentations, trying to match the faded images of the older pieces with the markings in the chest. "Four more." She glanced up at them.

"These look so old." Rich felt the pieces Birdie retrieved from the museum. "Look how faded and chipped the paint is."

Raina stood a few feet away with her arms folded, still in

the colorful leotard she'd danced in earlier that evening. "You know, we could just take a chainsaw to the bottom of that chest and get the stupid chess piece out. If it's even in there."

"Do you have a chainsaw?" Sophia asked.

Raina rolled her eyes.

"We don't want to ruin the chest," Rich said. "It must be worth a fortune, with the false bottom and the special locks. It's a museum piece."

"I agree with Rich." Louisa pulled out a chair and sat down. "We cannot break this chest. We're going to have a difficult time explaining where we got it as it is."

"What do you mean?" Ryan sat down too.

"We just brought an artifact back from the past and it's in perfect shape – and it may very well contain a priceless chess piece in a secret compartment. People will wonder how we found it." She yawned. "They'll probably call the newspaper and everything."

"Not if we're successful," Sophia said. "Does anyone have any idea where to look for the last four pieces?"

"Well, if our theory is correct, Marielle knows where they are," Rich said. They stared at him and he shrugged. "What? You're the ones who said it was her job to hide them. If that's true, then she knows where they are."

"Is this not what I've been saying?" Friedrich opened his hands wide.

"How do you suggest we ask her?" Raina asked Rich. "The last time we saw her, she was strapped to a stake in the courtyard."

"We have to go to her," Rich said. "Before dawn."

"Forget it." Raina retreated to her cot. "I'm not going anywhere. I'm done."

"It has to be Friedrich." Sophia spread her hand on the table. "Marielle will recognize him, and he's the only one who could get away with pretending to be a guard and speaking acceptable German."

Friedrich faced her. "My German is more than acceptable."

"Your German is excellent, being that you're a native speaker," Sophia said. "That's my point. But you may still sound odd to the people who lived back then."

"Birdie would have to go with him," Kayla said. "Right, Birdie? There's no way you're trusting him alone with the aventurine?"

She nodded and tried to sound braver than she felt. "You're right about that."

She didn't want to go back. She didn't want anyone to go back. But they were in so deep now, it seemed like the only way to find the missing pieces to the tangram and save Marielle. She couldn't let Friedrich go off by himself with the aventurine – he might never come back or he might lose it somewhere in the past. Who knew what havoc that would cause?

"Birdie should give me the aventurine." Friedrich stuck out his hand.

"Nice try," Birdie said. "No."

"We cannot all go parading into the courtyard to question Marielle." Friedrich slowly lowered his hand. "That would make things worse for her."

"And for us," Sam said.

"No, we can't," Birdie agreed. "And we can't go anywhere at all unless the aventurine cooperates."

"So, assuming it cooperates," Louisa said, "we'll need to hide while Friedrich goes to the courtyard."

"You honestly think they'll just let him wander right up to a convicted witch and thief?" Kayla asked.

Sam shrugged. "Only one way to find out."

"Do you really want to do this?" Louisa glanced up at Friedrich.

He nodded. "It is the only way."

The campers entered the deserted tournament field for the third time that evening, moving under cover of darkness and avoiding the puddles of light thrown by the spotlights. The night watchman was nowhere to be seen. Birdie wasn't surprised. Most of the props and materials from the pageant had been carted away, and there wasn't much left of Burg Rheinfels to guard.

They still wore period clothes, although Raina, whose brothers had convinced her to come along, had exchanged her dance costume for additional layers of skirts and scarves.

Friedrich drew to a halt when they reached the far edge of the field. "If our maps are correct, this path led to the dungeons." He shifted, pointing to the shadowy center of the courtyard. "Marielle should be right there."

Louisa glanced around. "We need to hide."

Friedrich led them to the perimeter of the old keep. "Crouch here, along the ruined wall. Stay alert – you never know who might be wandering around."

"This feels like a terrible idea." Raina crouched between

her brothers.

"You need to be quiet," Rich said, and when Raina protested, he held up his hand. "We all do. We can't get caught back there."

"Why didn't we just stay in the storeroom?"

"Because we already know there's a guard there," Rich replied. "Just cooperate, would you?"

Raina sunk lower to the ground.

Birdie met Friedrich's gaze.

"Give me the aventurine," he said.

"I'll hold on to it, thanks." The glass was cold against her palm, and the image of the dragon held tight.

Friedrich squinted at it. "It's not activating. Maybe if we get closer to Marielle?"

They wandered toward the middle of the courtyard, Birdie's hand outstretched to watch for any change in the glass. She could hear Raina complaining again from her place with the others against the ruined wall.

"Nothing?" Friedrich asked.

"Not yet."

Part of her wished nothing would happen at all, that they'd wind up giving up and going back to the storeroom. But she knew that was unlikely. They had to return the chess piece to Elisabeth's father to end this once and for all.

She crept forward, her eyes trained on the dragon in the glass. As they neared the middle of the courtyard, the speckles swirled and the glass grew warm. The air shimmered as the gold spilled across the surface and the lines of the dragon softened and dissolved. She stopped, waiting for an image to form.

Friedrich snatched the aventurine from her palm.

"Hey!" She lunged for the glass. "Give that—"

He snarled something menacing in German as the world around them changed.

Dozens of torches illuminated the courtyard, replacing the harsh, modern spotlights. A stone path bordered the keep, linking the buildings and stalls that formed the prosperous village inside the fortress walls. Live music replaced the silence of the ruin, floating softly across the courtyard, punctuated every so often by screams that traveled up the path from the dungeon.

There was no sign of Marielle or Peter. The post and stockades were deserted.

Birdie darted toward the others. It was a good hiding place, an oasis of darkness in the otherwise warmly lit space. She crouched next to Kayla.

"Where is she?" Kayla whispered.

Another scream carried up the path.

"They must have taken them to the dungeon for the night," Rich said. "To prepare them to be paraded out for the execution."

"We are not going to the dungeon." Louisa spread her arm in front of them like a blockade.

"We must." Friedrich had followed Birdie, and now stood tall before them.

Rich grimaced as he gently pushed Louisa's arm away. "He's right."

"I will not allow it." Louisa shook her head. "I am not dragging seven campers into a medieval dungeon."

"Of course not," Friedrich said. "I will go alone. You will

all wait here."

"How do you plan to get in?" Rich asked.

Friedrich glowered at him.

Rich rose and stepped out of his hiding place. "The dungeon will be guarded, but not as well as you think. The cells are underground, so it's almost impossible for the prisoners to escape. The guards won't be the top brass – it's likely they're in trouble for something else and got stationed there as punishment. Let's just say their morale won't be high."

Friedrich looked at Birdie. "You must come with me."

She laughed. "Why? You took the aventurine. What do you need me for?"

"You will be my reason for going into the dungeon." He glanced at Rich. "Get down. You must stay here and hide with the others."

Birdie snuggled in beside Kayla. "I'm not going with you either."

"I understand." He met her eyes, then gestured to the others. "Which one of them would you like to send down there with me instead?"

"No one... I..." Birdie stammered.

"That's what I thought. Now come on."

Her legs trembled. She couldn't let anyone else go with him. It had to be her. But she was furious at Friedrich for snatching the aventurine and at herself for letting him do it. And she was terrified of what she might see in the dungeon.

"We cannot stand here all night," he said.

Birdie took a deep breath and stood.

Friedrich looped his arm in hers and hurried down the

path away from the others. "Start crying, so it looks like you are upset."

"What? Why?"

"I will tell them you are Marielle's friend or something."

They neared the entrance to the dungeon, which was lit by torches. A guard sat outside.

"I can't cry on demand. You'll need another plan."

Friedrich yanked Birdie's arm and swung his leg out to knock her down.

CHAPTER THIRTY-ONE

"Hey!"

It was Sophia, her cry carrying over the melody in the courtyard and reaching Birdie as she struggled against Friedrich's grasp.

She didn't dare yell back and risk alerting everyone that intruders had entered the fortress grounds undetected. She listened, but heard no other sound.

Friedrich didn't notice Sophia's cry, or, if he did, he didn't seem to care.

Birdie barely got her feet under her again before they reached the guard at the dungeon's arched entrance. She stopped fighting Friedrich and stared.

The guard was gigantic and in desperate need of a shave as he lounged with his legs spread wide beneath his leather tunic. The helmet's nosepiece cocked sideways and his giant nose appeared broken, or at least badly mended.

In that instant, Birdie realized Friedrich had accomplished his actual goal, and it wasn't to pass her off as a visitor. He'd given the guard the impression he was dragging her toward the dungeon for some imagined crime.

"Was ist das?" The guard's deep, scratchy voice did nothing to soften his appearance as he looked lazily from Birdie to Friedrich.

Friedrich said something that Birdie didn't understand. The guard responded, and back and forth they went, continuing their discussion as if she were not even there.

It was infuriating. She wanted more than anything to lash out, to tell them both where they could go. But she was smart enough to know this was not the time, that any action on her part would get her strung up next to Marielle in the courtyard in the morning. So she stayed silent, waiting and, after a few more moments of conversation, the guard handed Friedrich a torch and waved them through.

"You can let me go now," Birdie said through her teeth as they passed under the arch.

Friedrich leaned into her ear. "Not a chance."

They crept along, moving deeper into the dark dungeon, drowning in the moans and cries of the prisoners further down the passageway. A middle-aged guard joined them, until Friedrich offered some words that appeared to ease his mind.

They continued on, ignoring the taunts from men trapped in cages, and the occasional screams of such anguish that Birdie's stomach clenched. She was grateful she didn't understand the words, as the emotions jarred her bones.

A song of sorrow rose around them, and the stench of unwashed humanity was so putrid that Birdie thought she might pass out before they reached Marielle. She used her free hand to cover her nose and mouth, but it did little good.

Poor Marielle and Peter in this place.

That thought alone pushed her to keep moving.

When they reached the end of the passageway, a guard pointed to a series of wooden grates that covered pits in the floor. Friedrich peered into each one with the light of the torch, pausing each time to search the dirty faces of the prisoners huddled below. At the third grate, he stopped and addressed the guard. *"Hier."*

The guard bent and shoved a huge key into a large iron lock and turned it. He slid the lock and unlatched the grate.

Birdie peered into the pit, her heart racing.

Marielle started, then stepped away, shaking her head back and forth. "Nein."

The lady's maid, who'd been so perfectly uniformed when she'd rushed into the storeroom, was now filthy, and her dress hung in tatters beneath the sack. Her hair, once neatly braided and hidden under a snow-white wrap, fell long and wild down her back.

Friedrich called to Marielle, and asked her a question in a commanding tone, as if he really were a guard of the fortress. She glanced at Birdie, who nodded ever so slightly. Marielle met Friedrich's gaze. She answered his question, hope mixing with the tears that filled her blue eyes.

Friedrich turned to the guard, who sneered at Birdie. Without another word, Friedrich placed his hand on the center of her back and shoved her into the pit.

Birdie screamed as Friedrich and the guard laughed.

Marielle did her best to break her fall, to catch her, but the shove had been so unexpected that they both collapsed backwards, hard, landing in what Birdie could only hope was mud on the dirty stone floor.

Friedrich snickered as the guard bent and re-latched the grate. He leered at them and Birdie could see the dark gaps in his mouth where teeth used to be.

"Friedrich!" she cried, no longer caring who heard her. "You cannot leave me here!"

She scrambled to her feet and peered up through the grate.

"Friedrich! You jerk! Get me out of here!"

Marielle slapped her slender hand over Birdie's mouth, her eyes wide as she motioned for her to be silent.

But it was too late. The guards must have realized something was not right with the new German guard, and a commotion broke out.

Friedrich shouted, and while Birdie couldn't understand him, she could feel the complete and total desperation in his voice.

Good. She nodded to Marielle, who dropped her hand from Birdie's mouth.

Although she could no longer see Friedrich or the guard, she could hear the fighting, the smacks and punches, the yelling.

And then she heard something else. Something that made her jump and her heart leap at the same time.

The whistle.

It blew, long and loud and desperate. Again and again,

echoing against the chamber walls, until there were no longer walls to catch the sound.

Marielle faded, the salty impression of her hand still tingling on Birdie's mouth.

And then they were alone, in the dark, Birdie at the bottom of what was now a steep stone ramp and Friedrich far from her, near the ruined entrance, clutching a burning torch, the whistle pressed between his lips.

"What happened?" Rich was out of breath as he reached them, the other campers close behind.

"You jerk!" Birdie clambered up the ramp. She brushed herself off and marched toward him, her legs aching from the fall. "You freaking jerk! Do you know what that means? How do you say it in German, Louisa?"

"What happened?" Louisa joined Rich on the dark pathway.

"What happened? What happened is he threw me into that pit," she pointed to the ramp behind her, "like a common criminal!" She held up her skirts. "I'm filthy!"

"It was the only way." Friedrich shrugged and tucked the whistle under his shirt.

"It was not the only way." Birdie shrugged animatedly and deepened her tone to imitate him. "Give me back the aventurine. You're the criminal. You're a thief!"

"Friedrich?" Louisa asked. "You took the glass?"

A white light blinded them all. *"Sie! Was machen sie da?"*

Birdie jumped at the booming voice and spotlight, and it took a moment to realize it was not the burly guard, but the night watchman.

They clung together and stared at him. He dropped the

beam of light to the ground and continued to speak, addressing Friedrich.

"What's he saying?" Birdie whispered.

"We're in trouble." Louisa kept her voice low. "He thinks Friedrich took the torch from the museum."

Friedrich extinguished the torch on the sandstone path and handed it to the night watchman.

The well-groomed man inspected it and then shook it at Friedrich as he spoke. Friedrich responded in German, and then waved for them to follow the night watchman back to the storeroom.

"Did you at least get to talk to Marielle?" Sophia whispered as they trudged down the path.

Birdie nodded.

"And?"

"And I don't understand German. Friedrich spoke to her and she may have told him where the pieces are, but I can't be sure."

Raina came up behind them. "Man, you smell awful."

The night watchman resecured them in the storeroom and left, latching the door with final-sounding authority. Everyone turned to Birdie and Friedrich.

"Don't look at me," she said. "I was a prop in this whole expedition, apparently."

"She didn't expect you to throw her into a pit, Friedrich." Louisa stood tall and folded her arms. "Was that necessary?"

"Yes." Raw satisfaction deepened his voice as he locked eyes on Birdie. "What were you thinking? Screaming in perfect English. You are a fool."

"Do you know where the pieces are?" Rich pulled

Friedrich's attention away from her.

"Marielle told me. Yes. But only Louisa and I can get them. The night watchman was clear that he did not want to see any campers out again tonight, or we will be reported and fired."

"You mean you won't tell us where they are?" Raina plopped down on her cot. "So much for being in this together."

"She's right. Why only Louisa?" Ryan asked.

"I do not want to get fired. Besides, do you speak German?" Friedrich waved his hand at each of them. "Do any of you? You haven't even tried to speak a word of German to us since you've been here. Not even a bitte or danke!"

Raina looked at Rich.

"Please and thank you," he translated. She nodded and laid down.

"No, we haven't," Ryan admitted.

"Well, Louisa does," Friedrich said. "If you came along, you fools would get us killed."

"But if you shimmer, we'll all go too," Ryan said. "And be trapped in here."

"We won't use the glass until we're far away," Friedrich said.

"How far?" Rich asked. "How long will you be gone? And what will you do when you find the pieces?"

"Open the chest and return the chess piece to Elisabeth's father," Friedrich replied. "Then this will all be over."

"No way," Kayla said. "The chest stays here with us. I don't trust you."

"I'm going to sleep." Raina closed her eyes. "Birdie, get out of those clothes and burn them or something, will you? The whole place reeks now."

"Sorry, Raina. It's not by choice. Louisa, will you help me change?"

She followed Birdie into the tunnel.

"Be careful," Birdie said, when they were out of earshot. "Friedrich is acting very strange. And I need the aventurine back. He still has it."

Louisa nodded. "I will be careful."

CHAPTER THIRTY-TWO

Friedrich and Louisa departed through the tunnel, promising to return as soon as they found the missing pieces. They were armed with the aventurine and the whistle, and still dressed to blend into Marielle's time. Louisa carried a plastic bag that held Birdie's ruined costume, which she planned to ditch in a trashcan at the edge of the parking lot to be collected with the waste from the pageant.

There was nothing left for the rest of them to do, and as the others settled on their cots, Birdie grew restless. "I'm going to wash my sneakers."

"How?" Sophia asked.

"I'll go through the tunnel. I saw the code Friedrich punched into the museum's security system. The bathroom is across the path from there."

"Keep an eye out for the night watchman," Sam warned.

"I will."

"I'll go with you," Sophia said, "to stand guard."

"Don't get caught." Sam picked up the old *Robin Hood* movie.

As they snuck to the bathroom, Birdie's stomach roiled with frustration at herself and the whole situation. She'd let Friedrich snatch the aventurine, and now leave with it. She'd let him treat her like dirt and failed to protect herself, even though she knew she couldn't trust him. And worse, she'd lost control of the situation.

She should be out there, searching for Marielle and the missing blocks, not in here, scrubbing her never-to-be-white-again sneakers in a period-themed restroom where the water wouldn't stay running from the spigot.

It wasn't fair. And it was all her own fault.

How could she be so stupid?

She shouldn't have brought the aventurine to Burg Rheinfels. She shouldn't have taken it out of Bruges. She should've put it back on the windowsill and let the next kid deal with it.

"Pump it again," she said to Sophia, who was operating the old-fashioned tap that pushed water into the basin.

She held each sole under the water and scrubbed it with paper towels and hand soap, careful to keep the inside from getting wet. They were the only shoes she had at camp, and one of only two pairs she'd brought to Europe at all. She needed them, and she needed them to not smell like centuries-old who-knew-what.

"Maybe your mom will buy you a new pair." Sophia eyed the sneakers as Birdie yanked several more paper towels from the dispenser near the door and wiped them dry.

She didn't reply. None of this was Sophia's fault, but she just couldn't bring herself to be friendly when she was feeling so mad. She pushed the restroom door open and checked the path.

"I wonder if Louisa and Friedrich found the blocks yet." Sophia glanced at the rising moon. "They've been gone a while."

Birdie motioned for Sophia to cross to the museum entrance. "I don't want to deal with that night watchman again."

When they reached the storeroom, everyone had ditched their costumes in a pile on the floor and changed into their street clothes. Birdie noted that, although they should be settling in for the night, no one wore pajamas. Even Raina, who was curled up on her cot facing away from them all, wore a T-shirt and jeans. Kayla was next to her on her own cot with her eyes wide open, staring blankly at the ceiling.

On the other side of the room, Ryan and Sam sat on their cots tossing a metal ball they'd pilfered from a costume. Sam nodded to them when they came in, but remained quiet.

No one had bothered to start the movie.

Sophia gestured toward Rich, who was at the table studying the maps, and Birdie followed her over to him.

"What are you doing?" Sophia slid into the seat next to him.

"We've been all over the place." He smoothed his hand over the map. "In the present and the past. But in the past, we've almost always been underground. Do you think

Friedrich and Louisa stayed underground or do you think they're in a building? I'd love to get into one of those old fortress buildings."

"I guess the real question is, where did Marielle hide the blocks?" Sophia leaned forward to study the map. "And is it far enough from here that we won't shimmer if they do?"

"The blocks could be anywhere," Rich said.

Sophia shook her head. "Not anywhere. The princess had to stay close to the keep and was under guard anytime she wandered farther than the gardens. And Marielle was limited to the fortress and Sankt Goar."

Rich regarded Sophia. "You're right. They were limited in their movements. They were limited in their contact with the outside world too, especially the princess."

"Which is why she needed Marielle to get the blocks out of the keep," Sophia said.

Rich turned the map slightly so Birdie and Sophia could see it. "Let's start with Elisabeth. We think she gave Marielle the blocks to hide. But what if she hid some herself too?" He pointed to the central keep. "She'd have been allowed in here, obviously, and out in the courtyard for special processions. She'd never be on this side of the fortress where the dungeon was."

"There were private gardens behind the keep in her time." Birdie pointed to them on the map. "She probably spent any time outdoors in that area."

"She'd know the gardener, and maybe the cook," Sophia said.

"What a sad life." Birdie stared at the map.

"She had a horse." Rich pointed to the stables. "So she

could've connected with the stable master."

"Frau Cheval told me Elisabeth only ever rode with a guard," Sophia said.

"If Elisabeth hid any blocks herself, the garden is a good possibility." Birdie thought about it. "She could have buried them there."

"I bet she buried two blocks there," Rich said, "and those are the blocks we found in the museum. They'd have been unearthed after the fortress was ruined."

"So we're back to square one." Sophia sat back.

"What about Marielle?" Birdie asked. "She had more freedom of movement."

"Yes, but even so, it was limited," Rich said. "We know she snuck off to the cave—"

"To meet her boyfriend," Kayla called from across the room. "I bet she gave a block to him."

They glanced over at her, but she was still staring at the ceiling.

"He was a baker boy." Birdie turned back to Rich and Sophia. "He could have taken it to Sankt Goar and hid it anywhere."

"Not anywhere," Sophia corrected. "Remember, everyone had a place and if people were out of place, other people noticed."

"So his house, his garden if they had one, the bakery," Birdie said. "He could have thrown it in the river for all we know."

"I doubt he'd have done that." Rich flexed his fingers. "I have a theory that Elisabeth planned to reunite the blocks when it was safe and retrieve the chess piece herself."

"You do?" Birdie asked. "I figured she'd just want to be rid of the thing." She thought of the aventurine.

"The chess piece was powerful and expensive," he said. "The princess probably recognized she could use it to her advantage at some point. Maybe even to run away. She was like a prisoner here, but she was shrewd enough to chase the prince away."

"If that's the case, Marielle would've told her where she hid the pieces," Birdie said. "Elisabeth would have insisted on it."

"Probably," Rich agreed. "And they'd need to be somewhere she could find and reunite them again."

"Okay, let's say we're right, that Peter took one piece to Sankt Goar, although that's kind of a long shot," Sophia said. "We're still missing three pieces."

"I think they're in the cave." Rich tapped an area at the edge of the map. "That's why Marielle ran there, to give the rest of them to Peter before they caught her."

"That's probably where Louisa and Friedrich went then." Sophia glanced at the tunnel entrance. "If Marielle told Friedrich where to look."

"She didn't have time to tell Friedrich much." Birdie wrinkled her nose at the thought of the dungeon. "And she may not have known about the blocks in the garden at all. The princess trusted her, but maybe not enough to tell her everything."

"We found them!" It was Louisa, out of breath and excited as she exited the tunnel into the storeroom. "We found two of the blocks!"

Friedrich slid into the room behind her, panting. "But

they saw us – the guards. The woods are crawling with them. They followed us into the cave. We had to use the whistle to escape."

"So you went back to the cave?" Ryan jumped off his cot and jogged over to the table. "And back in time?"

Louisa nodded.

"And we didn't shimmer." Kayla popped up on her cot and twisted so her feet landed on the floor. "Interesting."

"We were deep underground when it happened," Louisa said. "That's where the blocks were, hidden inside a crate."

Birdie and Rich exchanged glances.

Louisa came forward and dropped the two blocks on the table next to the chest. Sophia got to work, repeating the steps to pop the complicated latch. When the lid floated open, she pushed the fur lining aside and placed all the blocks inside, twisting and turning them until they were seated in the correct positions.

"They're part of the same set." Sam watched his sister work the puzzle with anticipation. "They're painted and carved exactly the same."

"There's some movement in the chest now." Sophia used her palm to rock the pieces. "There's definitely a false bottom. But there's no way to unlatch the mechanism without the other blocks."

"Did Marielle tell you where the rest of them are?" Birdie asked Friedrich. She could barely look at him.

"She didn't know."

"We do," Rich said. "Or at least we may have figured it out. They—"

"Yes." Birdie put her hand on top of Rich's, stopping him

from going any further. "We figured it out. And we'll tell you what we learned after you give me the aventurine."

The room fell silent.

Friedrich glowered at Birdie.

"Oh for goodness sakes, just give it back to her," Louisa said.

"Why should I?" He clenched his left hand, unconsciously signaling where it was.

"Uh, because it's hers." Kayla strolled over to the table to stand next to Birdie.

"That is pretty rich coming from you," Friedrich scoffed. "Besides, it's not hers. What does she know of the history of this place – or of anywhere in Europe? She has no business with it."

"That's not for you to decide, is it?" Rich stood and pushed his chair away from the table. "She found it and you took it from her. It's time to give it back now."

Friedrich stared at Rich and seemed to consider his options. He contemplated the others around the table before he spoke.

"Fine. But you are not to use it without my permission." He placed it on the table.

Birdie scooped it up and stuffed it deep into the front pocket of her jeans. "I can't make that promise. You've seen how it works. It decides when it will show us the past. I'm surprised it worked for you in the cave."

"Never mind that," Sophia said. "It doesn't matter. We need to find the last two blocks if we have any hope of returning the chess piece to Elisabeth's father. That's the only way to save Marielle and everyone else."

Friedrich checked his watch. "We're running out of time."

"What time is it?" Rich asked.

"Just past midnight."

Rich reclaimed his seat at the table. "Okay. This is where we think the last two blocks are hidden."

Those cute buildings with exposed wood on the exterior are common in traditional German villages. The construction style earned the name "half-timbered" because supporting logs were split in half so they could be used in two places. The cut sides of the logs face the lane, with plaster or masonry spread between, creating the classic half-timbered look. —Marty McEntire, *Europe for Americans Travel Guide*

CHAPTER THIRTY-THREE

"Go down to Sankt Goar?" Louisa flattened her hands against the table. "In the dark? Are you high?"

"The moon is up and it's bright tonight." Rich folded the map and placed it in the chest. "You were just out there. You know. You hiked all the way to the cave and back, and that's a tougher trail."

"It would be pretty cool to see the old village," Sam said. "The shops and stuff."

"You just said it's past midnight." Raina hadn't budged from her cot, not even to see the new blocks. "Nothing will be open."

"I can't guarantee the aventurine will show us the past," Birdie reminded them. "There's a chance we'd hike down there for nothing."

"But if there's a block there, and the glass wants us to

save Marielle, it may cause the shimmer when we get close," Kayla said. "That seems to happen a lot."

"So that gives us six pieces, assuming it's there. Where is the last block?" Friedrich asked.

"In the garden," Rich said. "You found two blocks in the cave, so there must have been three buried in the garden. They unearthed two after the fortress was destroyed, so that leaves one still there, at least in Marielle's time."

"Or Peter could have hidden two in Sankt Goar," Kayla said. "Marielle could have given him more than one to hide."

"To be honest, I'd rather sneak into the village than take on those guards again," Louisa said. "They're definitely looking for us. They're convinced the fortress is cursed with ghosts."

"So how should we do this?" Kayla asked. "I really don't want to wear a costume again."

"Me either," Birdie agreed, and Sophia nodded beside her.

"I don't think we need to," Louisa said. "Not to go into the village. It's late. If we go to the bakery, there shouldn't be anyone around except the night watchman and he's watching for fires."

"I'm confused. How would the night watchman get back there?" Ryan asked. "He didn't touch the glass, did he?"

Louisa shook her head. "Not our night watchman at the fortress. He's a security guard. In Marielle's time, villages had real night watchmen to watch for fires. There was nothing deadlier than a nighttime fire back then. An entire village could be lost."

Ryan nodded. "Same name, different guy. Got it."

"Okay, so if we're lucky we find the missing block, Friedrich blows his whistle, and we return to the fortress as fast as we can through the low tunnel," Rich said. "We'll leave the flashlights in there so we have them when we get back."

"I'm not going." Raina was still on the cot, facing away from them all.

"You'd rather stay up here in the ruined fortress all by yourself?" Rich asked.

"I'll be fine."

Louisa glanced at her cot. "I'm not sure how long we'll be gone, Raina."

"Whatever," she said. "I'm probably just going to sleep, anyway."

"Are you sure you'll be okay?" Rich asked.

"Just go already."

"Okay." He turned back to the others. "Let's do this."

As lovely as modern Sankt Goar was during the day, it held a special sparkle late at night. In the alley behind the main street, the street lamps dimmed, leaving the moon as the primary source of light.

Except for an occasional cat, the town felt deserted.

"Okay, where to?" Sam asked when they reached the train station.

"According to my research, there's been a bakery in the same building for hundreds of years," Sophia said. "Seems like a good place to start."

"I know where it is," Louisa said, "but we'll need to cross

Heerstrasse to get to it."

"The bars will still be open," Friedrich warned.

She nodded. "I know. But let's see if we can cross without being seen."

Louisa led them down the hill toward Heerstrasse, which was not deserted at all. Street-side tables tumbled out of several establishments, and they were crammed with people drinking, smoking, and laughing.

"The statue of the boys with the beehives used to be there." She pointed beyond the tables to the small town square.

"Wait. That's my mom." Birdie held up her arm to stop them all. "What is she doing?"

"Where?" Ryan asked.

Birdie pointed to a restaurant halfway down the block. "In the green shirt." Her mom was sitting at one of several metal tables, and she had a large glass of white wine in front of her. She was with a man Birdie had never seen before. They were sitting with another couple who were much older.

"Is that your dad?"

Birdie flinched. She shook her head.

"Then it looks like she's on a date," Ryan said.

She shot him a dirty look.

"What?" He laughed. "If it's not your dad, then—"

"Her dad is dead." Kayla walked up beside Birdie. "So shut up."

Ryan's face fell, and he held up both of his hands. "Sorry. Birdie, I had no idea."

Birdie opened her mouth to say something but the words wouldn't come. There it was, out in the open.

Kayla.

Again.

Sam cleared his throat. "Where is the bakery?"

"There." Sophia paused, considered Birdie, then shook off whatever she was thinking. She pointed across Heerstrasse to a slim stone building with wooden accents on the front and window boxes overflowing with flowers.

"Great," Kayla said. "How will we get over there without Mrs. Blessing seeing us?"

"Who's Mrs. Blessing?" Ryan asked.

"Birdie's mom."

"Your last name is Blessing? You should go by BB."

"We don't have time for this." Friedrich shifted his gaze from Mrs. Blessing to Birdie. "Follow me. We'll circle around and approach the bakery from behind."

Ryan's words echoed in Birdie's brain. A date? Was her mom really on a date? Could she do that? Her dad and Jonah had just died. It had only been a year. Was that the real reason she'd shipped her off to camp, so she could go on a date?

"Birdie, are you okay?" She'd fallen behind and Sophia waited for her to catch up.

"Did it look like my mom was on a date to you?"

Sophia smiled softly. "I don't know. You'll have to ask her."

"But I can't. She'd know we were out."

"Right." Sophia sighed. "Well, there's not much you can do about it then, is there? Let's see if the others found anything interesting."

They reached the far end of the village, where its few lanes converged and led out of town toward Bacharach. The moonlit river flowed just a few yards away, the water splashing against the bank in its rush upstream.

"Let's look around," Rich said. "I bet it isn't much different than it was in Marielle's time, except for the paving and streetlights. The street grid was the same."

Sam scanned the rear of a three-story building. "Where would Peter hide the block? What makes the most sense? Upstairs in the living quarters?"

"He wouldn't have hid it in a loaf of bread," Ryan said. "Or in the ovens, where it would burn."

"One problem. He didn't live here." Louisa shook her head. "He worked here. Nikolaus, the sentry with him the night of the attack? He lived here. It was his family's bakery. It still is, or at least they still use the family name." She pointed to a sign above the back door. It read BÄCKEREI BECKER.

"So does anyone know where Peter lived?" Sam asked.

"The block is not at the bakery now, if it ever was there," Friedrich said. "This is not the same building. The Rhine floods and the bakery would have been washed away and rebuilt many times since Peter worked here. A toy block made of wood would have been lost centuries ago."

"Remind me again why we thought it was a good idea to come down here?" Kayla turned to Birdie. "What about the aventurine. Is it doing anything?"

She retrieved it from her pocket, careful to hold it close so no one would take it from her.

"Well?" Friedrich leaned in to look.

She closed her hand around the glass.

"Nothing new," she said, but as she did, the glass grew warm. "Wait."

She sidestepped Friedrich and opened her palm. The gold was swirling again, swirling, swirling, as if unsure what picture to form. As it grew almost too hot to hold, the speckles slammed together to form the image of a toy block.

"You've got to be kidding me." She shook the glass as if it were an Etch A Sketch and she could erase the image. "We already know that—"

"Birdie, shush!" Sophia said.

She slipped the aventurine back into her pocket and felt its heat radiate against her leg.

As the world shifted, Rich's prediction came true. Not much changed. The river rushed by, only darker now, the water a black mass moving fast. The backs of the buildings lined up in front of them, although their sizes and shapes were askew.

It was very dark, though, and clouds covered a sliver of silvery moon that floated overhead.

"Geister!" came a cry in German. *"Geister!"*

Birdie nearly jumped out of her skin as the frantic voice cut through the night. Sophia latched onto her arm, holding tight. "What is going on?"

"Nein!" Friedrich waved his arms back and forth like a traffic cop trying to block a road. "Nein!"

Louisa sprinted toward a young boy who stood frozen in the alley, continuing to shout. She reached him quickly, secured him, and placed a hand over his mouth. She whispered something in his ear and the boy went limp, fear rippling across his face.

From his white uniform, Birdie guessed the trembling figure was a young baker boy. "What was he saying?"

"He thinks we're ghosts," Friedrich said. "He must have heard the rumors from the fortress."

"Ghosts?" Birdie rubbed her arm as Sophia released it.

"Sorry." Sophia stayed close to her. "He scared the crap out of me."

"Yes," Friedrich continued. "Geister means ghosts."

"What's he doing out here in the middle of the night?" Ryan asked.

"He is on watch," Friedrich explained. "He must have taken Peter's place."

"But he's just a kid," Ryan said.

The boy wrestled against Louisa's grasp. She whispered in his ear again, and after a moment, he nodded. She peeled her hand away from his mouth and allowed him to stand.

His gaze darted across the campers and then back at Louisa, who towered above him.

Friedrich approached him, his voice calm but firm. The boy nodded in reply but seemed incapable of speaking, as if his mouth had gone dry.

The village slept, so quiet that Birdie wondered if anyone else even lived there, if the boy's cries had been heard at all.

The boy reached into the side of his white jacket. He removed something, moving slowly, and held it up.

A toy block.

"No way," Ryan said.

"That's it!" Sophia clapped her hands, startling the boy. He threw the toy toward the river, hard, then took off running in the other direction.

"No!" Birdie cried as she pivoted to watch the small block fly through the air.

Ryan dove for it, jumping high. He caught it in midair, pulling it from the sky before it could fall into the river behind them.

"Nice catch!" Sam trotted over to meet Ryan beside the water.

"Thought I might have to go for a swim there." He chuckled nervously.

Rich came over and stared at the toy block. He ruffled his brother's shaggy hair. "I knew you'd come in handy someday."

Ryan pushed Rich, and they started to wrestle.

"That is enough," Louisa called, but she was smiling. "We must go. That kid will be back, and he will bring others."

"I feel a little bad." Kayla stared after him. "No one will believe he saw ghosts."

"Are you kidding?" Sam said. "They'll write another legend about it."

"How did you know he had the block?" Sophia asked.

Friedrich shrugged. "He was young. It was a toy. The aventurine reacted in this place so I made a guess. I figured there was a chance Peter gave Nikolaus a block to hide."

"That was Nikolaus?" Sophia asked. "But he was so little."

"No," Friedrich said. "That was Nikolaus's small brother."

"Poor kid." Kayla shook her head.

CHAPTER THIRTY-FOUR

"Let's get back to the fortress before anyone realizes we're gone." Louisa hugged the shadowy riverbank as she strode down the alley.

Ryan nudged Friedrich. "Do you want to blow the whistle? Speed the process up a bit?"

He shook his head. "Not yet. We cannot draw attention to ourselves in either time. We must get just below the fortress, and then I will blow the whistle."

"Maybe we'll go back on our own." Sam followed Louisa toward the far end of the block. "We found what we were looking for."

It was possible, but the air remained unchanged. "We haven't found everything yet." Birdie pulled the cooled aventurine from her pocket, checked its surface, and then put it away. "The toy block is holding tight."

A grinding sound wafted down from the top of the hill.

"We'll never get into the fortress now," Ryan said. "Look."

Burg Rheinfels loomed above the village and the river, larger by far than tiny Sankt Goar. Hundreds of torches lit the massive fortifications, and the formidable towers soared high in the night sky, framed by the sliver of moon.

"It's magnificent," Sophia breathed. "I never imagined it would be so beautiful."

"Or so huge," Ryan said.

They stared at the fortress. Birdie's heart ached when she remembered the pile of rubble it had been reduced to, a shadow of its glorious past. Even with all the descriptions and the tours, the artifacts and models in the museum, she couldn't have imagined, couldn't have understood, how imposing the fortress had been.

"The prince's flag is flying beside the family's." Louisa pointed to the highest tower in the keep. "They must expect the wedding to happen, for the dowry to be found in time."

"Watch the guards." Awe filled Rich's voice. "They're doing rounds along the tops of the walls."

Fast-moving clouds passed over the sliver of moon, giving Birdie a sense of foreboding. They shouldn't be here, in this time. She glanced down the alley, reassuring herself that they were alone. She shivered.

"Those guards will see us coming if we try to climb the hill," Ryan said. "They may see us already."

"He's right." Rich turned to the others. "We need to stay hidden if we can. That isn't a tourist attraction up there. It's an armed fortress and we're strangers."

"Worse." Kayla stared at the guards. "We're ghosts."

Friedrich motioned to the end of the alley. "Keep moving.

We need to get away from Heerstrasse before I blow the whistle. Otherwise, everyone in the present day will hear it and check to see where it came from. We cannot get caught down here."

Birdie thought of her mom sitting at the café, and the strange man. What would she say if she found her here, in Sankt Goar, in the middle of the night? It would be a disaster.

They stuck to the shadows until they reached the end of the block, where a dirt lane curled up the dark hillside.

"This is where I turned up to cross the tracks this morning." Birdie pointed to the overgrown hillside. "The trailhead should be about there in our time, in the parking lot of the hostel." She glanced at Friedrich. "We should be far enough away from the cafés here, don't you think? You should blow the whistle now."

To her surprise, he didn't argue. He fished the whistle from the front of his shirt. "You are ready?"

"Just do it," Kayla said.

Friedrich closed his eyes, and blew the whistle long and loud.

"What happened?" Louisa asked, panic touching her voice.

"Nothing." Rich made a slow circle.

It was still too dark, the only light coming from the cloud-covered sliver of moon and the torches atop the fortress walls.

"Nothing," he repeated. "We're still in the past."

"*Was?*" Friedrich's whistle dropped against his shirt as he opened his eyes, which grew wide at the sight of the fortress aglow at the top of the hill. He whirled around. The river flowed behind them, devoid of cargo ships or ferryboats. "Impossible!"

"Blow it again," Kayla urged. "Quickly!"

Friedrich's fingers fumbled as he set the whistle between his lips. He blew it, longer and louder than before.

The only reply was the deep, silent night around them, unbroken by streetlights or the whir of electricity.

"Why isn't it working?" Friedrich demanded, his sharp eyes cutting to Birdie.

On the lane below, a man shouted.

"The night watchman!" Louisa smacked at Friedrich's hand. "Stop blowing the whistle. You'll lead him right to us. We must hide!"

Their choices were few.

Below them, the broad river spread, its deep water offering only danger. Above them, a dense forest crawled straight up the hillside toward the fortress walls, which stood not ruined, but formidable, and under heavy guard.

More shouts rose, followed by the opening and closing of heavy doors and the footfalls of the villagers as they searched in the dark for the source of the piercing sound.

Rich took charge, as neither Friedrich nor Louisa seemed capable of deciding what to do next. "This way."

He stooped as he dashed through the brush up the hill toward the forest and, when he reached it, pushed into the trees. The others stayed close, following the path he cut. There was no hostel now, and the woods were far thicker than they'd been that morning, making it impossible to find even a deer path to follow. The canopy of leaves blocked the bit of light from the moon, and the ground was muddy beneath their feet.

Sam tripped on an upended root and sprawled forward into the underbrush.

"Here." Sophia bent to give him a hand.

On the lanes below, more shouts joined those of the night watchman, low German growls that frightened Birdie to her core.

"This way," Louisa said, regaining her courage as she plunged them deeper into the forest. "Hide."

She jumped behind a massive fallen tree, its exposed roots leaving a crater in the earth and creating a six-foot high barrier between the campers and the path they'd forged. They scrambled over the enormous trunk and ducked low.

Birdie crouched between Rich and Sophia, then peeked over the top of the decaying tree to get her bearings. The town was no longer a sleepy, dark place, but alight and abuzz.

On the lane below, a tall figure surged toward the place where they'd entered the woods, his dark cloak furling out behind him as he moved, a long-handled battle axe resting against his shoulder. A group of torch-bearing townsmen had collected around him as if marching off to war.

Solitary candles flickered to life in the houses as they passed, their shouts waking even the heaviest of sleepers.

"Try blowing the whistle again," Ryan whispered.

"Are you crazy?" Kayla whispered back. "He'll lead them right to us."

"Get down, Birdie." Rich tugged gently on the hem of her shirt.

She sunk low behind the log, her heart racing.

A bell clanged from the square, its slow rhythm like a clock counting out the hours. If anyone had slept through the commotion, they were sure to be alert and awake now.

"We really did it," Kayla mumbled.

A second bell rang, its tone lower and deeper as it drifted down from the top of the hill, answering the first.

"They've alerted the fortress," Rich whispered. Far above them, dogs began to bark.

"Shhh…" Louisa placed her finger to her lips.

The night watchman, flanked by the villagers, had reached the area just below the roots of the fallen tree. They pressed through the thick underbrush, the snap of the night watchman's thick cloak catching and releasing as he stalked through the brambles.

Birdie shrunk even lower, trying to make herself as small as she could. The heavy scent of burning oil filled her nose, and she felt the heat of the torches passing up and down the length of the fallen tree.

She didn't dare to breathe, even after the villagers moved on, climbing further up the hill and crossing several yards above them as they switchbacked through the trees.

Sophia softened beside her, as if relief were seeping from her soul.

Birdie did not relax. It would take just one man to feel their presence, to glance down at them from the switchback.

"Keep low," Louisa whispered.

"Hier!" A childish voice ricocheted through the night as the boy they'd met in the village leaped onto the fallen log. He waved his hot torch to light their upturned faces. *"Ich habe sie gefunden!"*

CHAPTER THIRTY-FIVE

Friedrich half-stood in time to take a surprise punch to the jaw from Nikolaus's brother. He tumbled backward, sprawling into the underbrush.

There was no time for anyone else to react. While they'd been concentrating on the men from town on the switchback above, the fortress guards had crept in around them.

The strong, gloved hands of a guard encircled Birdie's arms and in a flash she was yanked to her feet and clutched to his chest. He pressed the tip of a sharp dagger next to her pounding heart. She trembled against the rough leather of his uniform, which reeked of untamed sweat and smoke from a damp campfire.

Her gaze darted from Sam to Sophia, from Rich to Ryan, from Kayla to Louisa, all in positions similar to hers. Half of them were taller than their captors, but it didn't matter – the guards were well trained and strong, used to battles with much fiercer foes.

She focused on the roses embroidered on their tunics and their pointy helmets, certain they were part of the same regiment they'd encountered in the cave with Marielle and Peter. Kayla's guard looked very much like the one they'd called the Rottmeister.

Friedrich scrambled to his feet and pawed for the whistle, but a guard moved faster and secured him before he could retrieve it.

The activity had drawn the night watchman's attention, and he dashed down the hill, the townsmen on his heels. They appeared angry, surprised, and rather disappointed by the intruders.

The night watchman faced Louisa and spoke in a demanding tone. She bent her head to hide her face and refused to answer him, even when her guard rocked her hard.

It was Friedrich who spoke, blood trickling from his bottom lip. A cloud of gnats had formed around his head, but he was helpless to wave them away.

"Lass mich gehen," he cried. *"Ich bin ein Prinz!"*

His words elicited an amused grunt from the night watchman and caused the guards to pat them down. Ryan's guard plucked the wooden block from his pocket and held it high for the others to see. *"Was ist das?"*

Ryan sought to grab for it, but his arms were pinned.

Friedrich scoffed. *"Es ist ein Spielzeug,"* he said, *"für Kinder."*

The guards snickered and the night watchman frisked Friedrich down. He tore the whistle from his neck, examined it closely, then handed it to Nikolaus's brother.

The night watchman addressed the Rottmeister, pointing

toward the village, which was now alight with torches and lanterns. The Rottmeister, the bulkiest of the guards by far, shook his head and pointed up the hill to the fortress.

An argument ensued. She didn't understand the words the men used, but Birdie knew they were fighting over who would take the prisoners. She didn't need to guess who would win. The guards had caught their ghosts, and there was no way they'd let them slip away again.

She wondered what would happen if the aventurine activated now. Would it carry the guards forward too? Was it that strong? Or would they stay as shadows in the space between time, visible only to Birdie and the others?

Perhaps that was all ghosts were, living things trapped in time with no way to escape, no aventurine to solidify the date or anchor them in place.

Or maybe the guards would come back fully with the campers, smelly, overdressed, and furious. She closed her eyes and wished for the best scenario – that the glass would send the campers back now, leaving the guards empty-handed and stunned.

She opened her eyes and glanced around. They weren't going anywhere. The others seemed as resigned to their fates as she was, waiting to see what would become of them now that they were caught.

Nikolaus's brother tossed the whistle to a townsman, who looked at it with curiosity, then shrugged and wrapped his weathered hand around it.

The posturing continued between the townsmen and the guards. No one seemed in any great rush and Birdie wished they'd just get on with it already. Release them or kill them, but stop making them wait.

Ryan's guard tossed the toy block to the night watchman, who caught it handily. He considered it, then sniffed loudly. He mumbled something and threw it back to the guard as the other men laughed.

The guard scowled and jabbed the block back into Ryan's pocket, along with any embarrassment he may have suffered at holding the toy in his hand.

Having at last determined how to divvy up the meager spoils of the capture, the townsmen lumbered down the hillside toward the village, whooping as they went, leaving them at the mercy of the fortress guards.

The Rottmeister waited until the townsmen reached the lane before he started up the hill, pushing Kayla in front of him under the canopy of trees.

So this was it. They wouldn't die on a German hillside. They were going to the fortress. Birdie tried and failed to see a way out of the situation. She wasn't strong enough to overtake the guard who held her, and the woods were too thick to aid a fast escape.

She slid her foot forward to follow Kayla, but her guard tugged her back with a gap-toothed smile. He reached into her front pocket.

His fingers brushed the aventurine.

"Halt," he called as he examined the small treasure in his hand. He held the piece of glass high for the others to see, its golden speckles sparkling like fire in the torchlight, holding tight to the shape of the wooden block.

The Rottmeister paused, and seeing the aventurine, passed Kayla to another guard. He marched past the other campers and their guards to stand in front of Birdie. She lowered her gaze to the ground as Louisa had done and remained silent, even when he demanded something of her in German.

She sensed everyone holding their breath as they waited for her to respond. But she couldn't. She had no response. She had no clue what the Rottmeister had said, and responding in English was sure to be a death sentence.

The Rottmeister raised a hand to strike her.

"Stop it, you creep!"

Kayla.

Birdie peered at her through her lashes, as everyone else's jaws dropped.

"Let her alone, you big goon." Kayla leaned forward in the guard's grip. "She did nothing to you."

The Rottmeister dropped his hand and smiled the most frightening smile Birdie had ever seen, an evil quirk of the lips that didn't reach his dark eyes. He gripped the aventurine, swiveled on his heel, and marched to stand in front of Kayla.

Rather than bow her head as the others had done, she held her chin high, her hair flowing past her shoulders, her eyes sparking with anger. They stood at equal height, and she was not backing down, despite being pinned against the guard who held her.

For an instant, the world wavered.

Even the crickets stopped chirping.

And then, everything happened at once.

Kayla lifted her knee and used all the force she had to bring it up hard beneath the Rottmeister's tunic. He yelped and bent forward. As he did, the guard who held Kayla loosened his grip, and she used the surprise to push him away.

As she moved to run, Rich's guard dropped his grip to catch her, which allowed Rich to break free.

In the scuffle that followed, they each broke free as the guards tried to help each other secure the prisoners, but in the end, none of it mattered. The guards had daggers and training and recaptured them easily. The Rottmeister, recovered from the blow, his anger contained only by his iron helmet, took charge of Kayla himself, forcing her up the hillside, the others shuffling close behind.

It was a long, rough climb up a narrow deer path, the guards' leather boots tangling with the prisoners' sneakers on the uneven ground.

Birdie wished it were a dream. Her senses were on high alert – the pain in her shoulders from the guard's tight grip, the sting in her nostrils from the oil burning in the torches, the pounding of her heart from the fear of not knowing what would come next.

Except she did know. She could guess the Rottmeister's plan, and that was even more frightening.

The fortress entrance was no longer a modern electric gate, but a full-on drawbridge. Birdie eyed the arrow slits and murder holes with suspicion as they waited for the guards stationed inside to lower it.

She recognized the path to the dungeon but was helpless to change her fate. The fortress fell quiet as they marched along the path, and all Birdie could think about was what a waste it'd been to scrub her sneakers clean.

The guard at the entrance to the dungeon squinted in muted surprise, and then in genuine surprise, when he recognized Friedrich and Birdie. He exchanged a few words with the Rottmeister then stepped aside to let the regiment pass.

The stench of humanity greeted Birdie again and she gagged. Her eyes watered, and she prayed she could keep the pizza down and not make the stench inside the dungeon even worse.

They marched down the corridor, pausing to be pushed into cells. Friedrich was deposited into an above-ground cell close to the entrance, the bit of light from a nearby torch revealing a pack of nasty-looking men already inside.

It was quieter than it had been earlier, as if the inmates were saving their strength for another round of screaming and wailing with the sunrise. The silence unnerved Birdie more than the noise.

Kayla tussled with the Rottmeister again, earning her a gruesome cell close to Friedrich's, with heavily scarred women who looked like they'd never seen the sun. They grabbed for her as she stumbled inside and Kayla brushed them away, moving as far as she could into the back of the cell.

They pressed beyond the aboveground cells to the gaping pits, which offered only darkness and despair. They dropped the rest of the boys into one, and the guard bent to secure the latch.

Birdie didn't have to wonder where she was going. She knew. She'd been there before.

Sophia, Louisa, and Birdie were pushed into the hole with Marielle, whose face crumpled when she saw them, and she covered it with her hands.

CHAPTER THIRTY-SIX

Birdie had no way of knowing how much time had passed as they squatted in the putrid hole with Marielle, who awaited her fate with a stoic mix of dread and resolution. They'd found all but one of the puzzle blocks, but it didn't matter. Without the aventurine, they were trapped.

Why hadn't Friedrich's whistle worked?

Birdie combed her mind for a reason, for some solution – any solution – to their predicament.

Sophia was backed against the wall, staring up at the wooden crossbars that covered the hole. She'd been there a long time, so long that Birdie wondered if she'd fallen asleep standing up. She wouldn't blame her. Standing was preferable to sitting. Birdie was just too tired to care.

"I can get that open." Sophia nodded toward the grate. "I could spring the latch without a key. It's a super simple mechanism."

Birdie felt a ray of hope.

Louisa stood. "We must try to get you up there."

Sophia smiled, but there was no happiness in it. "It wouldn't matter. If I get it open, we couldn't all escape. They built the pit for shorter people but even so, at least one of us needs to stay in here to boost the others. Besides, we're at the dead end of the dungeon. We'd need to sneak past the guards and the other prisoners to get out."

"It should be Marielle." Louisa glanced at the lady's maid. "She knows the fortress better than any of us. The whole point was to save her life, right? If she gets away, we accomplished our goal."

"Not just Marielle," Birdie said. "Peter too."

Marielle glared at them, the frustration at being left out of the conversation plain on her face.

"We can boost Sophia up, too, so she can pick the lock on his pit." Louisa glanced up at the grate. "Could you do that?"

"If it's like this one."

"It's dangerous," Louisa said.

Sophia shrugged. "More dangerous that staying in this pit? Who knows what they plan to do with us, especially after Kayla kicked that guard."

"Okay. I will explain the plan to Marielle."

As Louisa shared their idea, Marielle shook her head and backed away. Her gaze flitted to Birdie and Sophia, then back to Louisa, whose voice was tinged with desperation. Marielle's eyes hardened.

She nodded and Louisa pulled her into a hug, but the lady's maid remained stiff and tramped away.

Louisa was right. It was dangerous. And unlikely to succeed.

But if they failed – again – at least they'd know they'd tried to save Marielle and Peter – and themselves.

She and Louisa knelt on the dirty floor and Sophia balanced on their knees. They lifted her like a cheerleader, the extra height giving her the boost to work the lock. It didn't take long. She forced the latch and flung the wooden grate open.

She hopped down from their knees. "Okay. It's open."

They boosted Marielle next, high enough to get her out of the pit, then Sophia. She gripped the edge of the hole and hauled herself up behind Marielle.

"Good luck!" Birdie whispered.

Sophia peered down at them through the open grate. "We'll come back for you!"

"Go!" Louisa waved her away.

Sophia nodded and moved silently down the corridor after Marielle.

"Now you." Louisa nodded toward the open grate.

"What?" Birdie faced her in the bottom of the pit.

"You must go too. You must find the aventurine if we're ever to escape this awful place."

"The Rottmeister has it."

"So find him."

"But I can't leave you here alone."

"You can and you will. Friedrich left you here earlier tonight, did he not?"

"I'm not Friedrich," Birdie said.

"Of course not. You're a good person and you can save

289

us all. Friedrich would hang us all to save himself."

Birdie couldn't argue with that.

"Do you want to live? Go, now, before someone comes."

Louisa clasped her hands and Birdie stepped into them. Louisa heaved her high enough to grasp the edge of the pit, then lifted onto her tiptoes to give her an extra boost.

It was just enough. Birdie climbed out and stared down at Louisa. "Thank you," she whispered. "I will come back for you. I promise."

"Go!" She waved her off and drifted away from the opening. "Close the grate. Do not get caught!"

Birdie hugged the stone wall, trembling as she made her way down the dimly lit passageway, sure at any moment she'd feel the heat of a guard's hands wrapping around her arms again or hear the screams of Marielle or Sophia being caught. She passed only one guard, but he was fast asleep, slumped against the opposite wall.

She held her breath as she slipped past him, wishing some other sound would cover her movements.

There was no sign of Marielle or Sophia. She reached low to replace the grate over the pit where Peter had been, hoping that closing it would draw less attention and buy them more time. It was pitch black in his pit, and she wondered if Rich, Sam, and Ryan were still down there in the filth.

She didn't dare to call to them. It was too dangerous and that guard could wake up at any moment.

She continued down the corridor and reached the cell where Kayla stood back against the wall, her eyes closed. The other women were curled together like rags, fast asleep.

"Kayla," Birdie said, the word barely audible.

Her eyes flew open, and she rushed on silent feet to the bars. She placed a finger to her lips and dug into her pocket. She pulled out the aventurine.

"How did you—"

Kayla shook her head to silence her. She passed the small piece of glass through the bars. "Get us out of here," she whispered, although Birdie wasn't sure if she'd spoken the words or merely mouthed them. "Make it work."

Birdie squeezed Kayla's fingers through the bars and watched as she slid back against the wall.

A second sleeping guard barked out a snore and she swallowed a cry. She slipped toward the entrance and held her breath as she peeked outside. The guard was gone, and Marielle and Sophia were nowhere to be seen along the torch-lit path. She made herself small and slipped into the night.

She rushed toward the tunnel to the storeroom, hoping if she got close enough to the chest and the toy blocks it would be enough to send her back. It was unlikely to work, she knew, but she couldn't stay out on the path. One glimpse of her modern clothes and even a civilian would drag her back to the dungeon.

She slipped through the tunnel into the storeroom and scanned the space for a place to hide. Her eyes grew wide when she saw Raina, cowering near a stack of barrels, wrapped in a long black cloak, only feet away from the sleeping guard.

Raina gasped. She used one hand to scoop up the front edges of her cloak and ran to her. They backed into the tunnel.

"Oh thank God!" Raina hugged Birdie hard but quickly stepped away. "Oh, you stink again."

"What are you doing here?" Birdie whispered.

"It was cold, so I grabbed this stupid cloak to wrap up in. I should have packed warmer clothes. I never dreamed it would get this cool at night."

"Focus, Raina."

"Right. Sorry. I was bored, so I figured I'd play with the puzzle. I watched Sophia work the lock, and it didn't seem that hard." She tugged the chest from beneath her cloak and held it out to Birdie. "And then I – shimmered, or whatever. By the way, I thought only vampires did that. Oh, wait. You don't think – we're not turning into—"

"You have the chest?" Birdie gazed at it in disbelief.

"Uh, yeah." Raina shook it lightly. "I just said that."

"Have you seen anyone else?"

"Anyone else? No, just you. And that guard. He has some nasty gas."

Birdie tamped down a giggle. If she started now, she'd never stop. Her legs shook as she hugged Raina again.

"Ugh!" Raina pushed her away. "Just – ugh."

Birdie released her with a smile. "We need to get out of here."

"You think?" Raina tilted her head toward the guard.

"How long have you been here? How long since you shimmered back?"

Raina shrugged. "I'm not sure. A while ago."

Birdie wanted to ask her more, to determine if she'd shimmered when they'd been in the village or later, after they returned to the fortress. "Did the guard see you?"

She shook her head. "He's been asleep. I didn't dare move and wake him. I've been hiding behind the barrels."

"Good." She considered the web of tunnels flowing out around them. "We have to get out of here. But to where?"

"Where's everyone else?"

Birdie grimaced. "You don't want to go there. Most of them are still in the dungeon."

"My brothers?"

Birdie nodded.

"We need to save them!"

Birdie put a finger to her lips. They needed time to work out a game plan, and waking the guard wouldn't help. "Yes. We'll save them. But we have to figure out how. We need to get out of here, get somewhere we know we're safe." Birdie considered it. "The cave?"

"Friedrich and Louisa said there are guards all over the woods."

"I'm sure they left by now."

"Why?"

"Because they caught their ghosts."

"That's why everyone's in the dungeon?"

Birdie nodded. She stole a small torch from a holder in the tunnel wall.

"Okay, but there better not be any bats this time." Raina drew the hood of the black cloak around her head and followed Birdie deeper underground.

They raced through the tunnels, crawling when they needed to, moving faster now that they were familiar with the route. They tumbled out several minutes later onto the forest floor. They didn't stop to catch their breath but sprinted through the dark night to the entrance to the cave.

When they stepped inside, they heard the whisper of voices.

"There's someone here!" Raina grabbed Birdie's arm and pulled her back.

"I know. And I think I know who."

CHAPTER THIRTY-SEVEN

Birdie and Raina crept along the cave's curved walls, prepared to flee. They kept to the shadows, the torch offering little more than a candle's glow. Birdie couldn't bring herself to extinguish it, to plunge them into total darkness, left to the mercy of their other senses as they inched their way deeper into the cave.

She thought about the animals that scurried through the chambers and prayed the noises she'd heard were not from a skittish raccoon.

A pool of light spilled onto the floor as they neared the dragon's lair and she raised her arm to stop Raina. They listened for voices again, and heard them, louder this time. American voices. The tension in Birdie's shoulders eased and she stepped into the light. "Oh, thank God."

Beneath the bright colors of the dragon, Sophia, Sam, Rich, and Ryan lounged in a circle on the floor, arguing.

Marielle and Peter huddled nearby, looking bewildered.

"You guys!" Raina flew to her brothers. "Birdie told me you were in the dungeon!" She glared over her shoulder. "Why did you lie to me?"

"Raina?" Rich sat back as she sunk down on the floor next to him. "What are you doing here?"

"Good question."

"So you came back, too?" Sam rubbed his chin. "Interesting."

Birdie's face lit with joy. "Sophia, you got them all out? You're amazing!"

Sophia jumped up and ran to her. She hugged her hard, then held her out to look at her. "We were trying to figure out how to rescue you. How did you get out?"

"Louisa made me go, too, after you and Marielle left. She's still back there, in the dungeon. We need to get her. Kayla too."

"Don't forget Friedrich," Ryan said.

Birdie wrinkled her nose. "If we must."

"But how?" Raina asked.

"That's what we were trying to figure out." Rich stared at his sister. "I can't believe you're here. Where were you hiding?"

Sophia released Birdie and whirled around. "You have to do it, Raina. You have to go to the dungeon to get them. You're the only one the guards haven't seen."

"Me? Forget it."

Sophia frowned. "It has to be you."

"I can't do it." Raina shuddered. "I've never been to the dungeon. How would I get them out, anyway? Steal the keys?"

"No one should go back to the dungeon." Rich sat forward. "The most important thing now, with all due respect to Marielle and Peter, is to get back to the future. That's the only way we'll all be safe."

"How do you propose we do that?" Ryan asked. "That guard took the aventurine."

"And Kayla stole it back." Birdie reached into her pocket. She let it sit on her palm, cool and still. "That's why she caused the commotion out on the hill. She passed it to me in the dungeon."

Ryan's eyes grew wide. "No way!"

"Why didn't you guys break Kayla out, too?" Raina's attention was still on Sophia.

"There was no time. The boys were in the same pit as Peter. That's the only reason we could get them. And I checked, but the lock on the cells is different from the one on the pits. I couldn't open Kayla's cell without a tool."

Rich stared at the glass in Birdie's hand. "It still shows the block. We need to find the last piece. I wish we could talk to Marielle and Peter and ask them about it."

Marielle and Peter sat a few feet from the rest of them. Peter had clasped Marielle's hands in his lap and from time to time they whispered to each other in their own language.

"Wait. Do you have the map you drew?" Birdie asked.

"I didn't bring it."

"Map?" Raina retrieved the chest from the folds of the cloak and opened it. "Which one do you want?"

"Where did that come from?" Ryan gaped at the chest.

"Dumb luck. I was holding it when I shimmered."

Rich grabbed the map he'd drawn and unfurled it with the wave of a hand. He set it on the floor in front of Marielle and Peter. "Bring the chest here."

Ryan dug into his pocket and pulled out the block they'd found in the village. "Sophia, here."

She knelt and placed the block into the indentation. The bottom of the chest rocked as she pressed it down.

"So close," she said. "One more."

Rich gestured to the puzzle in the chest, then to the place where the missing block would go.

Peter and Marielle exchanged glances.

Rich pointed first to the garden on the map, then to the edge of the map that led to Sankt Goar. "Hier?"

Peter's eyes widened.

Marielle grew excited. She leaned forward to study the images on the blocks, then tapped on the map as she glanced around frantically.

"She's looking for something to make a mark with," Birdie said.

"Do you have a pen in that magic chest?" Ryan asked Raina.

"Nope."

Rich scooped a handful of pebbles from the floor and placed one on the map.

Marielle snatched the pebble and moved it a few inches to the right, next to the wall of the brewery. "Hier."

Rich let out a breath. "It's here. At the fortress. You'll need to get it, Raina." He glanced up at his sister. "You're the only one with the right clothes, and Marielle and Peter are fugitives."

"It's a cloak." She removed it with a swirl. "Any of you could wear it."

They stared at the heavy cloak dangling from her outstretched hand.

"You should do it," Sophia said to Rich. "You studied the map more than any of us."

"She's right," Ryan agreed. "You'd know your way around with your eyes closed."

Rich took the cloak from his sister, shook it loose, and wrapped it around his broad shoulders.

"That will not work." Ryan eyed Rich's sneakers. The cloak fell almost a foot too short.

"Birdie?" Rich seemed sorry for what he was about to say. "It'll fit you. I can show you where to go on the map. You've been in the keep before, so you're familiar with the area."

"What will the rest of you do?" She accepted the cloak from his outstretched hand.

"Marielle and Peter should stay in the cave." Rich glanced at them sitting together on the floor. "That seems like the safest place for them, since they're still wanted for stealing the dowry. We should have a little more time before the guards realize we're missing."

"The rest of us will follow you," Sophia said. "At least to the end of the tunnel. Then we'll hide and wait. If you find the last block, we'll be right there to deal with it. And if you don't…"

There was no need for her to continue. They all knew the consequences if she failed.

"What about the others?" Raina asked.

Ryan grimaced. "They're not going anywhere."

"I know that. But they're in danger."

"If we do this right, they won't be in danger anymore," Birdie said. "And we'll be home before dawn."

Rich signaled to Marielle and Peter to stay where they were as he picked up the chest and cradled it like a football under his arm. With the plan in place they moved quickly, retreating from the cave through the woods and tunnels. They were nearly at the storeroom before they stopped.

Sophia straightened Birdie's cloak. "Be careful."

"And quick," Rich warned. "We don't know how long until the guards realize their prisoners escaped."

Birdie slipped out of the tunnel and into the chilly air of the courtyard, where only a few torches still burned. The music that floated in the breeze several hours before was gone.

She steeled herself as she tightened the cloak, which fell just long enough to brush the ground and hide her sneakers. The weight of it on her shoulders felt comforting, the broad hood protective.

The only noise in the quiet before dawn was the shuffle of her feet on the sandstone path. Her eyes, already accustomed to the gloom in the tunnel, adjusted quickly to the dark night. She could see well enough to spot a small gate that separated the brewery from the keep and led to the gardens beyond.

The gardens were lush, the plants in full bloom, the bounty a fragrant mix of herbs and flowers, lettuces and early vegetables. The air smelled of upturned soil and parsley and dill.

She made a beeline for the brewery wall, where a tall trellis crawled with vines. She was fairly certain it was the spot Marielle had pointed to on the map, although she wondered how the lady's maid knew the toy block was there. Perhaps she'd been with Elisabeth in the gardens on the day she hid it.

It didn't matter. Birdie just needed to find it. She dropped to her knees on the cool earth and used her bare hands to explore the soft dirt beneath the trellis, to examine the heavy posts that held it steady.

It was impossible to know where Elisabeth had hidden the small block, or if she'd protected it from the elements. Birdie wasn't sure what she'd find, if she could find anything at all.

A clue, she supposed.

She peered at the sliver of moon that now shone on the opposite side of the clear night sky, the clouds having drifted away on the wind.

She rose to her feet and made a slow circle, glancing around the gardens. Where could it be? She pivoted again searching for something – anything – among the leafy plants that would lead her to the toy block.

The third time around, she noticed a bit of disturbed earth just past the ragged end of the trellis, beside the brewery wall. She skidded to it, falling to her knees and pushing the loose dirt aside with her bare hands.

Her fingers lit on something rough.

She burrowed deeper in the loose soil and tugged at the object buried there. She yanked it from the ground and held it to the moonlight.

A pouch, a leather pouch, no larger than a change purse.

She wiggled her dirty fingers to loosen the piece of twine that cinched it closed, then flipped the pouch upside down. A simple wooden block tumbled into her palm.

Birdie rocked back on her heels, and almost howled with delight. She put the toy to her lips and kissed it, then dropped it back into the pouch.

She stood, relief washing through her. She'd done it. They'd be okay. The others would be saved.

She shoved the heavy cloak aside and pulled the aventurine from her pocket. She held it up, expecting it to grow warm, to swirl, for the world to shimmer. She'd found the last block, completed the task, finished the quest.

But the aventurine remained cool to the touch and the image of the toy block held steady. The keep still towered against the night sky, the flags snapping from the towers.

She cursed and pulled the cloak tight.

"Did you get it?" Sam jumped up when she reached the others in the tunnel.

"I found it. I have it."

"Then why are we still here?" Ryan asked.

"Open the chest." Sam nudged Sophia. "Finish the puzzle. Hurry!"

Rich placed the chest on the ground in front of Sophia. Her hands trembled as she unlocked it.

Six of the seven pieces were there, fitted into the indentations.

This was it. Birdie removed the last block from the leather pouch and held it up for the others to see.

"Just do it!" Sam urged.

Birdie placed the small wooden block inside, wriggling it into the last open space. She glanced up, waiting for the world to change.

The others did the same, but the air remained still.

"Nothing." Ryan peered into the chest. "That was the last piece. Why isn't it working?"

Sophia studied the blocks for a few moments. "Hmmm." She tilted her head to one side. "Does that look like a dragon to you?" She plucked three of the pieces out and reconfigured them until the etchings on their surfaces lined up to create the image of a dragon.

"It's an exact match," Sam said. "Amazing. But why didn't it open the secret compartment?"

"And why are we still here?" Ryan pressed.

Sophia grinned. "Because that's not the puzzle."

"What are you talking about?" Sam said. "You just solved it."

"No." She shook her head. "I just put the pieces together in the right order. This is how you solve the puzzle."

Sophia spread her hand across the surface of the blocks and pushed down firmly until something beneath them clicked. She twisted the puzzle until it clicked again. As it did, the front of the chest popped open, revealing a deep drawer.

"The hidden compartment," Sam said. "Just like you predicted!"

"What's in it?" Rich bent forward. "Please tell me there's something in it."

Sophia spun the chest to Birdie. "You do it."

Birdie eased the drawer open. She lifted a piece of fur and peeked underneath, then beamed at Rich. "There's something there alright." She removed the fur lining.

"Oh, wow." Rich teetered back on his heels.

There, resting in the drawer, was a magnificent chess piece – a knight on horseback rearing high, covered in gemstones.

Birdie gathered it from the drawer and balanced it on her palm.

"Holy crap," Ryan said. "That thing is spectacular."

"Look how it shines." Sophia's eyes were wide. "Even in this light."

"Jewels," Sam whispered. "Diamonds, sapphires, rubies. There are others, but those are the most valuable."

"This knight grants wealth, privilege, and power?" Ryan's hand hovered over the precious piece.

"That's the legend," Sophia said. "Some call it the knight's blessing and some call it his curse. Others say you need to reunite all the pieces of the chess set to gain its power. No matter what the legend says, this chess piece has been missing for centuries."

"And there you are, holding it in your hand." Sam met Birdie's gaze with wonder.

"Take it." She handed it to Sam. "Everyone take a turn holding it. If it brings good fortune, we need all we can get. In case you haven't noticed, we're still in the past. We haven't shimmered back yet."

They each held the piece, examining its intricate design, admiring its jewels. When they finished, Birdie wrapped it in the fur. "Now, we need to figure out how to get it to

Elisabeth's father."

"Why?" Raina said. "Marielle and Peter already escaped."

"But they're not free," Rich explained. "They won't be free until we remove all suspicion from them. We have to return this chess piece."

"It may also be the key to returning to our time," Birdie said. "If we return the lost object, then maybe we'll be free too."

"How do you know they won't murder us for having it?" Ryan asked.

"I don't," Birdie said. "That's why Friedrich should be the one who returns it."

CHAPTER THIRTY-EIGHT

"Birdie, you cannot be serious," Raina said. "Do you hate him that much?"

Birdie thought about that for a moment.

"Birdie!" Sophia said.

"Okay, okay. It's not because I hate him. Friedrich needs to be the one who returns it because he's the only one who is both male and speaks German. He can say he found it across the river near the Loreley. They're likely to believe him because of the problem with the villagers and the bees. They'd be suspicious of the rest of us because we're so obviously not from here."

"So how do we make that happen?" Sophia asked. "Friedrich is in the dungeon, and he's dressed like he works at the mall."

"There's a guard uniform in the storeroom," Raina said. "It was hanging on a hook against the wall."

"Okay, good. But Raina" – Birdie faced her – "you need to break him out of the dungeon."

"Me? You can't be serious! Why do you want me dead so bad?" She shimmied away from her.

"We don't, Raina." Rich sighed. "I hate it, but Birdie's right. You're the only one the guards haven't seen. They think we're still in the pits. If they catch any of us, the gig is up."

"What if I get caught?"

"They shouldn't suspect you of anything," Rich said. "They have no reason to. Just do not speak, whatever you do. Pretend you're dumb."

"Shouldn't be too hard," Ryan said.

"Knock it off." Rich shot him a look that wiped the smirk from his face. "This is serious. Deadly serious. If she fails—"

"Let's not think about that." Sophia patted Raina's knee. "You won't fail, right?"

She didn't respond.

"Okay," Sophia said. "Let's get that uniform."

Birdie returned from the storeroom swiftly, having snuck past the sleeping guard to grab the uniform and a helmet from the wall, along with an empty cask and a sack of cherries. She shrugged out of the cloak and passed it to Raina, who layered the uniform under it, smoothing the front so it wouldn't appear bulky.

"Will this really work?" she asked. "I'm huge."

"Like a charm." Birdie slipped the helmet into the bottom of the cask and covered it with cherries. "Use the cherries to distract the guards and the prisoners. The helmet is for Friedrich, to help him hide his face."

"What should I do with the cask?"

"It's for Louisa. She's all the way at the far end of the dungeon. When you reach her, toss the cask down to her. She'll know what to do."

"This is never going to work."

"You can do it, Raina." Rich leaned in for a quick hug. "I believe in you. Now go, before it's too late."

Ryan reached into his pocket and retrieved a thin piece of iron. "Give this to Friedrich, for the lock. He should be able to jimmy his cell and Kayla's."

Raina's face fell as she took it.

Ryan gave her a weak smile and a gentle push toward the end of the tunnel. "Good luck."

The minutes passed slowly as they waited in silence. Birdie clutched the chess piece as Rich paced the length of the short tunnel.

"She'll be okay," Sophia reassured him as he neared them again.

His eyes grew hard and he turned back toward the entrance.

"Raina doesn't like being told what to do." Ryan watched his brother drift farther away. "She usually does the opposite. We can't be sure she'll pull this off."

Birdie thought of her brother, Jonah. He'd been the same way.

Sam stood and shook the loose dirt from his pants. "I need some air."

"Sam—" Sophia began but he held up a hand to silence

her. "I need some air." He brushed past Rich and disappeared out of the tunnel entrance.

"There's nobody out there," Birdie reassured Sophia. "He'll be okay."

"Do you think we'll ever go back?" Ryan blurted. "I mean, we've been here a long time now. What if the aventurine's magic is all used up?"

Birdie's stomach flinched.

"Don't say that." Rich had neared them again. "Just… don't."

Shuffling at the tunnel entrance drew their attention. Rich spun to look as Birdie jumped to her feet.

"Nein!" Friedrich surged into the tunnel in the guard uniform and helmet. He held Raina clamped close to his side.

"We have to get her!" Raina pushed at him but he held firm. "We can't just leave her in there!" She dug her shoes into the dirt floor but he yanked her along.

"Let her go," Rich growled.

Friedrich stopped short, his eyes growing wide. He released Raina immediately.

She stumbled away from him. "He wouldn't let me get Kayla." She shot Friedrich a dirty look and then bent forward, hands on her knees. "He dragged me out of the dungeon before I could even give her the lock pick!"

"What? Why?" Birdie glanced behind them. "Where's Louisa?"

"I gave her the cask." Raina straightened. "I'm hoping she got out, but Friedrich—"

"There was no time." Friedrich announced. "The sun is

rising. We must leave the fortress or risk capture."

Birdie shook her head. "No. We're not leaving the fortress, and we're not leaving Louisa and Kayla behind."

"As head counselor—"

"For God's sake, dude." Rich clenched his fists.

Birdie rushed to Friedrich and pushed the chess piece into his hands. "Here. You can end this."

"You found it?" He gaped at the knight.

"We did. And now you have to return it."

"Can't we just keep it?" His mouth hung open in awe at the jewels.

Outside, a bell tolled, producing a low, slow rhythm.

"No, we cannot just keep it and we did not just spring you from the dungeon to have you make off with the chess piece. You have to give it to Elisabeth's father. That's the only way to end this and save us all."

Friedrich wrapped his hand around it and scowled. "I should report you all. You left me in that dungeon to rot! I saw you go by and you didn't even try to get me out."

"You mean like you just did to Kayla?" Raina placed her hands on her hips.

"Report us where? You're free now." Rich stood tall in the tunnel. "So suck it up and do what Birdie says."

Outside, the bell continued to toll.

Further away, trumpets blared.

"That's some wake up call." Sophia glanced toward the tunnel entrance. "No one in the fortress could stay asleep with that racket going on."

"What do you want me to do?" Friedrich muttered as he turned to Birdie.

"You need to find Elisabeth's father and return this to him. Tell him you found it across the river in the grottos near the Loreley."

"That is a great story." Friedrich's eyebrow twitched.

"I know."

"There is just one problem. How will I find Elisabeth's father and, if I do, how do I get close to him?"

Sam ran back into the tunnel. "Uh, that won't be a problem. He'll be at the execution."

"What execution?" Rich said. "Marielle and Peter escaped."

"Kayla's."

CHAPTER THIRTY-NINE

When they reached the end of the tunnel, Birdie's breath caught.

The courtyard teemed with people as it had during the pageant, but the shops and stalls were real and the window boxes overflowed with flowers. The intimidating keep soared toward the heavens, gleaming white, its flags rippling in the breeze that swirled up the hillside from the untamed river far below.

Trumpets blared as dawn arrived. Bedraggled villagers shuffled through the main gate, eager to watch the show. Birdie recognized the night watchman and several of the men from the night before.

Friedrich exited the tunnel first. Birdie followed in Raina's cloak, while the others ducked behind an empty stall along the stone wall.

"I don't think I can do this, Birdie." Friedrich slowed

abruptly and she nearly ran into him. "Look at all these people. What if they think I'm an imposter?"

"You are an imposter." Birdie peered at him from under the hood of the cloak. His face had gone ashen. She shoved him toward the courtyard, but he was frozen to the spot.

"Oh, don't you dare tell me you're getting cold feet now." She shook her head slowly. "No way. This is it, buddy. You got what you wanted. You get to return the chess piece." She shoved him again, harder this time. "Get out there."

As she spoke, the Rottmeister led Kayla into the courtyard. Her modern clothes had been covered by a plain sack cinched at the waist with a length of rope. Her hands and feet were bound, and she struggled to stay upright as he pulled her along.

"It's the guard from last night," Birdie breathed. "He's leading her out himself!"

That did not appear to ease Friedrich's mind. He stepped back to stand beside her.

The crowd murmured, growing louder as Kayla passed through them. They yelled at her, spitting as they growled words Birdie was glad she couldn't understand.

Kayla held her head high, her blond hair flowing loose in the chilly morning air.

When they reached the pyre that had been built for Marielle, the Rottmeister ordered two guards to secure her.

"You must do this." Birdie faced Friedrich and gave him another push toward the crowd. "If you don't save her, she will die. And you'll have to answer to her grandparents. What will you tell them? That you let them murder her like a common witch?"

"If we get back."

"We will go back," Birdie said. "But you must return the chess piece. That's the only way."

"I am not sure what I would say to her grandparents."

"Seriously, Friedrich?"

He shook off the thought. "Okay, okay. But if they put an arrow through my heart for this—"

"Just make it good," Birdie ordered with a final shove.

And make it good he did.

Friedrich regained his composure as he stumbled away from Birdie and into the middle of the courtyard, as if he'd been practicing for this moment his whole life. A ripple passed through the crowd and they hushed. The other prisoners, who'd been chained together and brought up from the dungeon, watched Friedrich in silence.

Louisa was not among them and, when Birdie glanced over her shoulder, she saw that she'd joined the others behind the stall. Raina had done it. She'd freed everyone but Kayla.

Birdie backed toward them.

"Thank God you got out," she whispered to Louisa.

"You're telling me." Louisa gazed at her around the edge of the stall. Birdie could tell she was shaken.

In the center of the courtyard, Friedrich stretched to his full height, raised his chin, and spoke.

"What's he saying?" Birdie whispered and Louisa translated.

"My liege!" Friedrich cried as he turned in a slow circle to allow every person in the crowd to admire him. "I bring important news."

Elisabeth and her father had been escorted by their

personal guards and were seated on a dais high above the throng. Elisabeth wore a long gown not unlike the one Louisa had worn at the pageant, and her hair was piled high upon her head in elaborate braids set off by an embroidered hood. She was a tiny woman, not more than a girl really, her diminutive size accentuated by her father's substantial girth.

"And what is this news?" her father asked without standing. He sounded bored and crooked a finger to signal the guards to ready their arrows.

Friedrich lowered to one knee and bowed deeply. "My liege. I bring news of the missing dowry."

The villagers gasped as both Elisabeth and her father rose to their feet.

"And what is this news? Out with it, boy!"

"'Twas not the lady's maid who stole the dowry," he cried. "'Twas another, far more wicked, a stranger from across the mighty Rhine, a stranger who has none other than the evil Loreley by his side!"

The gasps grew louder and longer.

"Who is this stranger of whom you speak?" Elisabeth's father asked, using his hands to tamp down the noise from the crowd.

At the edges of the courtyard, the guards took a step closer to Friedrich.

"A devil who crossed the river to destroy the fine village of Sankt Goar three fortnight ago." Friedrich dared a nervous glance at the advancing guards. "Only to be heroically thwarted by the humble baker boys!"

Marielle and Peter appeared at the edge of the crowd, across the courtyard from Birdie and the others.

"They tell me it was the baker boy who aided her," Elisabeth's father said. "A common thief!"

"'Tis a lie, sir!" Friedrich cried. "For I have crossed the treacherous waters to find the scoundrel and make the end of him with my own sword!"

He reached into his uniform. As he did the guards around Elisabeth's father drew their weapons.

"Worry not, I bring no weapon. Only this."

He placed the chess piece on the palm of his hand, slowly unwrapping the fur that surrounded it. As he did, its brilliant jewels sparkled like a magic token, catching every ray of morning sun.

The crowd gasped again and then, slowly, began to cheer.

Elisabeth sunk back into her seat and clasped her hands in her lap.

Her father nodded to one of his guards, who ran down from the stage and retrieved the chess piece from Friedrich's outstretched hand.

He examined the piece, holding it to the sunlight.

"'Tis true," the guard announced. "It is the missing piece."

"Bring this hero a pint!" Elisabeth's father called as the crowd cheered and the guard marched across the courtyard to hand him the treasured chess piece. He held it high for the crowd to see. "We have much to celebrate! Now, on with the execution!"

Birdie gasped as the war drums pounded.

The trumpets called again, deafening in their proximity.

Kayla caught her eye, fear passing over her face.

"Do something!" she cried.

CHAPTER FORTY

Birdie scrambled for the aventurine and held it out in front of her.

The crowd chanted over the drums, growing louder, the energy and excitement in the courtyard building.

The Rottmeister advanced with a glowing torch held high in the air, smiling wickedly at Kayla, his grizzled face alive with the taste of revenge. When he reached her, he turned to the crowd, pumping the torch into the air with such force that the spectators began chanting his name.

He paused and met Kayla's eyes. Then he bent the torch toward the timber beneath her.

Birdie's hands trembled so violently she nearly dropped the glass.

"Do something!" Sophia cried. "He's lighting the fire!"

Birdie surged forward, desperate to get closer to Kayla. But the crowd was too thick, too agitated, as they knocked against each other to witness the spectacle. She clasped her fingers around the aventurine and held it tight, fearing it would slip away and be forever lost beneath their stamping feet.

She rushed forward again, using her shoulders to break through, but the villagers jostled her back until she was where she'd begun, standing next to the others.

The kindling crackled as the flames licked the wood.

"Now!" Birdie cried, her eyes filling with tears. "We did what you wanted us to do! Take us back!" She dropped to her knees and opened her hand wide.

Why wasn't it working?

Sophia knelt beside her as the tears spilled down Birdie's cheeks.

"Birdie!" Sophia grabbed her arm and squeezed it hard. "Birdie, look. The sparkles! They're moving!"

In the center of Birdie's palm, the aventurine grew warm.

The sparkles swirled, barely moving at first, then picking up speed as the glass grew so hot against her skin she had to pull the edge of the cloak across her hand, slipping the dark cloth under the glass.

"Oh, thank God." Birdie collapsed against her.

"It's working!" Ryan cried.

The image of the toy block dissolved into a sea of gold.

The chanting crowd faded, slipping through time like sand through open fingers, leaving nothing but an impression, an imprint, behind.

And then, they were back.

The drums were replaced by the forlorn whistle of an early morning barge passing through the gorge.

They were positioned as they'd been centuries before – Friedrich in the center of the courtyard, still on one knee, Kayla several yards away where the pyre had stood, and the others near a crumbled pile of stone that had once been a mighty wall. Louisa fell to her knees beside Birdie and Sophia.

"You saved us." Tears coursed down her cheeks. "We're back."

Birdie grasped the aventurine. It was growing cold. She slid it into her pocket, her fingers trembling. She could barely breathe.

That had been so close.

Too close.

"What time is it?" Sam stared at the sunrise across the river.

"Early." Friedrich brushed sand from his knee as he stood. He hesitated, staring at the place where Elisabeth's father had been, as if trying to secure the memory deep in his mind.

He was disheveled, the leather tunic too short for his frame, his blond hair sticking up in odd places and his skin smudged with dirt. Birdie could only imagine how dreadful she looked if he was such a mess.

Then he strolled toward them. "You must get cleaned up and eat something before your parents come." He gestured to the path that led to the storeroom. "And then, I never want to see any of you ever again." He pointed at Birdie. "Especially you."

"The feeling is mutual, Fred," Kayla called to him as she rose awkwardly to her feet. Birdie saw her legs quivering from across the courtyard. "Now, would someone mind untying me?"

Sophia left Birdie's side and jogged to her. "Oh, Kayla, let's get you out of those ropes."

Raina dropped to the ground and sat like a pretzel. She stared blankly at the silent courtyard. "Did that really all just happen?"

No one said anything.

Sophia struggled to untie the knots that bound Kayla. They were both shaking, but somehow she managed.

"We must go." Louisa's voice cracked as she spoke. "Back to the storeroom."

They didn't bother to hide from the night watchman, although he was nowhere in sight, anyway. They entered the storeroom through the main door, sliding the latch open from outside and filing down the stairs.

Everything was exactly as they'd left it, down to the empty pizza boxes at the end of the table.

"I need sleep." Raina collapsed onto her cot. "This has been one massive nightmare."

Sophia sat on her cot and reached for her phone.

"What are you doing?" Sam asked.

"I want to see what happened to Marielle."

The others gathered on the nearby cots and waited in silence while she searched for information.

Sophia smiled as she looked up at them. "Nothing at all. She married Peter, who's still mentioned as a hero because of the bee incident, but there's no other mention of her at all."

"That's probably a good thing," Louisa said.

Birdie exhaled. "So it's over."

"Not quite," Sophia said. "There's more. The article mentions a guard, a towering stranger, who returned an invaluable, enchanted chess piece and then disappeared into thin air – stolen from glory by a spell." Sophia glanced up from the phone. "A spell cast upon him by an evil witch who was about to be burned at the stake."

"That would be me." Kayla bowed on her cot. "You're welcome, Fred."

"And, get this!" Sophia laughed. "There's a statue of him in Sankt Goar!"

"Oh, I've got to see that." Kayla lay back on the cot and closed her eyes.

Friedrich puffed his chest.

"So everyone lived happily ever after," Ryan said.

"Even us." Raina yawned. "If we can ever get some sleep."

"Yes, go to sleep." Louisa stretched out on her cot. "We can all sleep for a bit. The sun rises early this time of year, so we still have several hours until camp ends."

"Wait, what about Elisabeth?" Sam asked. "What happened to her?"

Sophia scrolled through her phone.

"Nothing changed." She sounded surprised. "Apparently, her father was so grateful to have the chess piece back he didn't make her marry Prince Gunzelin. He brushed the canceled wedding off by accusing the prince of being in league with the rogue who stole the dowry."

"Nothing changed?" Friedrich sat down hard on his cot.

"Sorry, Fred," Kayla said. "Guess you'll have to be

satisfied playing a prince at camp, because your life is exactly the same."

He scowled.

"Chin up." Rich slapped him on the back. "At least you got a statue."

CHAPTER FORTY-ONE

In the end, it was Frau Hamel who woke them, throwing open the heavy wooden doors and calling down the stairs as she entered the storeroom.

She brought food, which was the only thing in the world that could have enticed Birdie to crawl off the cot. She was exhausted. They all were. Everything that happened a few hours before seemed like it happened days ago or in a dream.

Frau Hamel was not happy. She spoke to Louisa and Friedrich in German before switching to English so they all would understand.

"It smells like pigs live in this room," she barked, her accent heavy. "You were to be awake and cleaning up the bedding and cots an hour ago. This is unacceptable."

Birdie had grown used to the smell, but she couldn't disagree about the general state of disarray.

Ryan stirred on his cot but didn't open his eyes.

"I am sorry, Frau Hamel." Friedrich leaned down to pick up a thin blanket that had fallen from a cot to form a puddle on the floor. "It was a…" He paused, searching for the right words. "A long night. We will clean up."

Frau Hamel nodded briskly and turned an expectant gaze to Louisa.

Louisa shuffled across the storeroom to the long table, which was now piled high with pastries and yogurt containers.

"And you, Louisa?" Frau Hamel demanded.

"I am done." She picked up a pastry and examined it. Her braids were frayed and dark circles swam under her eyes. "You can find someone else for the next camp session." She plopped the pastry into her mouth and reached for another one.

Frau Hamel inhaled sharply and stormed up the steps. "Your parents will be here in thirty minutes. I expect this storeroom to be clean and each of you to be out at the curb waiting for them before they arrive."

She left the doors open, allowing the sunshine and fresh breeze to filter through the storeroom.

No one said a word in her wake.

Birdie was just amazed it was morning. Morning had arrived, right on time, as if nothing had happened at all.

They groaned and grumbled their way through breakfast, the sugar from the pastries doing little to erase the fog of sleep. Raina didn't bother to join them – she stayed curled up on her cot, her breath slow and steady as she continued to doze. At some point Friedrich gathered his things and slipped away, although Birdie didn't realize he was gone until Ryan spoke.

She patted her front pocket to make sure the aventurine was still there.

"So this was something, huh?" Ryan said.

Sam chuckled. He rubbed his round face. "Yeah."

"Are you guys going back to the States now?"

"No," Sam said. "We're just getting started. We have a few more stops in Germany and then we're off to France. I'm not sure how anything will compare to this, though."

"I'm going home to Ohio," Kayla said. "And I can't get there soon enough."

"What about you?" Sam asked.

"Munich." Ryan reached for another pastry. "By train."

"How about you, Birdie?" Sophia asked.

She thought about it. "Prague. And don't ask me anything about it because I know nothing."

"Prague is a beautiful city," Louisa said. "It's… very old and historic."

They all exchanged glances.

"Great," Birdie said.

"You may want to lose that glass before you get there," Kayla said.

"I know. I just need to figure out how."

They cleaned up and gathered their things, not wanting to leave the mess in Louisa's hands as Friedrich never returned. When they were done, they made their way to the curb, squinting against the bright sun.

Sam and Sophia's parents were the first to arrive.

Sophia hugged Birdie before she left. "Stay in touch, okay? I put my number in your pack."

Birdie nodded. "Definitely."

Mrs. Blessing came next, pulling up in the rental car. "Good morning!" she said, her eyes bright.

"I need a shower." Birdie slid into the front seat and leaned against the headrest. She waved to the others still waiting on the curb and closed her eyes.

Her mom rolled down the windows. "Yes. Did you guys pull an all-nighter or something?"

Birdie didn't hear the question. She'd already nodded off.

They'd made their way through the tricky underpass and onto Heerstrasse before Birdie started, realizing she'd fallen asleep. She opened her eyes.

"Why aren't we parking in the lot?" She glanced over her shoulder. They'd already passed it.

"Herr Mueller said we could park in front of the hotel to load our bags."

"Are you allowed to drive down this street?"

Her mom checked the clock on the dashboard. "For ten more minutes, anyway. After that, it becomes a pedestrian zone again."

As her mom navigated down the narrow street, Birdie recalled how the village had looked the night before. They passed a row of empty tables, and she remembered seeing her mom with the strange man at the café.

She opened her mouth to ask her about it, then closed it. In her exhaustion, she'd almost given herself away. She sat back and watched the town crawl by.

"Mom, stop!" She sat up straight in her seat.

"What is it?" Mrs. Blessing hit the brakes hard.

There, in the center of the small town square, stood Friedrich.

He was admiring a statue, but it was not the statue of the baker boys that had stood there when Birdie and her mom arrived, its beehives affirming their heroic tale.

Instead, Friedrich gazed up at a stone form, almost true to life atop its pedestal, of a gangly guard holding a treasured chess piece high in the air.

"Do you know that boy?"

"He was one of our camp counselors." She dug in her daypack for her camera.

"What's he doing?" Her mom tilted her head to get a better look at him through the windshield.

Birdie leaned out of the window and snapped several photos.

Friedrich took no notice.

"Funny, I didn't notice that statue before."

Birdie smiled. "Neither did I."

"Okay, well, did you get the photo you wanted?"

Birdie nodded.

"Good. Let's go get you cleaned up and get our stuff. We can't miss our flight to Prague."

ABOUT THE AUTHOR

Heidi Williamson loves to travel, study history, and write stories. When she's home, she's based in Pennsylvania. When she's not home, she spends time exploring beautiful places, both in the United States and abroad.

www.birdieabroad.com

If you have a moment, please consider adding a rating or review for this book wherever you bought or borrowed it. Ratings and reviews are so important for independent authors.
Thanks!

CPSIA information can be obtained
at www.ICGtesting.com
Printed in the USA
BVHW081052230123
656900BV00002B/22